Praise for *Hounded*

"David Rosenfelt deftly works in wry humor, a love of dogs, and New Jersey gangsters in *Hounded,* his highly entertaining twelfth legal thriller featuring attorney Andy Carpenter."

—Associated Press

"Heartwarming . . . This is an entertaining, feel-good read, populated with Jersey gangsters, ruthless criminals, and likable protagonists. Longtime fans and new readers alike will be charmed by wisecracking, canine-loving Andy." —*Publishers Weekly*

"Great summer entertainment, a page-turning mystery with a lot of good laughs along the way." —*Portland Press Herald*

Praise for *Without Warning*

"[Rosenfelt] excels at creating fascinating plots and telling his stories with crisp writing that's a pleasure to read. The plot of his new book has a relentless sense of urgency that captures readers' attention early on and never lets go." —*RT Book Reviews* (4 stars)

"Spooky. Creepy. Edgy. Shuddery. What more could anyone want? . . . Highly recommended for readers craving that elusive 'something different.'"

—*Booklist*

Praise for *Dogtripping*

"A book that will make you laugh, cry, and want to adopt a dog from the nearest shelter—all on the same page. David Rosenfelt's extraordinary narrative style makes it fantastically easy to read in one sitting; in fact it's difficult to put down . . . It's funny, poignant, and at times, downright sad. In short—it's wonderful."

—*Examiner.com*

"Rosenfelt very well could be the funniest American author alive today. . . . He's charming, likable, self-deprecating, self-aware, and utterly hysterical."

—Associated Press

Praise for *Unleashed*

"Terrific . . . How does Rosenfelt manage to construct such clever and complex plots, tie them all together, make you love Andy more with every novel, and bombard you with nonstop humor, all at the same time? Only Rosenfelt can pull off that kind of quadruple play. His is an absolutely unique mystery/comedy talent. Do not miss *Unleashed*. Don't miss any of them."

—*Examiner.com*

"Books in the Andy Carpenter series are more leisurely, character-driven pleasures. . . . Rosenfelt has had plenty of time to hone his protagonist's wiseass humor and refine his oddball cast, which, alongside millionaire defense attorney Carpenter, includes four octogenarian computer whizzes, a taciturn bodyguard, and a brainiac accountant."

—*Booklist*

"Rosenfelt demonstrates again that he's a master storyteller in this immensely enjoyable new Andy Carpenter novel. His writing is crisp, his plot unfolds at a rapid clip, and his characters are people you'd like to hang out with. Surprises in the plot and gripping courtroom scenes make it difficult to put down."

—*RT Book Reviews* (4 stars)

"A fun read. Andy is still a joke-a-page lawyer."

—*The Daily News* (Memphis)

HOUNDED

ALSO BY DAVID ROSENFELT

ANDY CARPENTER NOVELS

Unleashed

Leader of the Pack

One Dog Night

Dog Tags

New Tricks

Play Dead

Dead Center

Sudden Death

Bury the Lead

First Degree

Open and Shut

THRILLERS

Without Warning

Airtight

Heart of a Killer

On Borrowed Time

Down to the Wire

Don't Tell a Soul

NONFICTION

Dogtripping: 25 Rescues, 11 Volunteers, and 3 RVs on Our Canine Cross-Country Adventure

HOUNDED

David Rosenfelt

MINOTAUR BOOKS
NEW YORK

This is a work of fiction. All of the characters, organizations, and events portrayed in this novel are either products of the author's imagination or are used fictitiously.

www.minotaurbooks.com

The Library of Congress has cataloged the hardcover edition as follows:

Rosenfelt, David.
Hounded / David Rosenfelt. — First edition.
p. cm. — (An Andy Carpenter novel ; 12)
ISBN 978-1-250-02474-9 (hardcover)
ISBN 978-1-250-02475-6 (e-book)
1. Carpenter, Andy (Fictitious character)—Fiction. 2. Attorneys—Fiction. 3. Ex-convicts—Crimes against—Fiction. 4. Orphans—Fiction. 5. Dogs—Fiction. 6. Domestic fiction. I. Title.
PS3618.O838H68 2014
813'.6—dc23 2014005818

ISBN 978-1-250-05515-6 (trade paperback)

Minotaur books may be purchased for educational, business, or promotional use. For information on bulk purchases, please contact the Macmillan Corporate and Premium Sales Department at 1-800-221-7945, extension 5442, or write to specialmarkets@macmillan.com.

First Minotaur Books Paperback Edition: July 2015

10 9 8 7 6 5 4 3 2

Dedicated to Dr. Sean O'Donnell and the amazing staff at Miles Hospital. They are the reasons Andy Carpenter lives on.

HOUNDED

Pete Stanton figured he was the poorest person in the room.

Of course, it was always possible that he was wrong. Maybe the servants had been allowed to attend, since it was their boss who was being eulogized. Having had no experience with servants, Pete was not in a position to venture an educated guess about that. And if he asked the guys at the precinct, chances are they wouldn't know either.

One after another the speakers spoke about what a wonderful woman Katherine Reynolds was, and what a caring and compassionate life she led. She was a philanthropist, and a litany of charities that benefitted from her largesse were cited. Jokes were told about her eccentricities and unique character traits, but all were gentle and ultimately meant to praise.

This was a memorial service, not a roast. The deceased had died weeks earlier, and the funeral had been small and private. This was a chance for everyone else to pay their respects.

Based on the speeches, Katherine Reynolds was a woman without a flaw, and Pete figured that's how it should be. If you're not coming back, you should get a good send-off.

Pete looked over at Katherine's husband, Carson Reynolds, stone-faced as he listened, dabbing occasionally at his eyes. He was trying to read something in Reynolds's face, but there was nothing there to read. Certainly Pete had no way of knowing that Carson Reynolds was the happiest man in the place.

The happiest woman, also undetected by Pete, was actually sitting just three rows away from him. Her name was Susan Baird, and she herself was less than a year a widow. Having known Katherine Reynolds quite well, she knew that at least seventy percent of the spoken praise was total bullshit, and the rest hyperbole. But her death moved Baird up the ladder from mistress to girlfriend, so she was fine with whatever might be said at this service.

Pete had already decided that there was nothing for him to learn when he felt his cell phone vibrate. He saw that it was a text message from Danny Diaz, and it was marked "urgent."

He got up and left the service.

No one seemed to notice or care.

"We have to leave," Danny Diaz said.

He was trying to say it as casually as he could, but he knew that his son, Ricky, would see through it. Ricky was just eight years old, but it had been at least three years since Danny was able to fool him.

"Where are we going?" Ricky asked.

"I'm not sure. On a trip, like a vacation."

"When?"

"Now. Right now." He was trying to keep his voice calm; there was no reason to transfer his anxiety to his son.

"We going to see Mom?"

Danny didn't know how to respond to that; he certainly didn't want to get Ricky's hopes up if things didn't work out. "I'm not sure yet, Rick. You know where your suitcase is?"

"In the closet."

"Okay. Well, put as many of your clothes in it that can fit, all right? Can you do that for me right away?"

"Can I take some toys?"

"Just a couple. We want to keep room for clothes."

Ricky pointed. "Can Sebastian come?"

He was referring to their six-year-old basset hound, sleeping soundly on a doggie bed against the wall. While Ricky was sensitive to increased energy levels in the house, Sebastian was unmoved by it, or pretty much anything else.

Danny had forgotten about Sebastian. "We'll come back for him," he said, with no conviction whatsoever.

Ricky saw through the lie and shook his head. "I'm not going without Sebastian."

"Okay. Sebastian can come."

Ricky began to gather his things, throwing a couple of Sebastian's toys into the bag as well. He instinctively knew that they were not coming back, though he had no idea why. Danny went down the hall to his own room to do the same.

Ricky heard the doorbell ring, and for some reason it worried him. Moments later, Danny came into the room. "You okay in here?"

"Yeah, Dad. Who's at the door?"

"I'll see. But meanwhile, you stay in the room, and don't make a sound, okay?"

"Why?"

"Just do this for me, Ricky. Not a sound, and don't come out until I tell you to."

"Dad . . ."

But Danny was gone, closing the door behind him.

It was probably just three minutes, though it seemed much longer, before Ricky heard the two really loud sounds. They sounded like firecrackers, the ones he heard last July Fourth, when he and his mom and dad had gone to the park. These sounds were so loud that they even woke up Sebastian, who looked around, puzzled, and then nodded off again.

Another five minutes went by, and Ricky didn't hear anything, though he had his ear pressed against the door. His father had told him not to come out of the room, but that was an edict that couldn't last forever, could it?

So Ricky waited five more minutes, and then opened the door slowly, and went to the top of the steps, looking down. "Dad?"

No answer, no sound, no sign of his father. So he took another few steps down, calling out again, but not getting a response.

So Ricky went down a little farther, and peered around the landing. He was only eight years old, but what he saw then would stay with him if he lived to be a hundred.

And like any eight-year-old would do in that situation, he ran back upstairs, and started to cry.

It's all come down to this," says Edna. "All the hours . . . all the work . . ."

I could, if I were so inclined, point out the irony of that statement. Edna has been in my employ for fourteen years, and "work" is something she has successfully avoided for fourteen of those years.

But I don't mention that, because I am Andy Carpenter, The Considerate One, and because Laurie Collins is staring daggers at me, knowing what I'm thinking.

The truth is that even if Laurie wasn't sending me this silent threat, I wouldn't say anything. This is too important to Edna, and I don't want to do anything to spoil her moment.

We are in the coffee shop at the Brooklyn Marriott Hotel, home of the American Crossword Puzzle Championship. The entire hotel has been taken over by the people running the tournament, the participants, and the friends and family of both. It is one of those rare sporting events that I didn't know existed, probably because bookmakers don't take bets on it.

There are four of us at the table: Edna, Laurie, Sam Willis, and myself. Sam is my accountant, and he also helps me on cases that require his considerable computer expertise. I am somewhat lacking in that area; until recently I thought rebooting a frozen computer meant twice kicking the damn thing across the room.

We've only been here for three hours, but it's been a long three hours. Spectators are only allowed in the back of the room while the competition is going on, so we opted to stay here. It turns out that even though watching people doing crosswords ranks somewhat below a Springsteen concert as exciting entertainment, waiting in a coffee shop for it to end has got to be worse.

Edna has entered the tournament for the first time this year, and the evening session ended about twenty minutes ago. She has introduced us to some of her competitors, and I've been impressed by their smarts and dedication. You really need a vast knowledge base, sort of *Jeopardy* on steroids. And there is considerable pressure; the clock is always running, and a mistake can be devastating. These people have an expertise and a talent, and what they do is not at all easy.

Edna repeats her oft-stated frustration that the prizes and media interest aren't greater. "Hockey players make millions, and there are only 500,000 of them in this country. There are fifty million people who do crossword puzzles. And what you have here, right here in this room, is the cream of the crop."

I don't point out that the number of people who do something doesn't necessarily make it a spectator sport, or generate a fortune in salaries. If it did, then instead of the Super Bowl, we'd all be watching the World Procrastination Championships, and instead of the World Series, we'd be tuning in to the International Masturbation Invitational. Actually, that might get a huge Nielsen rating.

Edna is tired and stressed, having been at it all day, and she is actually in eleventh place out of two hundred contestants. She feels she has a chance to move up in tomorrow's final day. "At this point, it's all about stamina and handling the pressure," she says.

"Mmmm," I say, since I'm not really paying attention. I'm looking toward the bar, which is unfortunately far away. The table we got was the only one open when we came in, and it's on the other side of the room from the bar. That wouldn't be a big deal, except for the fact that the only TV in the room is behind that same bar.

"Something wrong, Andy?" Laurie asks.

She's having fun with me, since she knows why I'm staring over there. The NBA final between San Antonio and Miami is on, and even though I'm not from Texas or Florida, I'm interested in the game for three reasons:

1. I bet on it.
2. I bet on it.
3. I bet on it.

I didn't bet a lot, just two hundred dollars. Since last time I looked I had thirty million of those dollars, I'm doing it more for the competition, to demonstrate that I know more than the odds makers. For the last decade, it has not been going well.

"I'm just looking for crossword celebrities," I lie. "Hey, you guys look thirsty. Anyone want a drink?"

I've been heading back and forth to the bar to get drinks for almost two hours now, so I could catch the score of the game on the television. This is not the place to get sloshed, so we've been having Diet Cokes. But by lingering at the bar each time, I've been able to catch quite a few plays.

Since everyone has already taken in so much liquid that they're about to float away, they finally draw a line and decline another drink. "How about pretzels?" I ask. "They've got some great-looking pretzels over there."

At that moment, a group of three people comes in to the coffee shop, and as they are walking past our table, one of the men sees Edna and stops. "Great job, Edna," he says. "Good luck tomorrow."

She just smiles nervously and nods, and he walks on. "Do you know who that was?" Edna asks. Then, not waiting for an answer, she says, "That was Norman Thomas."

"Wow," I say. I don't have a clue who that is, but Edna is obviously impressed, so I pretend to be as well.

Laurie, who is somewhat less into pretending than I am, asks, "Who is Norman Thomas?"

"The best puzzler in U.S. history; the Babe Ruth of crosswords. And he just told me I did a great job."

"That's terrific, Edna. Now kick his ass tomorrow," I say. "I'm going to the restroom."

I start to walk toward the restroom near the bar, when Laurie stops me and points to one much closer to our table. "There's one over here, Andy."

Since my goal is to get another look at the television, I shake my head. "I tried that one. The urinals are a little high. You wouldn't understand . . . it's a guy thing."

I head toward the restroom, which is actually a necessary stop because of all the Diet Cokes, stopping briefly at the bar to check out the status of the game. On the way back, I make a longer stop, and while I'm watching, my cell phone rings.

The caller ID says "Paterson Police," which means it's my friend Lieutenant Pete Stanton. He's the only Paterson cop who would call me, all the others would prefer to shoot me. As an obnoxious defense attorney, I'm not a department favorite.

"Hey, Pete," I say.

"Where are you?"

"At a crossword puzzle tournament."

"Wow, life in the fast lane."

"At some point I need to slow down," I say. "But right now I'm having too much fun."

"Laurie with you?" he asks.

"Yup."

"I need you both down here."

"Where?"

"Thirty-third. Between eighteenth and nineteenth. Leave now."

"What's going on?"

"Danny Diaz got himself killed."

"Shit, I'm sorry," I say. "But what do you need me for?"

"I'll tell you when you get here. Just make sure you bring Laurie."

Click.

I don't know much about Danny Diaz.

All I know is that Pete arrested him, probably five years ago, on an assault charge. He served some time in prison, but when he got out he was fairly successful in turning his life around. Pete took an interest in him, and I think he works as a mechanic, or something like that.

Pete actually mentioned him a few months ago, when Diaz's wife left him. I'm not sure of the details, and I really had no reason to be interested. But I do know that Pete liked him a lot, and has a pretty close relationship with Diaz's son.

What I don't know is why he wants me to come down to the scene. "It doesn't make sense," I say to Laurie in the car. "Even if they've arrested someone, why would Pete want me to represent the suspect? If he thought the person was innocent, why arrest him in the first place?"

"We'll know soon enough," Laurie says.

"And why would he make it such a point that you come, unless you're going to be involved as well?" Since Laurie is a former cop and my private investigator, perhaps Pete thinks that I'll need her expertise for whatever he has in mind for me.

It's fair to say that I'm not happy about this. I sure as hell don't want a client, but I have trouble saying no to friends, and Pete is a good one. "No," I say.

"What are you talking about?" Laurie asks.

"I'm practicing saying 'no' to Pete."

"Maybe he won't be asking you to do anything. A friend of his died; maybe he just wants another friend there to comfort him."

"You think he wants me around for comfort? For moral support? Me?"

She thinks for a few moments, then, "You're right. Keep practicing."

"No, Pete," I say. "Pete, no, I just can't. No means no. Pete, which part of no don't you understand?"

We arrive at the Thirty-third Street block that Pete directed us to, and it's not hard to tell which is Danny Diaz's house. While the houses are all basically the same size and shape, and are separated only by narrow driveways, one stands out from the others. This is mainly because there are at least ten police cars, lights flashing, in the street in front of it.

As is the case in all major crime scenes, a whole bunch of cops are outside, standing around and waiting for something to do. A number of them are handling crowd control, though the neighbors that have gathered seem to be standing peacefully behind barricades.

But the real action must be going on inside, and that's where Laurie and I start heading, at least until we run into one of Paterson's finest. His name is Sergeant William Costello, a genial guy who has a smile for pretty much everyone but me.

I embarrassed him on the witness stand about four years ago. He deserved it, but he sort of never saw it that way, and mentioned to me about six months later that he was pondering ripping my eyes out and feeding them to his cat. Somehow, a close friendship never sprang from that.

"Where do you think you're going?" he sneers. Then, when he sees Laurie, he brightens. They know each other from back when she was on the force. "Pete called and asked us to come down," she says.

He looks at us both, then says to Laurie, "You. Not him."

Laurie looks at me, as if for guidance, and I say, "Go ahead. I'll wait out here with Wyatt Earp."

Laurie goes inside, and I wait there for five minutes, with Costello frequently looking over at me as if he's afraid I might take one of the barricades, slip it into my pocket, and walk off with it.

Laurie finally comes out, and she's with Pete. She waves to me, but they don't head in my direction; instead they go next door to another house, with Pete carrying what looks like a small suitcase. I don't know what is going on, but it's a safe bet that whatever it is, I'm not a crucial part of it.

Costello looks over at me again, and I say, "You are doing one hell of a job. I've never felt safer."

After another ten endless minutes, Pete comes out of the house next door, and walks over to me. "Come on," he says, and as I follow him past the barricades, I offer Sergeant Costello my sweetest smile.

"What's going on?" I ask Pete.

"I need you to do me a favor."

"What is it?" I say, as we're approaching the house. Before he can answer, I hear a dog barking.

"Did Diaz have a dog?" I ask.

"He did."

"And you want me to take it?"

"I do."

The request is not a surprise, and an easy one to grant. My former client, Willie Miller, and I have a dog rescue group called the Tara Foundation, named after my golden retriever. Unless Diaz's dog is Cujo reincarnated, we can find it a great home with no problem.

"I can do that," I say. "No need to worry."

"Well, there's more to the favor," Pete says. "Actually, quite a bit more."

We reach the front door of the house, and enter. "What else?"

"I think I'll let Laurie tell you about it."

Before I get a chance to ask him what the hell he is talking about, we turn the corner of the foyer into the den. Standing there is Laurie, and in her left hand is a leash, at the end of which is a basset hound.

But for the moment, I'm more concerned with what is in her right hand. It's another hand, much smaller, which is attached to a small arm, which in turn is attached to a small boy. The hand, arm, and boy are all human.

Uh-oh.

"Andy, this is Ricky," she says. "And that's Sebastian."

I don't say anything; I just turn and look at Pete. "It's a pretty big favor," he says. "I will definitely owe you one." Then, to Laurie, he says, "Call me and let me know how things are going, okay?"

She nods. "I will."

Pete then leans over and gives Ricky a kiss on the top of his head. "See you soon, Ricky."

"Bye, Uncle Pete."

"Ricky and Sebastian are coming home with us for a while," Laurie says.

"ARE YOU OUT OF YOUR MIND?!" is what I'm thinking. What my mouth winds up saying is, "Great. Good to meet you, Ricky."

We head for the car, me carrying a suitcase that I assume contains Ricky's clothing, but for all I know it may have another child in it.

The day has taken an unexpected turn.

The ride home is fairly uncomfortable.

I try to make small talk with Ricky, but he's not very responsive. And I can't ask Laurie what the hell is going on while Ricky is there. Sebastian, for his part, is sound asleep. Stretched out on the backseat, he looks like a horizontal fire hydrant.

Ricky also falls asleep just before we get home, so Laurie carries him into the house. It's up to me to get Sebastian and the suitcase in, which is no easy task, but I finally get it done.

Tara, who pretty much goes with the flow, looks at me curiously when I bring in Sebastian, and they sniff each other for a minute or so. Tara is used to me bringing home strange friends, so she takes it in stride. I have no idea if Sebastian is house-trained, but I grab two leashes and take him and Tara for a walk.

Usually our walks are at least twenty minutes, but I cut this one down to ten, because I'm anxious to talk to Laurie and find out what is happening. Sebastian does what he is supposed to do, which gives me hope that he's house-trained after all.

We get back to the house, and Laurie is waiting for me downstairs. "Ricky is up in his room," she says.

"Ricky has a room?"

She nods. "The one next to ours. I'm sorry we didn't talk about this before, Andy, but I knew you wouldn't refuse Pete."

"What are you talking about? I was practicing refusing him in the car, remember?"

"That was about taking on a client. This is different; you would have agreed."

"What exactly would I have agreed to?"

"Pete has a good relationship with people at Children's Social Services. He's going to work it out so that Ricky can stay here while his future is being decided, rather than being put into the system right away."

"What kind of a time frame are we looking at?"

"Not very long," she says.

"You're saying that, but you really have no idea, right?"

"Right."

I pause a short while to take stock of the situation. It's obvious that this boat has sailed, so even if I wanted to resist it, there is no way I would get anywhere. I mean, the kid already has a room, and he is currently sleeping in it.

"So I can't swear around the house anymore?" I ask.

She smiles. "Andy, you hardly ever swear."

"I know, but it's comforting to know that I could if I want to."

"Write it out and slip it to me in a note," she says. Then, "Andy, he found his father's body."

I fully realize that I'm being selfish in being unsure about this arrangement, but selfishness has always been my default reaction. "Poor kid," I say.

"Yes."

"I was talking about me."

She smiles again; it is a smile for which I simply do not have a defense. "So was I."

"Do they know who killed Diaz?"

"I don't think so," she says. "But I really didn't get into that with Pete. He was focused on helping Ricky."

"I guess it could be worse. Pete could have had a client for me, and it would have meant me going back to work."

"God forbid."

"So what do we do now?" I ask.

"My friend Rosie Benson is a child therapist. I'll give her a call tomorrow, and hopefully she can tell us how we handle this. But my guess is we just have to make Ricky feel secure and loved. He's lost two parents in a very short time."

"Where is his mother?"

"According to Pete, she's his stepmother. But nobody seems to know where she is," she says.

"Poor kid." Now I say it with a little more feeling.

"You talking about him this time?" she asks.

"I am."

I pour Laurie and myself glasses of wine, and we sit and talk some more. Tara and Sebastian hang out with us, sound asleep. They don't seem to need wine to relax and unwind.

About an hour later we go up to bed. Laurie stops at the open door to Ricky's bedroom, and we look in. He appears to be asleep, or at least he's not moving or making a sound.

Laurie walks over to his bed, leans down, and kisses him lightly on the head. She walks back toward me, then stops and gives me a hug so sudden and intense I think she might be practicing a frontal Heimlich maneuver.

I hold on to her and realize that it is the first time I have ever seen Laurie cry.

I wake up at six-thirty, because I hear noise in the house.

As I get up, I remember about Ricky, and the fact that he's in the room next door. Somehow I had forgotten all about it during my sleep, but it comes flooding back to me.

Laurie is not in bed; she must have gotten up without my realizing it. That's fairly unusual; typically I get up first, bring us both coffee, and then take Tara for a walk. I've got a feeling we're about to enter a period in which nothing is typical.

I look in Ricky's room, but he's not there. No one is in the kitchen either; all I see are a couple of empty plates with crumbs on them sitting on the table. Apparently, the rest of the house has been up for quite a while. I hope that's not a sign of things to come.

I follow the sounds, which now seem to be muffled laughter, to the den, and look in. Tara and Sebastian are on the couch, and I can make out a human hand and bare foot under them. They are smothering Ricky, and based on the sound, he is loving it.

"Where's Ricky?" Laurie asks, to no one in particular. Then, when she sees me walk in, she smoothly switches that to, "Andy, where's Ricky?"

"I don't know," I say. "Maybe we should ask Tara or Sebastian."

Laurie asks them the question, but they don't seem inclined to respond. Finally, Ricky's head peers out from under them.

"There he is!" Laurie yells in mock surprise.

Now that the "where's Ricky?" question appears to be solved, I'm moving on to, "Where's coffee?"

I get coffee for myself and Laurie. I am a creature of habit, and by this time I am always in the den, watching the *CBS Morning News*. I used to watch the *Today Show*, until they came up with something called "The Orange Room." Basically, they go there to tell us what people are tweeting to the Today Show Orange Room. People who would take the time to tweet to the Today Show Orange Room are among the people in the world whose opinions interest me least, so I stopped watching it.

When I get back, though, the TV is on and Ricky has already chosen the station. Unless the *CBS Morning News* has switched to an all-cartoon format, I'm going to have to acquire new habits.

But he's engrossed in it, so it gives Laurie and me a little time to talk. We don't have that much more so say than we did last night, although apparently Laurie has spent enough time with Ricky this morning to pronounce him "a great kid."

Laurie is just waiting until a decent hour to call her therapist friend, Rosie Benson, and she points out that for the time being at least, we can't both be out of the house at the same time, unless we take Ricky with us. She asks if I had any plans for the day.

"I was hoping to go down to the police station and strangle Pete."

"He did the right thing in calling us," she says, and looking in on Ricky, I have to admit that she is right. He is in a much more comforting and welcoming environment than he would have been if he'd just been brought into the child welfare system, as well intentioned as the people running that system might be.

Once I'm showered and dressed, I head down to the police station to see Pete. In addition to torturing him about asking us to take Ricky and Sebastian, I want to find out if he has a long-term plan, and if he has discussed it with the proper children's agencies.

I had called ahead to make sure he would be available, but when I get there, the desk sergeant tells me that Pete has been called into the captain's office.

"He said he'd be available," I say.

"Well, he ain't."

The sergeant has no idea how long the meeting will last, and has no intention of making any effort to find out. It's another demonstration of defense attorneys being less than revered by police officers, even though I consider us to be quite lovable.

After a half hour, I decide I am not going to wait anymore, even though I basically have no place to go. "Tell him I'll see him tonight," I say.

"Do I look like a message taker?"

"Now that you mention it, you don't look bright enough. But do your best."

I call Laurie, and she tells me that she is going to meet with her therapist friend that evening, after regular office hours. She would need me to watch Ricky.

"I was going to talk to Pete tonight at Charlie's," I say.

"That's not going to work."

"Laurie, if I can't go to my favorite sports bar, drink beer, and talk drivel with my friends, then the entire system is breaking down."

"You can bring Ricky," she says. "Be good for him to get out and spend some time with you."

"Bring Ricky to a sports bar?"

"It's a restaurant," she points out. "Buy him a burger and come home early. You'll have fun. Just try not to swear, drool, or leer at women."

"You're taking all the fun out of it."

You like hamburgers?" I ask.

We're on the way to Charlie's and Ricky has been quiet. He seems uncomfortable with me, and I'm certainly uncomfortable with him, so I come up with the only question I can think of.

"They're okay," he says, without enthusiasm.

"Charlie's has the best hamburgers."

"They're okay," he repeats. I think he's still talking about hamburgers in general and not those at Charlie's. I'm afraid if I ask him to confirm that, the conversation could get bogged down.

"What do you like?"

"Fried chicken."

"Good. Because their fried chicken is even better than their hamburgers. It's not greasy, you know?"

"I guess. . . ."

That's pretty much the extent of the conversation. I'm careful about what to say, because I'm afraid he'll starting asking me questions about his father. I cannot imagine what this kid has gone through, or how he can manage to cope with it.

Laurie calls me on the cell. Just before she left the house, Pete called to talk to me, and she told him I was on the way to Charlie's. He said he'd meet me down there. Then, "How's it going with you and Ricky?"

"Good. He likes fried chicken; grease doesn't seem to be much of a factor. Hamburgers are okay."

When I get to Charlie's, Vince Sanders is already sitting at our regular table. Vince is a friend, but not exactly a ray of sunshine. Exposing Ricky to him could legitimately be called child abuse.

Vince stares at us as we walk to the table, his mouth open in shock. "Vince, this is Ricky Diaz," I say, with an emphasis on "Diaz." Vince is editor of the local paper, and the murder of Ricky's father was on the front page, so he should be able to put two and two together. "Ricky, say hello to Vince Sanders."

"Hello," Ricky says.

"Hey, kid. You want something to drink?"

"Sure. What is there?"

"You got a fake ID?"

"Vince . . . ," I say.

"I just figured maybe a light beer," Vince explains.

Pete comes into the restaurant and walks toward the table. He looks stressed about something, but makes an effort to brighten up when he sees Ricky there. "Hey, Rick, how's it going? These guys treating you okay?"

Ricky nods happily when he sees Pete, offering up a smile that had so far been reserved for Laurie. I guess Vince and I don't bring out the best in kids.

Pete leans over and whispers to me, "You and I need to talk."

"You got that right."

I'm not sure when we're going to have that talk, since we clearly can't do so in front of Ricky. So instead we just watch some sports and order hamburgers. Ricky orders a chocolate milk, which causes Vince to cringe and ask, "What is that? Milk, like with chocolate in it?"

The door opens and two men come in, both of whom look familiar to me. Pete sees them as well, and he seems to tense up as they head toward our table. He stands up and says to me, "Come on."

"Come on where?"

"Follow me. Vince, hang out with Ricky for a few minutes."

I get up as well, and we take three steps toward the door when the two men reach us. By now I recognize them as two of Pete's colleagues on the force. "Hey, Pete," one of them says. "We need to talk with you."

"So talk."

"Let's do it outside."

Pete nods and starts to follow them. I'm sort of frozen in place, which is generally my default position in life. "Come on," Pete says to me.

"What's going on?"

"You need to be there," he says, clearing up absolutely nothing in the process.

I follow them outside, and there are three uniformed patrolmen waiting for us. One of the detectives who had entered the restaurant starts reciting the Miranda warning, signifying an arrest, but there doesn't seem to be anyone there to arrest.

Then I realize that they are talking to Pete, and he doesn't seem at all surprised by it.

"What the hell is going on?" I ask, but for the moment no one answers me.

"I'm sorry, Pete, but we need to cuff you."

Pete nods his assent to this, and puts his hands behind his back to facilitate them doing so.

"What are you charging him with?" I ask.

"What is your role in this?" the detective asks me.

"He's my attorney," Pete says.

"So what is the charge?" I repeat.

"Pete Stanton has been charged with the murder of Danny Diaz."

I know you understand the system," I say to Pete, before they take him away. "But it's a different system when you're on the other side. So do not say one word without me present, okay? Not one word."

He nods. "Got it."

"I'll follow you down there."

He shakes his head. "No, there's nothing you can do tonight. I'll get processed, and that takes time. And you can't leave Ricky with Vince; he's been through enough."

It is Pete's attempt to lighten the situation, but the strain in his face makes that impossible. Having said that, he is right about my inability to do anything tonight. "Okay, I'll be there first thing in the morning."

They put Pete into a waiting squad car, and I go back into the restaurant. Vince and Ricky seem to be engaged in an actual conversation, and when I get there, Vince says, "Hey, this kid knows more about sports than you do. Of course, this napkin knows more about sports than you do."

"Thanks, Vince. Ricky, we have to leave."

"We do?" Ricky asks, clearly not relishing the prospect. "Where's Uncle Pete?"

"We do. Uncle Pete had to go. We'll see him later. Vince, call me . . . we need to talk."

He nods; Vince is no dummy and can sense something is wrong.

Ricky says, "Goodbye, Uncle Vince."

Uncle Vince?

Ricky is quiet again on the way home, which gives me time to think, and that turns out to give me time to get angry. I'm sure they have what they consider good reason to arrest Pete, but there is no way he's guilty. He's as good a cop and human being as anyone I know, and him being put in cuffs and taken away is not how he deserves to be treated.

As we pull up at home, Laurie is arriving as well. She gets out, and I can see by her face that she knows what's happening. "I was listening to the news on the radio," she says, not wanting to reveal more in front of Ricky.

We go inside, and while she is getting Ricky ready for bed, I take Tara and Sebastian for a walk. When Laurie and I have something serious to talk about, we often do so while strolling in the park with Tara. It's a little jolting that Ricky's presence prevents that, but nothing I can't deal with.

By the time I get back, Ricky is in bed, and Laurie is waiting for me in the den, two glasses of wine already poured. "Were you there when it happened?" she asks.

"I was. They took him right out of Charlie's."

"Did Ricky witness it?"

"No, the actual arrest was outside. Ricky doesn't know what happened."

"Good," she says, obviously relieved. "Now tell me everything you know."

"That won't take long. I don't know a thing."

"You have to represent him. You know that, right?"

"Of course."

I haven't had any interest in taking on new clients for a very long time, the inevitable result of substantial personal wealth, and very substantial personal laziness. But I do not have to be convinced to help Pete; he is as good a friend as I have ever had.

"In fact, let's get it started." I call Hike Lynch, the lawyer who helps me out when we actually do take on a case. He is an outstanding lawyer, but as downbeat a human being as there is in the hemisphere. Fortunately, I get his machine, and his message is, "This is Hike. Assuming I'm not dead, I'll call you back. If I am, I won't. Whatever."

I assume that he's alive, and leave word for him to be at the office for a meeting tomorrow at noon. I then call Sam Willis and tell him the same, and for good measure I throw in Willie Miller.

I also call Edna, but don't reach her either. I leave a message for her about the meeting. I feel guilty that I never called to ask how the tournament came out, but with all that has been going on, it just slipped my mind. I say on the message that I want to hear all about it, and to some degree I do. I just have a lot of other, more important stuff to worry about right now.

I leave it up to Laurie to call Marcus Clark, for a couple of reasons. For one, she is the only person who can understand the few words that he says. But more importantly, like everyone besides Laurie, I am scared to death of Marcus. I actually think he could beat me up, or much worse, through the phone.

Everybody we reach agrees to meet at my office at noon. It's going to be a long night tonight; I basically have no idea why Pete was arrested, or what any of the facts are. We're going to have to hit the ground running; the first days of an investigation are usually the most important. But I can't get started until I have information, and that won't happen until tomorrow at the earliest.

"We're going to be really busy," I say to Laurie. I then add, pointedly, "Both of us."

She knows that I'm talking about the situation with Ricky. My role in this is obvious, and so is Laurie's. She's my lead investigator. Ricky's presence is going to be difficult to accommodate with all this going on.

"We'll make it work, Andy."

"So which one of us can't attend the meeting tomorrow? One of us has to be home, and we can't bring him with us. Taking him to a sports bar to meet Vince is shaky enough; having him sit in on a meeting about defending the man charged with killing his father would be a bit much."

"We'll have to arrange some kind of child care. Andy, these next few months can affect his entire life."

"Okay . . . then why don't we have the meeting here instead of my office?" I ask.

"That's a great idea. Thank you; I'll make the calls."

I shake my head. "I'll take care of it. I won't be doing much sleeping anyway."

Pete's a big boy who can take care of himself, but I still feel for him. He's in a position that is as scary as it gets, and no one is immune to the fear.

I know what he is feeling, but I don't know what he is thinking. Most importantly, I don't yet know what he knows.

It is definitely going to be a long night.

I'm out of bed at six a.m.

I should be tired, because I've slept very little, but I'm not. I'm anxious to get started; it's not a feeling I've had concerning work in a very long time.

Laurie and Ricky are both still asleep. So I head out to the jail, and on the way I call Hike to give him his first assignment. I ask him to find out who has been assigned to the case in the prosecutor's office. A police captain getting charged with murder does not happen every day, and the media is already all over it, so I assume it will be one of the senior people. But I'm going to need to deal with them very soon, so I have to know who it is.

I'm not unfamiliar with the jail or the process, but this time it's a little different. Defense attorneys rank just below terrorists in the eyes of most law enforcement officers, and the ones who man the jail are no exception.

So the desk staff delights in making things as difficult as possible, with today being a notable exception. Once the sergeant hears that I am Pete's attorney, I am treated almost like a human being. He doesn't go so far as to offer me coffee, but he does tell me where the vending machine is. It's a machine I'm already familiar with.

Within ten minutes, I'm brought into a room to talk with Pete. It's record time; I don't think I've ever gotten to see a client in under an hour before. The other departure from protocol is that

Pete is not cuffed or restrained in any way; he's simply sitting at a table in a private room, waiting for me. There is an armed guard who brings me there, and one stationed outside the room, but it is still a sign of deference and concern for Pete that even I appreciate.

Usually, in first meetings like this, I can see the fear etched in the client's face, often accompanied by bewilderment, and sometimes embarrassment. I don't see that in Pete; his attitude is one part concern, three parts determination.

He gets to one area of the concern right away. "How's Ricky doing?"

"Good," I say. "Seems like a terrific kid, and pretty much likes everyone except me."

"You're an acquired taste."

"So I've been told. Talk to me."

"Are you my lawyer?"

"No, I'm here because I have a jail bridge game with the inmates, been doing it for years. I asked to talk to you because one of the players got paroled, so we need a fourth."

"I need to formally hire you, to pay you."

He is technically correct; there is no lawyer-client confidentiality until he hires me. "Okay, give me a dollar."

"They took everything away."

"So give me a verbal IOU for a dollar."

"You got it." Then, "Andy, no bullshit now; I've got very little money to pay you."

"I'll more than make it up by not having to buy you beers at Charlie's while you're in here. Now will you tell me what is going on?"

"Danny was working as a police informant; he's been providing information for more than three years."

"Information about what?"

"Various criminal enterprises. He'd always been tied in, even though as far as I know he'd been on the right side for a while.

Ever since he got out. I don't think he's come up with much information, but I'm not sure, since I wasn't his contact."

"What does this have to do with you?"

"Apparently he informed on me," he says.

"For doing what?"

He shrugs. "I don't know yet, but I guess we'll find out soon enough."

"You knew you were going to be arrested yesterday," I say.

He nods confirmation. "Yeah. The chief called me in on the morning of the day Danny died. He told me that Danny had given some information on me, that he couldn't discuss it, but that an investigation was ongoing. Then, the morning after the murder, he said that in light of the circumstances, they were putting me on paid leave."

"That's all he said?"

"Yeah. He wouldn't have been allowed to say more. It's policy."

"So how did you know you were being arrested?" I ask.

"Just a feeling I had. I've been around long enough that I can sense things when I talk to people. I was the walking dead."

"So you don't know what they have?"

"I don't. But whatever it is, it's either wrong or manufactured. Because I did not kill Danny."

"Who did?"

"I don't know," he said. "Danny had texted me, said he needed to see me right away, that we had to talk. I think I got there right after he was shot, but I didn't see anyone. I searched the place, but the shooter was gone. Then I called in for backup."

I nodded. "Okay. I'll keep you posted, and we'll get more into this when I see the prosecution's case. In the meantime, Ricky is fine. You think Social Services will let him stay with us?"

"Have Laurie speak to Donna Williams down there. She's a friend, and she knows the story; I talked to her yesterday. She also knows Ricky is better off with you."

"Will do."

"Then get me the hell out of here," he says.

"I'm about to start working on that now. We've got a meeting at the house. Arraignment will be in a day or two."

"Do we have a shot at bail?"

I shake my head slightly. "Not a great one, but we'll go for it." I know he understands how unlikely it is.

"Marcus going to be at the meeting?" he asks, smart enough to want Marcus on his side.

"Of course."

"Marcus costs money. Money I don't have."

"We starting with that again? It's money I do have."

"You're never going to let me forget that you did this for me, are you?"

I smile, for the first time since I've been here. "Not a chance in hell."

I basically have nothing to tell you," I say.

I'm aware that this is not the best way to get a group fired up and raring to go, but at this point I really don't have a choice.

Hike, Sam, Willie, and Marcus have come to the house, as requested, to begin the process of defending Pete. Laurie is here as well, but she lives here, and Ricky, who for the time being also lives here, is upstairs playing with some toys that Laurie got him.

"Pete doesn't know much either, at least not about the evidence. He knows that Danny informed on him for something, but doesn't know what it could be. That leads me to assume that they believe the motive was revenge, but that wouldn't be enough to make an arrest."

"So what can we do now?" Willie Miller asked the question, and I'm not surprised that he's anxious to get started. I met Willie when he had already spent seven years in prison for a crime he didn't commit, and I defended him successfully in a retrial. Of all people, he would be the most upset about Pete facing the same fate he suffered.

Willie does not really have a role to play here, but he usually finds a way to be helpful. He's a black belt in karate, and knows how to handle himself very well. He's tough as nails; not Marcus tough, but a good guy to have on our side.

"Really nothing," I say. I just wanted to get everybody together to tell you to be ready, that we want to hit the ground running. "We'll get the information soon enough in discovery. Hike, did they assign a prosecutor yet?"

He nods. "Richard Wallace."

On balance, that's good news. Wallace is one of the few prosecutors I have a good relationship with. He's honest and fair, and actually was mentored by my father, when he ran the prosecutor's office. Wallace will be relatively forthcoming and easy to deal with concerning discovery, which can occasionally be a contentious procedure.

Having said that, the only negative about Richard Wallace handling the case is a significant one. He is a tough, smart adversary, and remains unflappable in the face of my courtroom bullshit. When it comes to prosecutors, I prefer weak, dumb, and completely flappable. Unfortunately, that's a rare breed.

Edna walks in and says, "Sorry I'm late." She sits down and opens a pad to take notes, a surprisingly business-like approach. Maybe the tournament experience has changed her.

We take a little more time to set up the structure, which is no different than always. Hike will work with me, Marcus with Laurie, and Willie will freelance if we need him. Sam is an entity unto himself, and will wait to see if we need his computer skills.

I adjourn the meeting, after telling the group that we will be using my house as our headquarters, rather than the office. I move to the den and call Richard Wallace. He takes the call, starting with, "Andy, I figured you'd be the one Pete would turn to."

"Turns out Clarence Darrow is dead."

He laughs. "No wonder I haven't seen him around the courthouse lately." Then, "Haven't seen you there in a while, either."

"That's the way I like it. Can I come down?"

"Sure. I was just going to lunch," he says. "You hungry?"

"No, but if the county is buying, I'll eat like a pig."

"You're on."

He picks a restaurant called the Bonfire, which is much closer to my house than it is to his office. He's not being gracious or accommodating by making this choice; it's more about his not wanting to be seen dining with an adversary.

I get up to leave, but before I can do so, Edna comes in and closes the door behind her.

"Can we talk?" she asks.

"Sure, but I'm heading for lunch with Richard Wallace in a few minutes."

"I won't be long. I'm going to stay through this case, because I care about Pete, but then I'm going to be resigning."

"Why?" This has truly taken me by surprise.

"I finished eighth in the tournament, Andy. Eighth."

I'm not sure if she considers that good or bad, but I think it's fantastic, so that's how I react.

It turns out, she agrees. "No one has ever finished that high in their first year. They're talking about me as newcomer of the year."

"Can you make any money doing this?" I ask.

"It's not about the money."

We talk a bit more and decide to revisit it after Pete's case is completed, though she says her mind is made up. As I'm leaving, she once more reiterates her desire to do anything she can to help Pete.

Richard is waiting for me in a back booth at the restaurant, reading through a file. He looks up and smiles when he sees me, and we shake hands.

"That for me?" I ask, pointing at the file.

He shakes his head. "No, unlike defense attorneys, we prosecutors can walk and chew gum at the same time. This is another case."

"There is no other case," I say.

He nods his understanding. "Yeah, this is not going to be fun."

The waiter comes over and we order. Once he's gone, I say, "You can't think that Pete Stanton is a murderer."

"Until two days ago, I would have thought it more likely that I was. I've always considered Pete a friend."

"So why did you take the case?"

"First of all, it was explained to me that if I turned it down, people high up would be very upset."

"Why?"

"It's very high profile; apparently some people are dumb enough to think I will represent the county well."

"You could have said he was your friend, and gotten out based on that conflict."

He nodded. "Yeah, I probably could have. It would have hurt me internally, but I could have handled it. But I also want to make sure he gets a completely fair shake."

"He will."

"I know," he says. "I'm glad you're on it. But you know I'm always in it to win, and you've got an uphill climb."

"What have you got?"

He shakes his head slightly, as if sorry to report the news. "A lot; you'll start getting discovery this afternoon."

"Give me the highlights."

He shakes his head. "Let's not ruin our lunch."

When I get home, I witness a truly frightening sight.

Ricky and Marcus are in the den, playing some kind of board game. It makes me uncomfortable knowing I'm on the same planet as Marcus, but he and Ricky are yukking it up, and actually smack hands with each other in a high five. It is the first time I have ever seen Marcus hit someone that did not result in hospitalization, or worse.

Evidently Ricky is that rare kid who takes to everyone, except for me.

Edna and Laurie are in the kitchen, and Edna is regaling her with all the details of her impressive tournament finish. I get to hear about it as well, and then Laurie says, "Edna has offered to help out around here with Ricky."

"Great, Edna. Thanks. Can that start now?"

I tell them that I want to head back to the murder scene with Laurie, and have arranged with Richard Wallace for access. Edna is fine watching Ricky, so Laurie tells him that Edna will be there. Apparently, Ricky likes Edna as well, because he's totally okay with it. Between her and his good buddy, Marcus, he's seems pretty content.

Laurie and I head back to what used to be Ricky's house. Actually, it probably still is; I would think he will inherit it. I make a mental note that I need to check into whether Danny left a will. As long as Ricky is in our care, I should be protecting his rights.

One of the first things Laurie and I always do when we start a case is go to the scene of the crime. It gives us a good feel for the investigation that will follow, much better than just using the photos that have certainly been taken.

I generally like to wait until I have gone over the discovery, since I would then know what the prosecution alleges took place. But I'm so anxious to get going on this that rather than just wait for the discovery documents to arrive, it seems more productive to begin the process now.

The scene is quite different from what it was the other night, and not just because it's daylight. There are no crowds around, no police barricades, no cars with flashing lights. Except for the yellow police tape around the house, and one officer standing on the porch, you'd never guess that a person was gunned down here so recently.

The cop had received instructions through Richard's office to let us enter, and we do so. It doesn't take a trained detective to tell where Danny was standing when he was shot: there is a large bloodstain about twelve feet from the front door.

"Do we know whether he was shot in the back?" I ask.

"No, he took two bullets in the chest. Pete mentioned that the other night."

"So it's likely he wasn't running away. He probably let the killer in, otherwise he would have been shot nearer to the door."

"Ricky was up there in his room," she says, pointing. "At some point we might have to ask him what he heard."

"That can be your job."

"What did Pete say about what he saw when he arrived?"

"He said the door was slightly ajar. He pushed it open and saw Danny lying there. He started to back out of the house to call for backup, then realized Ricky might be inside. So he went back in, and heard Ricky upstairs, crying. He called for backup after that."

"Did he search the house?" she asks.

"He did, but didn't find anyone. He thinks the shooter might have gone out the back door."

We walk to the back of the house, and see telltale fingerprint powder all over the door and windows. If they lifted any prints that didn't belong to Danny or Ricky, we'll find out when we get the discovery.

We go out the back door. There's a small backyard, which borders on the equally small backyard of the house behind it, on Thirty-second Street. At night it would have been easy for somebody to get away undetected, especially since no one would have been looking for them.

On the way home, I ask Laurie what therapeutic advice Rosie Benson gave her. The thrust of it is that Ricky's reaction will not be entirely predictable; he could bury the trauma for a length of time, only for it to suddenly present itself. Or it could just be a slow process. Either way, we are to be loving and welcoming and sensitive, none of which are qualities for which I am particularly well known.

"What if he asks me questions about what happened?" I ask.

"It's important you be honest with him, Andy. Be gentle and supportive and loving, but tell the truth."

"The truth?" I ask, trying not to moan.

She nods. "But make sure you really hear the question; people sometimes have a tendency to expand their answers to include things that the child hasn't asked about. Be very specific."

"Expanding the answer will not be my problem," I say. "Did you find out if he has other family anywhere?"

"He does not, except for his stepmother, whose whereabouts are unknown. Andy, for the moment we are all he has."

Hike is waiting for us when we get home, and fortunately he is not with Ricky. Compared to Hike, exposing Ricky to Marcus and Vince is like letting him hang out with Mr. Rogers and Captain Kangaroo.

Hike has brought the initial discovery documents, which Richard Wallace had sent to our office. There isn't that much, just one boxful, and that amount of paper will increase dramatically as the weeks go by. Every time there is a significant murder case, a forest dies.

Evidence takes time to get processed in, and this case is literally unfolding in the moment. But what is here is not good.

Danny had indeed been a police informant, although the activities he was informing on are not in these documents. Apparently, he had implicated Pete with one of his reports, just before he died.

Danny had expressed concerns for his own safety, explicitly revealing a fear that Pete was a threat to exact revenge on him. While the prosecution does not have to prove motive, the jury likes to hear it, and this very definitely fills the bill.

There is also a neighbor's statement in which he claims that Pete was on the scene shortly after the shots were fired, and in fact he was. The timing of that will have to be carefully scrutinized, and we'll attack it in cross-examination.

The most damaging evidence, at least as far as these documents go, has to do with the murder weapon. It was tied to a shooting murder a year ago in Paterson, one in which a woman named Carla Kendall was killed. Pete was one of the first to arrive on the scene and investigated the case. The murder weapon was never found—at least that is what Pete reported—and no arrest was ever made. But if ballistics are to be believed, that's the weapon that killed Danny Diaz.

Even worse, a pair of gloves was found tucked beneath the backseat of Pete's car. On those gloves was gunpowder residue, and the conclusion investigators reached was that Pete fired the shots while wearing the gloves, and then quickly hid them away.

It is a powerful case, which explains why an arrest was made so quickly. And it's early on, so likely to get worse.

Laurie and Hike read through the documents as I do, and they of course come to the same conclusion.

We've got problems.

The discovery information tells us some of what we're up against.

But it also says something far more revealing. Pete isn't just an innocent man wrongly accused. He is an innocent man wrongly accused because someone specifically set it up that way.

If Pete is not guilty of the murder, which is something I am positive about, then he's been set up to take the fall. The gloves hidden in his car make that an absolute fact: they had to have been planted there, with the gunpowder residue on them.

I call Pete, and he denies putting them there, so the person who did so would have known that it would be seen as significant evidence of Pete's guilt.

On one hand, this is very bad news, in that it means we're against a smart, determined enemy, in addition to the prosecution. But it also presents an opportunity, in that the conspirators must have a reason for doing what they're doing to Pete. So we can search for them, and we can also search for that reason. If we achieve either goal, we win.

Of course, Pete's occupation makes the task more daunting. He's a cop, and has been one for many years. That means there is no shortage of people, in and now out of jail, who have a reason to hold a grudge against him. And those people are by definition criminals, and dangerous.

Of course, the best person to tell me who those people might be is Pete himself, so I head back to the jail. Once again I'm treated with deference when I arrive and ask for Pete; maybe I am likable after all. I make a mental note to bring and hand out lollipops next time I come.

I get to the room first, and Pete is brought in a couple of minutes later. "It's a weird feeling being happy to see you," he says.

He's saying that as the casual insult we as friends always hurl at each other, but this one has some meaning behind it. As Pete's lawyer, not only am I the one true friend he has in his current predicament, but I am his lifeline to the outside world.

If he is going to hear any good news, he knows that I am the one that will deliver it. It's the same way with all my clients, and it's not a position I relish, because good news in these situations is always in short supply.

"It's nice to be loved for who I am," I say.

"Yeah. What have you got?"

I describe the prosecution's case against him, or at least what we've received so far. I'm not really into face-reading, but even if I was, I wouldn't be able to venture a guess this time. I don't see anger, or fear, or even frustration. All I see is someone listening.

When I finish, he says, "It's a setup."

That simple sentence illustrates one advantage I have with Pete that I don't have with other clients. He's a detective, an investigator; this is his profession. Not only will I not have to take the time to explain every nuance to him, but he'll be a valuable resource for Laurie and me to call on.

I nod. "So it appears."

"There are a lot of bad guys that don't like me."

"There are a lot of good guys that don't like you," I say, in a misguided attempt to bring sports bar banter into a decidedly unsports-bar environment. "We just have to figure out which guys would go to these lengths to bring you down."

"Right. I'm going to have to think about this."

"Yes, you are. And while you're thinking about it, consider two categories."

"Which are?"

"People who have a grudge against you for something you did in the past. But also current cases: people who want you out of the way to stop you from doing something to them in the future."

He nods. "Good point. There are a bunch of people in that first category who might be my future roommates."

He means that many of the people who would have reason to seek revenge are in prison, mainly because of his efforts. "I know that," I say. "Once you give us names, we'll track down where they are now."

"I'll get right on it," Pete says. "And you should talk to Stan."

He means Lieutenant Stan Phillips of the Paterson Police Force. He was Pete's partner for years before Pete got promoted up to captain.

"He can't stand me," I say. I once won a case by basically demonstrating that Phillips conducted an investigation incompetently, rendering certain key evidence inadmissible. "The extent of his conversations with me for the past five years has been to call me an asshole."

Pete smiles. "He tells it like it is, that Stan. He'll talk to you; I'll get the guards to let me call him. He'll be as good a source for coming up with suspects as I am."

"And you'll mention that he shouldn't shoot me?"

He shrugs. "I'll do my best, but Stan makes his own decisions."

There's no way around it: I am lovable.

It's not a status I've gone out of my way to achieve; it has come to me naturally. I'm charming, fun to be with, kind to animals . . . basically I bring joy wherever I go.

And it can be a burden. Sometimes I admit I would just like to be Andy Carpenter, Ordinary Person, not Andy Carpenter, Mr. Wonderful. But I grin and bear it, because that is who I am.

Yet occasionally, impossible as it may be to believe, I will run into a person who fails to grasp that essential truth, who seems not to want to bask in my reflected wonder.

Lieutenant Stan Phillips of the Paterson Police Department is such a person. If I didn't already know this, his verbal greeting when he sees me waiting for him in the precinct lobby would have tipped me off. "Well, looks like the wind is blowing in a lot of garbage these days."

I'm not feeling particularly tolerant of that attitude, in fact I'm not at all in the mood for this crap, so I smile, turn, and start walking toward the door. "Where are you going?" he asks.

"To speak to my client about finding someone more cooperative to aid in his defense."

"Damn, you're a pain in the ass."

"Is that an effort to be conciliatory? Because if it is, you need some work on your technique."

"You made me look like a clown and let a guilty guy walk." He's still bitter about my blowing up his investigation with him on the stand.

"First of all," I say, "the jury said he was not guilty, and they were right. Second of all, I didn't make you look like a clown. You are a clown. I just peeled away a few layers of bullshit so everybody could see it."

He stares at me for a few moments, probably to decide whether to kill me, or talk to me. What I have on my side is that he is Pete's friend.

He makes his choice. "You want to talk about Pete?"

"That's all I want to talk about."

"Come on," he says, and turns and heads for his office, with me following. It's a win for me, though I don't think I'm going to see him at Andy Carpenter Fan Club meetings any time soon. It's just as well; they're overcrowded anyway.

On the way to his office, we pass by Pete's, which I have been in a bunch of times. It's closed, the shades are drawn, and there is KEEP OUT tape blocking the door. It doesn't surprise me, but it pisses me off.

Phillips sees me looking at the door, and then we make eye contact, sharing our common feelings about what has happened to Pete. We don't hug, but it's a bonding moment.

When we get to his office, he hands me a legal pad that was on his desk. "This is all I have so far. There will be more."

"What is it?" I ask.

"A list of scumbags who could be setting Pete up. I left off the two-bit guys who wouldn't have a clue how to go about it."

"This is great," I say, impressed by how fast Phillips has put this together.

"In cases where I know where the guy is, I wrote that down. A bunch of them are still doing time, but I included them anyway."

I guess he thinks I don't understand that, so he adds, "Cell phones. They're so easy to come by that half the inmates spend most of their time ordering pizzas."

I briefly look at the list, and then say, "I'm going to have questions about some of this."

"You ask, I'll answer," he says, and then writes something on a piece of paper and hands it to me. "It's my cell phone number; you can call me twenty-four/seven."

"Thanks, I will."

"Just get Pete out of this. He is good people."

I nod my understanding, and start to put the list into an envelope that he hands me. Then, I ask, "So if you had to pick one person on this list, gut instinct, who do you think it is?"

"I put him on the top. Tommy Haller."

Humans are creatures of habit, a basic truth that Alex Parker has always known.

It's a mostly helpful trait; it helps one organize one's life, often allowing order to cut through the chaos.

Of course, there is a negative side to it, way worse than simply limiting one's experiences to the tried and comfortable. When habits are observed and chronicled by someone wishing to do harm, the practitioner of the habits becomes vulnerable. This most often takes the form of financial fraud; when a person becomes predictable, bad things can happen.

Parker is a student of habits, most often those of strangers. He doesn't choose the people he observes; they are assigned to him. But once he has spent a few weeks with a particular subject person, he can literally predict virtually everything they will do in the course of a day.

Alex is not interested in the finances of his subject. He is not looking to use their credit cards, or tap into their bank accounts. Alex's method of operation is to find a person's most bland, commonplace, everyday patterns, and then kill that person with his own habits.

He followed Daniel Stockman for five weeks, slightly longer than usual, but not substantially so. It's not that Stockman was unpredictable; rich people are as susceptible to habit-forming as their less wealthy counterparts. But Stockman was smart, and he was careful.

Almost as careful as Alex.

It took four weeks for Alex to decide which habit to focus on, and to feel comfortable with the scenario. Stockman had breakfast every Monday morning with five other men, all business leaders of considerable personal wealth. They ate in Lucy's Diner, a busy, nondescript place that Alex felt they chose so they could appear to be "regular people."

They were not. They were rich and privileged, which by itself did not make them evil, not in Alex's eyes. In fact, Alex was anxious for the day to come when he himself was rich and privileged. He was getting there already, at a rapid pace.

Unwittingly, Daniel Stockman was about to help make it happen even faster.

Alex had become a regular at the diner, going there twice a week for breakfast. He was there every Monday, at the same time as the businessmen met for breakfast, as well as every Thursday. He did not want his presence there to be seen as in any way unusual.

Alex was not surprised that in the weeks he watched the men have breakfast, each one of them ordered the same thing every single time. Habits.

The one thing that Stockman ordered that was unique among the group was orange juice. He had it every time, and none of the others did. And best of all, at least as far as Alex was concerned, the orange juice often sat on the counter between the kitchen and the bar, waiting to be picked up by the server. It sat there an average of four minutes, but never less than two.

Once the juice was brought to the table, it was no longer a viable target. There were too many men sitting there; any diversion that would do the trick would have to be large, and therefore attention attracting. That was simply not Alex's style.

But while the juice was sitting on the counter, it was fair game. It was even easy for Alex to approach it; there was a wastepaper basket in front of it and slightly to the left. Alex would have a reason to go there, to deposit a piece of trash.

That's not all he would deposit.

He tried it on the fourth week, but had to abort the operation. The server picked up the juice and food slightly faster than usual, and he was approaching as Alex was about to make his move. So instead he just put the trash in the can, and went back to his table.

On the Monday of the fifth week, the coast was clear, and Alex smoothly dropped the small pill into the orange juice. He was positive he was unobserved in the process, and he went on to the bathroom before returning to his table.

If the men took their usual amount of time at the breakfast, the pill would take effect about the time they were getting the check. But on that day they got up slightly earlier than usual, so it wasn't until he was outside and nearing his car that Daniel Stockman fell to the pavement.

The commotion reached into the restaurant, and Alex went outside along with everyone else to see what had happened. They were already administering CPR to Daniel Stockman, which Alex knew was a complete waste of time.

The newspapers would publish stories in which his colleagues and family members professed shock, since Stockman had been a runner and the picture of health. They would go on to report that the autopsy results revealed that Daniel Stockman died of a massive heart attack.

And those results were correct: the cause of death was in fact a heart attack. But unless the autopsy was performed within one half hour of death, an obvious impossibility, there would be no way to know the cause of Daniel Stockman's heart attack.

The cause was the little white pill, and Alex Parker.

Arraignments are very boring, and usually inconsequential.

They are basically a formality. The charges are read, though everyone already knows what they are. The defendant pleads not guilty, which also comes as absolutely no surprise to anyone. Bail is set or not set, again with the decision basically preordained, and a trial date is scheduled, albeit tentatively.

There is nothing that takes place that couldn't be accomplished between the judges and the opposing lawyers in thirty seconds, if it were done in an office. But it's in court, with all the trappings, so it moves way too ponderously.

It's the setup that makes it so anticlimactic. A crime has been committed, and the state is about to try to take away a man's freedom, or even his life. All the important players are put into a room for the first time, and it's a human reaction to expect fireworks, or at least drama.

And it's a human reaction to be disappointed when there is none.

One thing that the arraignment does accomplish is letting me know what the media interest in the trial will be. Whenever a cop is accused of murder, the case is followed pretty closely. Today's strong turnout by the press is an indication that this case will continue that tradition.

Richard Wallace and three members of his team are already in court when I arrive with Hike and Laurie. He walks over to me and we shake hands. "This is not going to be fun," he says.

"That is the last thing you're going to say in this court that I'll agree with."

He smiles. "I would expect nothing less. We have any reason to talk later?"

He's asking if Pete and I would consider plea bargain negotiations. "Zero."

He nods. "That's what I figured, though I'm not sure whether I wanted to hear it or not."

"Pete wants the trial at the earliest possible date," I say, because it's true.

Richard nods. "Okay." I'm sure he's surprised; quick trials are not usually the approach the defense takes.

But Pete made it very clear to me that he wants this behind him, and even though I don't think it's in his best interest to rush, he insisted on it. He has more confidence in me than the current situation warrants.

I hear a noise, turn, and see guards bringing Pete into the room. His hands are cuffed in front of him, which annoys me no end, but in the short term there is nothing I can do about it. Long term, I'm going to shove those cuffs down the state of New Jersey's throat.

Pete has a thin folder under his arm, which he gives to me when he sits down, doing so awkwardly, because of the cuffs. "It's the list of possibles you asked me to come up with. I'm sure I'll think of more."

"Good."

"Did you talk to Phillips?" he asks.

"I did. He's a fun guy. But he gave me a list as well."

Pete knows the drill very well, so I don't have to prepare him for what is to come. Very often clients are excited to be out of jail and have the world paying attention to them, and they think that something good could happen. Pete knows better, which for his lawyer is a relief.

Judge Cynthia Matthews is presiding, and unless some conflict develops, it is very likely that she will be on the bench for the actual trial. I'm fine with that; she's smart, fair, and in the past has been willing to tolerate my courtroom style more than most.

The charges are read, and Pete is asked how he pleads. He answers "Not guilty," in a voice that is firm and confident. I'm glad about that, though legally his tone of voice is of no consequence. It's of some small importance only because the media will report on it, and the future jury is out there hearing about this through the media.

Once that is out of the way, I request that bail be set. Richard immediately responds that the seriousness of the crime dictates that my bail request be denied. Precedence is firmly on his side; murder defendants very rarely get released on bail.

"Your Honor," I say, "Captain Stanton has had an exemplary career as a public servant. He has never once been charged with a crime; there has never been the hint of any wrongdoing on his part. We will demonstrate he has been wrongly accused here, but that will take some time.

"He is innocent until proven guilty, and he will never be proven guilty. To deprive him of his freedom in such a situation is unfair and unnecessary."

Judge Matthews turns to Richard for a response. If he has any sympathy for Pete, one would not know it by his words. He argues effectively that Pete should be considered both a threat to the community and a flight risk.

I quickly respond. "Your Honor, I would propose a very substantial bail, and the defendant can be subject to house confinement, with an ankle bracelet to monitor his movements. But there is one more thing, Your Honor. Are you familiar with the name Frank McCoy?" I see Richard grimace when I mention the name.

"No, I am not," she says. "What does Mr. McCoy have to do with this case?"

"Sergeant McCoy was a Newark police officer, convicted on corruption charges, and sentenced three years ago to ten years in prison. He was murdered six months into his sentence."

"And your point is?"

"My point is that prisons are a dangerous place for police officers. Some of the inmates are only there because of Captain Stanton's efforts to protect the public."

Richard interjects. "Is Mr. Carpenter suggesting that New Jersey does not have the ability to protect the defendant?"

I turn to Richard. "I would imagine that Sergeant McCoy's family would be somewhat skeptical of that ability. But let's assume for the moment that the prison authorities would take the necessary steps to keep Captain Stanton safe. How much would that cost? And would he have to live in solitary confinement? Is that a fair reward for arresting criminals?"

Turning back to the judge, I say, "House arrest and electronic monitoring should be more than sufficient, but if it would make the court feel more secure, the defense would be willing to pay for guards at the defendant's house. And we would find a significant bail to be appropriate and acceptable."

I can feel Pete staring at me, but I don't turn to look at him. Instead, I continue, hoping to close the deal. "The defendant would be confined, the public safety would be ensured, and there would be no expense to the government. It is the textbook definition of a win-win."

I consider asking that he be allowed to stay at my house instead, but I'm afraid the state would then make Ricky leave, since living with his father's accused murderer might not be viewed by Children's Services as ideal.

Richard renews his objections, and Judge Matthews takes a few moments to consider her decision. "Very well," she finally says. "The defendant will be confined to his own house, with electronic monitoring, and round-the-clock police guards, paid for by the defense."

Richard, accepting the defeat, says, "Your Honor, a search warrant is being executed on the defendant's house this afternoon. Therefore we would request that he remain in custody until tomorrow."

"I was going to suggest tomorrow anyhow," she says. "To that end, Mr. Wallace, please provide the court by tomorrow morning a full plan for how the house detention would be executed."

"Yes, Your Honor," Richard says.

Judge Matthews continues. "Bail is set at $750,000."

She adjourns the proceeding, and Pete immediately says, "Andy, I don't have $750,000. I'm short about $749,000."

"Really?" I ask. "What have you been doing with all the money you haven't been spending on beer and hamburgers?"

"Andy, what the hell are you doing?"

"I'm loaning you the money, interest free. Assuming you don't skip bail, I'll get it back. If you do skip bail, I'll hunt you down and shoot you like the animal that you are."

"Andy, I can't let you do this."

"If the situation was reversed, would you do it for me?"

"Not a chance in hell."

"Good. That proves I'm a better person than you." As the guard comes over to take him, I tap him on the shoulder and say, "Hang in there. You're out tomorrow."

Tommy Haller is, at his core, a very successful businessman.

He started an operation from scratch, found a product that there was a demand for, and brought that product to market. He has managed to maintain and increase his market share, and is known to be fiercely competitive.

It would be fair to say that Tommy is living the American dream, if not for the fact that the products he sells are hard, illegal drugs. And if not for the fact that he often eliminates his competitors by killing them.

Organized crime in northern New Jersey has long been dominated by Dominic Petrone, but Petrone is aging, and his grip is loosening. On his worst days, Petrone, while responsible for countless illegal activities, including murder when he deems it necessary, is Mother Teresa compared to Tommy Haller.

Petrone has never shown much enthusiasm for the drug trade, and that reticence allowed others to move in. At one point the main operative in the area was one Carlos Quintana, a truly psychotic killer whose demise I helped organize, in order to prevent my own. It was not my finest hour, but it allowed me to continue to have hours.

With Quintana out of the picture, others rushed to fill the vacuum, especially with Petrone not inclined to stamp out competition, as he had in the glory days. Haller proved the most resourceful and ruthless, and he gradually ascended to the top by killing off his challengers one by one. He is brutal and apparently without conscience, though marginally more reasonable and level-headed than Quintana was. And most importantly, unlike Quintana, he is smart enough to manage to peacefully coexist with Petrone.

Tommy Haller is at the top of the lists prepared by both Pete and Phillips as someone who is most likely to exact revenge against Pete. About a year ago, Pete arrested Tommy's brother, Jimmy, on an assault charge. It seems that Jimmy was in a dispute with a customer who found himself unable to pay for goods received.

Jimmy, clearly not the sharpest tool in the Haller shed, attempted to buy his way out of difficulty by offering Pete a substantial bribe. The effort earned him an additional felony charge, but the importance of that paled somewhat when the assaulted customer subsequently died of his injuries.

Pete's testimony at Jimmy's trial helped the state of New Jersey put him away for a sentence of forty years to life, and it came as no surprise to anyone that brother Tommy had expressed some displeasure with Pete's efforts.

"I think it's unlikely that Haller is behind this," Laurie says.

"Why?"

"Not his style; there's way too much finesse involved. If he wanted to go after Pete, he'd just try to put a bullet in his head."

I basically agree with her, although I can't be close to sure, since I've never had the pleasure of meeting Haller. We travel in different circles: he doesn't attend crossword puzzle tournaments, and I avoid drug kingpin conventions.

"I need to talk to him," I say, regretting the words even as I am saying them.

"Why?"

"To get a sense of him; to decide if he's worth looking into. We don't have a lot of time, or a lot of people, and we can't chase down blind alleys."

"So you're just going to go talk to Tommy Haller," she says, her tone indicating she considers me out of my mind.

"I'm going to try."

"*We* are going to try" is how she corrects me. "There is no way you are doing this alone."

"I hope the 'we' includes Marcus," I say.

She nods. "Of course it does. I'll call him."

While she does that, I have a little time to think about how to allocate the limited time and resources at our disposal. It's a more difficult task in this case, because we have three distinct, and very different, directions that we must take.

First is the traditional defense: we must try and prove that Pete is innocent of the crime. If we can do that, which is going to be a tall order, then nothing else matters.

Second, we can try to figure out who actually committed the murder. To do so, we will need to dig into Danny Diaz's life, and his death, and reveal who had the motive and opportunity to kill him.

Third, and this is the area that Tommy Haller falls neatly into, we need to figure out who set Pete up to take the fall. There is no question that the answers to questions two and three will be the same, but we can go after that answer from both directions.

Laurie comes back into the room and says, "Marcus will be here whenever we need him."

"What did he say?"

"What did Marcus say?" Laurie asks, somewhat incredulously. Marcus never says anything, beyond a well-placed grunt or two.

"Does he know Haller?" I ask.

"I don't think so."

"Is he worried about dealing with him?" I ask.

"Marcus? You're asking me if Marcus is worried? If Marcus was worried, he wouldn't be Marcus. He'd be Andy."

It isn't easy to make an appointment with Tommy Haller.

There's no phone number to call where the receptionist answers and says, "Drug-land . . . may I help you?" Haller doesn't seem to have an admin setting his schedule, at least not one I know how to reach.

Whether or not he has any information to provide, I can't imagine he'll be interested in talking with us. The defense has no ability to force potential witnesses to submit to a deposition, but even if we did, it wouldn't apply to a situation like Haller's. At this point we couldn't begin to demonstrate that he has any relevance to our case.

I call Lieutenant Phillips and ask where I can find Haller, and he asks, "Why would you want to find Tommy Haller?"

"So I can talk to him."

"Who might your next of kin be?"

That doesn't sound particularly encouraging, but I persist and he tells me the address of the place where Haller is known to work out of, sort of his headquarters. It's on Bergen Street in Paterson, an area that is not for the faint of heart. Which is a problem, because my heart is considerably fainter than most.

Bergen Street runs up to and dead-ends at the Passaic River. It's an area that used to flood frequently, as a good rain would make the river overflow. They finally did something to mitigate that, so the people who live and work there did not need access to canoes on a regular basis.

Because it's a dead end, the only way out is to reverse the way in. When I'm in situations that involve any kind of physical danger, I have a tendency to focus on the "how to get out" part. This address is not a great setup for that, especially since Haller's location is at the very end of the street, right on the river.

I drive, with Laurie in the passenger seat and Marcus in the back. As we get close, I appear to be the only one of us who is nervous, though Laurie seems to be on alert. I look back at Marcus, and he is either meditating, or asleep.

We arrive at Haller's at ten o'clock in the morning. Marcus tells me to park halfway down the block, at least a hundred yards from Haller's place. I have no idea why, and I don't ask. In situations like this, Marcus's decisions are not to be questioned. At least not by me.

I tell myself that this is no big deal. Even though Haller has a reason to hate Pete, he's still something of a long shot to be involved in the current case, and that actually lessens the danger here. We'll ask a couple of questions, he'll deny them, and we'll leave. No harm, no foul.

There are three steps leading up to Haller's door, in what was probably once a two-family house. A very large individual sits on the top of the steps, back against the wall, just to the side of the door. He watches us as we walk up the street, probably wondering if we are coming all the way to him. I imagine very few uninvited people do that.

When we reach him, it's clear that he is even larger up close than he seemed at a distance. He's borderline enormous; I actually think he could swallow me without chewing more than once or twice.

He doesn't say anything, just stares, so I feel obligated to break the ice. "We're here to see Tommy Haller."

"That right?" he asks.

"That's exactly right," I confirm.

"What for?"

I clearly have no interest in telling him why we're here, so I say, "We're from Publishers Clearing House. He's won a substantial prize."

"Get lost, assholes."

I don't take kindly to anyone calling Laurie an asshole, but basically that is what he has done. Either Marcus or I is going to defend her honor, and I figure I'll let Marcus take first crack at it.

Marcus doesn't seem to have taken offense, but nor does he seem intimidated. He motions for us to follow him, and he starts walking up the steps. The Enormous One at first seems surprised, but then starts to rise to intercept Marcus.

What happens next is a blur, so fast and so barely perceptible that if I didn't see the result, I would question whether it happened at all. Marcus makes a quick movement; it seems like he flicks out his elbow. From my vantage point, I don't see it hit anything, but I hear a crunching noise.

Enormous no longer is getting up, in fact he sits back down in the same position he was in before, back against the wall. The only difference is that he is no longer conscious, which is fine with me. He's actually more fun to be with this way.

There are two windows in the front of the building, and they are shaded so that one cannot look in from the outside. But there is the chance that someone inside has seen what transpired, and Marcus seems to take that into consideration. Rather than knock on the door, he puts his ear to it, listening.

I don't hear anything, because my heart is pounding so loudly that it's hard to hear over it. Marcus seems to hear something, though, because he hesitates, as if trying to figure out his next step.

As steps go, it turns out to be a beauty.

Marcus kicks forward and up, and it's amazing to watch. His foot hits the door so high, it's actually over his head, yet he doesn't seem to launch himself in the air to do so, and he maintains perfect balance coming down. The Rockettes have never kicked that high, and I hate to use this word describing Marcus, but they've also never looked so graceful.

It is as if the door explodes, crashing forward, leaving an empty space where there once was a door. We move forward, following Marcus, as he steps on the fallen door into the room.

As I also step on the door, it seems unsteady, and I realize with some horror that there is a person under it. I know that because I can see a foot sticking out, and a voice obviously attached to that foot is screaming in pain.

Marcus steps on an area that sounds like where the voice might be coming from, and the voice stops. It is only then that I actually look into the room, and it is nothing like what I expected. It's modern, with chrome office furniture, and artwork on the walls. It all seems so out of place that I feel like we stepped into a different dimension by accident.

Tommy Haller is sitting at a desk; I recognize him from photos. If he's upset by what he's witnessed, he's not showing it. "You Marcus Clark?" he asks.

I assume he isn't talking to Laurie or me, but Marcus doesn't seem interested in answering, so I fill the breach. "In the flesh," I say. "He's a personal friend of mine; we're very close."

Haller doesn't look at me; he can't seem to take his eyes off Marcus. "I heard of you," he says. Then, maybe thinking we hadn't understood, or were questioning the veracity of his statement, he repeats, "Yeah, I've heard of you."

"Great," I say. "That makes us all feel closer. Let's talk about Pete Stanton."

Haller continues to ignore me, reminding me in the moment of every girl I went to high school with. He stares at Marcus, while slowly reaching into a drawer and taking something out. It's a gun, which would not have been my first choice of things to come out of that drawer. For example, I would have preferred M&M'S.

He points the gun at Marcus, who does not seem to consider this a negative development, or a positive one. "You know what this is?" he asks Marcus.

Suddenly there is a loud firecracker sound, and the gun goes flying out of Haller's hand and onto the floor. He looks as stunned as I am, which is way up on any stun-o-meter that might be measuring the event. We both look to the other side of the room, where Laurie is holding her own gun, and pointing it at Haller.

There's no other conclusion to be reached other than she literally shot the gun out of Haller's hand, a feat the Lone Ranger would be proud of.

"The next one goes in your head, asshole," she says. Laurie, if I haven't mentioned this before, is not to be confused with a delicate flower.

At that moment, Enormous staggers into the room, having somewhat recovered from whatever Marcus did to him. He looks groggy, and when Laurie says, "Sit down," he sees the gun and eagerly heads to the nearest chair.

"You just made a big mistake," Haller says to Laurie. The net effect of that statement is that Marcus seems to edge slightly toward Haller, the first movement of any kind since we settled in. He isn't crazy about anyone threatening Laurie, and Haller is smart enough to pick up on it.

"Okay," Haller says, raising his palms in a gesture of surrender. "What do you want?"

I jump in again. "As I mentioned, we want to talk about Pete Stanton."

"That piece of shit ain't getting out of jail alive. I got people in there."

"Is that why you set him up for the Diaz hit?" I use words like "hit" to demonstrate my street cred; I am as cool as they come.

"What the hell you talking about?"

"Why did you hit Diaz?"

"Who is . . . is that the guy Stanton iced?"

I didn't come here for a confession, or for Haller to unburden his soul to us. I am here looking for a reaction, so that I can judge whether it is real or not.

This is real.

It's clear that Tommy Haller had nothing whatsoever to do with killing Danny Diaz, or setting Pete up to take the fall for it.

But at least we had a fun morning.

Edna is helping Ricky with his homework when we get home.

That is unusual in itself, since it's almost July, and school doesn't start until September.

The mystery is cleared up when Edna speaks. "What's a four-letter word for 'king of the jungle'?"

"What are the letters?" Ricky asks.

She points. "See this? The first letter is an 'l.'"

Ricky thinks for a moment, then brightens. "Lion!"

Edna looks up at us and says, "The kid is good." Tara and Sebastian, who are lying on a blanket together munching on chewies, don't seem terribly impressed.

Edna turns back to Ricky and says, "Now we need a three-letter word for insect, starting with a 'b.'" Before he can answer, she looks up at me and says, "Oh, Richard Wallace called; he said it's important."

Laurie starts to praise Ricky for his crossword puzzling prowess, while I head to the phone to call Wallace. I usually have instincts regarding when I'm about to hear good or bad news. Unfortunately, those instincts are only correct on the bad side; good news never seems to arrive when anticipated.

This time alarm bells are going off in my head; prosecutors don't call during the pretrial phase to share happy defense news.

The only question, as I dial the phone, is how bad this is going to be.

Wallace gets on the phone immediately and gets right down to business, another bad sign. Within moments, the signs are no longer important; the ominous words take over.

"There is a new development, Andy. I wanted to tell you myself before it hits the media."

"What is it?"

"We executed the search warrant on Pete's house. The officers found heroin—street value over a hundred grand."

I don't know what I expected, but it wasn't this. "That's insane, Richard."

He doesn't seem inclined to take my word for it. "It's real, Andy."

"I would be involved with drugs before Pete would," I say, and I mean it. Pete is about the most antidrug person I know. In fact, I once did him a favor and defended his brother on a drug charge. I got him off on a technicality, but the scare got him to turn his life around. I saw firsthand Pete's attitude about the subject; his using or dealing heroin is not within the realm of possible reality.

"I'm sorry, Andy, but it gets worse. Diaz had informed on Pete that he was dealing. So it goes directly to motive. It's all in the discovery."

"I haven't seen that yet."

"I know," he says. "It's on the way to you. Because it involved an informant, I had to navigate some police politics before I could share it. But it's there."

"It's bullshit, Richard. This whole thing is bullshit. I don't know how the drugs got there, but they're not Pete's. And they're not evidence of murder. If there were drugs in that house, they were planted there by someone other than Pete."

"One way or another, they're getting in, Andy."

I know he's right. The judge might not consider the discovery of the drugs admissible, but that won't deter Richard. He'll just add a charge of drug possession, and then the jury will hear all about it.

I'm not going to get anywhere talking to Richard. Not only wouldn't any arguments I make be productive, but if I want to make them effective, it's best I not preview them to the opposition.

I get off the phone and signal for Laurie to come into the kitchen, out of earshot of Ricky. I relate to her exactly what Richard said to me. She is stunned, but in typical Laurie fashion, does not waste time saying so. Her focus is on how we can counter this.

"This changes things, Andy. We've been thinking too small."

"I know. It's well-financed to the point that they're willing to throw away a hundred grand worth of heroin to help build their case."

"And they're smart; this has been planned and executed remarkably well. This is not a Tommy Haller–type operation; this is out of Tommy Haller's league."

"And Diaz was in on it," I say.

"How can you be sure?"

"Diaz informed on Pete for drug dealing, and then drugs were found in Pete's apartment. The two have to be connected. Either Diaz was part of the frame on his own, or he had no choice."

Laurie nods. "And what he didn't realize was that his own murder was going to be the clincher against Pete."

"I guess it's time to hear what Pete thinks."

"Where is he?"

I look at my cell phone to see what time it is. I used to wear a watch, but I'm a techie now. "Guards should be bringing him home right about now."

"He's going to be upset."

"Yeah," I say. "Maybe you should tell him."

She smiles. "You can handle it."

I head over to Pete's house, which is about a ten-minute drive from mine. It's a trip I am sure I'll be making quite a few times, and it certainly beats driving to the jail.

Pete is already home, and I find him sitting at the kitchen table with a uniformed officer, who I don't recognize. Pete introduces him as Kevin Bogart, and Bogart gives me a smile and a big handshake.

"Kevin's going to be doing the eight-to-five shift," Pete says.

Kevin smiles again and says, "Easy duty."

"Where are you going to be stationed?" I ask.

"Right outside the front door," he says.

"Would you mind going there now? I need to talk to my client."

"Sure," Kevin says. "No problem." He is one agreeable guy.

Once he leaves, Pete asks, "What's up?"

"They searched this house yesterday."

He frowns. "I know. I'll be straightening everything up for two days."

"You notice anything missing?"

"Like what?"

"Well, they walked out of here with about a hundred grand worth of heroin."

"That better be a joke," he says.

"I wish it was."

"Andy, this is nuts. Where did they say it was?"

"I don't know yet. I'm sure Wallace is going to add it to the list of charges, so he can get it admitted as motive evidence."

"Motive for what?"

"Murder. Danny informed on you for drug dealing."

Pete just sits there for a few moments, a stunned look on his face. It's the first time I've seen him appear overwhelmed by events. Finally, "I don't know what to say."

"I can understand that. We are up against some wealthy, smart people who want nothing more than to put you in jail and leave you there for a long time."

"So we need to figure out who, and we need to figure out why."

"Right. And it all starts with Diaz. I want you to write out everything you know about him. Leave out nothing; email it to me."

"If he said I was a drug dealer, then I might not know anything about him at all."

"He may have been forced to do so; we won't know that for a while. But one thing is for sure: he knew the people who have done this to you."

"I want to know everyone Danny Diaz spoke to on the phone. Cell phone, home phone . . . every call in and out."

If Sam Willis were worried about delivering the information to me, he's hiding it well. "No problem."

"How far back can you go?" I ask. Sam can access pretty much anything online, and since everything in the history of the world is now online, that makes him a valuable guy. The fact that he is not legally entitled to do much of what he does makes him even more valuable.

"How far back do you want to go?"

"Since birth, but I'll take the last couple of months."

"Give me twenty-four hours," he says.

"I'll be happy to give you twenty-four hours, as long as we can start them twelve hours ago."

"Okay . . . I'm on it."

"I want whatever the phone company has got. If he ordered a pizza, I want to know the toppings."

"They don't record the content of the calls, Andy. They just know when they were completed and how long they lasted."

"We clearly have too much privacy in this country," I say, but I have a hunch that Sam thinks I'm serious.

Sam goes off to do his computer magic, and as he walks out,

Laurie walks in. I would make the 'Sam for Laurie' trade any day of the week, but I have a feeling that today is going to be an exception. It's because of what she has in her hand.

A Frisbee.

"Feel like going to the park?" she asks.

My mind is racing. "The park? Are you crazy? It's seventy degrees out."

"Does that mean it's too hot, or too cold?" she asks.

"Whatever. It certainly isn't Frisbee weather."

"I thought we'd take Ricky, Tara, and Sebastian to Eastside Park for a little while. He's been cooped up in the house too long."

"House-cooping is good; I just read a study on it somewhere. I only wish I had known about it when I was a kid."

"We'll be back in an hour or so; you can use a break. And it'll be good bonding time for you and Ricky," she says.

"Tell him to come in here and watch the Mets game with me."

"Did you also see the study about women being more in the mood for sex after throwing a Frisbee in the park? It was in *USA Today*."

Laurie and I have abstained since Ricky came to live with us. "No, I missed that."

"The statistics show it to be a real turn-on. Never having actually played Frisbee with a man, I can't confirm or deny that."

"What did *USA Today* say happens when the woman is rejected on her Frisbee proposal?"

"It's quite clear on that," she says. "Icicle-city."

"I'll race you to the park."

So we go to Eastside Park, Laurie, Ricky, Tara, Sebastian, and me. Within five minutes, we're throwing the Frisbee on the lower level near the baseball fields, and Ricky and Laurie seem to be enjoying it. Tara and Sebastian have absolutely no interest in the process, and when Ricky throws it near them, trying to get them to jump at it, they just lie there and look at him like he's nuts.

For myself, Frisbee-throwing has never really had much appeal.

I like games that have a beginning and end, and you keep score and come up with a winner. If there's no winner, how can you mock the loser?

The game of Frisbee, as best I can tell, consists of throwing it, and catching it. If you miss, you pick it up and throw it again, with no apparent penalty. I'm therefore not sure what the incentive is for catching it.

But it's a beautiful day, and being in the park with our rapidly growing family is not unpleasant. I also recognize that there are going to be very few relaxing moments coming up; the intensity of preparing for trial simply does not allow for them.

We take a long detour on the way home and stop at the Fireplace, a restaurant on Route 17. I get hamburgers for Ricky, Tara, Sebastian, and myself, and a salad for Laurie, and we eat at an outdoor table. It's the happiest I've seen Ricky, and that is definitely good to see.

I spill half a cup of soda on my shirt, which sends Ricky and Laurie into absolute spasms of laughter, pointing and generally mocking me. Ricky is laughing so hard that his orange juice starts coming up through his nose, causing even more laughter. It's nice that my misfortune can bring such joy into people's lives.

All in all, the day gives me a glimpse into what life is like for normal human beings, which will help me if I ever attempt to become one.

Ricky goes to bed soon after we get home. Laurie gives him a choice of who should tuck him in, Laurie or me, and he chooses her without hesitation. It's hard to blame him; I would make the same choice.

Tara and Sebastian are completely wiped out from the excitement and exertion of the day. I'm not sure why lying on the grass is any more tiring than lying at home on a dog bed, but it apparently is.

Laurie and I have a glass of wine, and listen to some music, and then we go to bed. I am happy to report that those *USA Today* people really have their act together.

Veterinary medicine is a huge industry. This year, in the United States alone, people will spend more than twelve billion dollars to provide medical care for their pets. And that number rises every year, both here and abroad. People often brag about how much they spend on their pet's ailments as a badge of honor, as if it is proof of their love for their dog or cat.

A substantial portion of that is spent on drugs. In fact, almost eighty percent of all dogs receive medication each year. It is certainly no surprise that the drug companies have taken full advantage of this opportunity, and have jumped in with both feet. Research into animal drugs reaches an all-time high every year.

But obviously, all the terrific care and medications in the world ultimately are not enough, and our pets' lives eventually come to an end. The vast majority of pet owners wind up having them euthanized, after they've determined that the animal no longer has an acceptable quality of life.

Euthanasia obviously also requires the administering of a drug. Most commonly, the animal is given a sedative injection, and then a lethal drug is injected into a vein. It can be stressful for both animal and grieving owner.

Daniel Mathis set out to find a better way. Mathis is a highly regarded research chemist for Blaine Pharmaceuticals, a small to midsize company that found a niche in veterinary medicine, and the firm has fared quite well.

The founder and owner, Stephen Blaine, cashed out, selling his business to a private buyer. A new chief executive, Mitchell Blackman, was installed, but except for some minor cost-cutting, life went on as before. Certainly Daniel Mathis did not notice any change; he was valued by Blaine, and by the new owners.

Mathis had seen the euthanasia area as one of special promise. He submitted a proposal to Blackman in which he would set out to develop an easier, stress-free way for a stricken pet to be euthanized. It would not require any injections at all, but would be a pill that could be given conventionally, even in a treat.

Best of all, Mathis was confident this could be accomplished using natural compounds, already found in the body. He believed he could find a combination that would cause the animal's heart to simply stop beating, with no pain or suffering. And because the compounds would be natural, they would be inexpensive to produce, thus yielding substantial profits.

And he did it. In a clinical trial, the compound was developed, produced in limited quantities in pill form, and given to a sample of animals who were at the end of their lives and ready for medical euthanasia. And it worked, better than Mathis even expected. The end for the aging and afflicted animals was painless and stress free; they simply silently and permanently went to sleep, essentially as the result of a sudden and massive heart attack.

Blackman was of course very pleased with the progress that Mathis reported, and they planned a slow rollout of the drug, starting in major markets, and expanding into smaller ones. International would come later, once it was established in the U.S. The rollout was at least a year away, since more testing was necessary.

Mathis had one concern, which was that the drug could have human application. Many human drugs are also widely used by veterinarians, especially antibiotics and pain medications. The only difference in production is that the composition of animal meds is not required to be as precise.

But this drug was different. Human euthanasia has always been a hotly debated topic among medical professionals, bioethicists, etc. This drug would make suicide much easier to accomplish, and therefore could create controversy. Mathis discussed it with Blackman, and they agreed that they would have to get their legal ducks in a row before moving forward. It was another reason that the rollout would not be commenced quickly.

Once the first phase of testing was completed, even the limited production of the drug was halted. There were seventeen pills remaining unused, and Mathis considered destroying them, but was advised by his legal team that he should keep them secure in his office.

And then came that horrible day, almost a year ago, when he discovered that they were gone, along with the records of his work. He went straight to Blackman, and they agonized over what to do. Blackman thought that he might be mistaken, that the pills could have been destroyed. Or more likely, the pills and records were misplaced, and would turn up later.

Also, Blackman pointed out with some accuracy, they could not be sure the drug would work the same way on humans as on animals. Not all drugs did, and certainly no human tests had been conducted. Perhaps the natural compounds would be harmless to humans. Mathis was positive that his drug would be equally lethal in humans, as it was in animals, but Blackman was not convinced.

Mathis went along with the ultimate decision not to say anything. He believed it to be a business decision; if the worst happened and these pills fell into human hands, the revelation of the company as the source could provoke lawsuits large enough to destroy the company ten times over.

So Mathis did and said nothing.

Except worry.

Emails have ruined my life.

Okay, that may be an exaggeration. Maybe they haven't ruined it entirely, but they've certainly had a very negative effect on it.

First of all, they control me. My computer beeps whenever I receive an email, and I am incapable of ignoring it. I can't help but going over and checking it out, despite the ninety-nine percent probability that it's going to be of no interest to me.

Sometimes it's a banker in Nigeria, trying to figure out a way to get me eight million dollars, or it's a company trying to sell me something, or it's my bank or credit card company telling me my statement is available for viewing.

Those things are uninteresting, but much preferable to the emails from people I know. Those are the ones that have caused a complete overhaul in my entire social structure.

Prior to emailing, my relationships were built on leaving messages on people's phone machines, and having them leave messages on mine. That way we could stay in touch, without ever having to actually interact.

But email messages are different. They have actual content, with questions that require answers. Often they send me links to long articles, or seemingly endless videos, which I feel an obligation to read and watch.

Even though it seems technology driven, all of this has the effect of adding depth to relationships, or at least it does to mine. Unfortunately, I'm not a big fan of depth in relationships; I like to keep my friends in the shallow end of the pool.

Then there are the acronyms, collections of letters that I never understand, but that apparently represent words too long to type out. My least favorite is LOL, which I have come to understand means "laugh out loud."

I used to think the emailer was instructing me to "laugh out loud," which struck me as rather arrogant. But I was then informed that it means they are laughing out loud as they type. Somehow I have trouble picturing that, because I have never actually read anything remotely funny that was followed by an LOL.

This morning I am extra vigilant listening for the email sound, because I want to know everything that Pete knows about Danny Diaz. And it shows up bright and early; I guess wearing an ankle monitoring bracelet promotes a strong work ethic.

According to Pete, Danny Diaz had a rough life. He grew up in Paterson's inner city, raised by his mother, who Pete believes was in this country illegally. Danny's father was not in the picture, and he had no siblings, so Danny was left alone when his mother died in a car accident.

The seven-year-old Danny was bounced around through the system, in various foster situations, and once he turned eighteen set out fending for himself. Not trained in any vocation, he did mostly odd jobs, and it was a struggle to get by.

Danny married Sophia, but she died in childbirth, leaving him to take care of their newborn son, Ricky. At that point, his lack of money took on a far greater importance. He began to discover that some of his friends, who were working somewhat outside the confines of the justice system, were finding food and shelter easier to come by.

Danny eventually went that route as well, and after a couple of years wound up as a low-level employee in the Dominic Petrone crime family. He was mostly doing collections from people who found themselves in the unenviable position of owing Petrone money. Apparently, he was noticed and liked by higher-ups, though it was unlikely that he came to the attention of Petrone himself.

Collections aren't always the smoothest part of that kind of operation, and Danny committed and was arrested for an assault on a resistant client. The arrest was made by Pete Stanton, and during the investigation Pete had occasion to meet Ricky.

He also took a liking to Danny, and felt empathy for him in his situation. So he went out on a limb, pulled some strings with a friendly and understanding prosecutor, and got Danny a six-month sentence, followed by probation. Part of the deal, in addition to Danny "going straight," was that he would function as an informant, should he become aware of criminal activities.

No one believed for a second that Danny would inform on anyone in the Petrone family; to do so would be akin to jumping from a plane without a parachute. And Danny had to be extra concerned with self-preservation, as he remarried, this time to Juanita, thereby growing his family even more.

It was not a perfect union from the beginning. Pete first became aware of trouble in Danny and Juanita's marriage about six months ago, which was about four years after Danny got out of prison. It eventually culminated in Juanita abruptly leaving. Danny did not talk about it to Pete, but Pete suspected she was using drugs.

Danny did openly express a hope and belief that Juanita would come back. But as far as Pete knows, she never contacted Danny or Ricky, and he has no idea where she is now.

Pete was not Danny's contact if he had information to provide, and his sense was that Danny did not have much of it, since he had taken a job as an apprentice in an auto body shop.

Why Danny would have informed on Pete is not something that Pete has knowledge about, but he assumes that Danny was under intolerable pressure from some outside force to do so. I find Pete's forgiveness and understanding of Danny's actions to be remarkable, even if that forgiveness and understanding are posthumous.

Laurie comes in and reads the email, and her initial reaction concerns Ricky and his future. "Is anyone trying to find his stepmother?"

"I don't know; I'll ask Pete's friend at Children's Social Services. But it shouldn't be hard if she wants to be found."

"What do you mean?"

"The murder has made national news, and that's only going to increase as the trial begins. She'll either see it, if she hasn't already, or someone will tell her about it."

"I know she's not his biological mother, but I still don't understand how she could leave that child."

I don't know the answer to that, so I don't try and come up with one. My unexpressed view is that if she'd walked out on him, maybe it would be in his interest for her not to come back. If he gets adopted, he at least can be sure that the adopted parents want him.

Instead I steer the conversation back to the information about Diaz. "The good news is that he was working for Dominic Petrone, and the bad news is that he was working for Dominic Petrone."

"What do you mean?"

"Well, his connection to them means that he was involved with some rather dangerous individuals, which gives us a lot of people to point to as possible guilty parties. If he was hanging out in a convent with a bunch of nuns, our options would be more limited. This goes toward reasonable doubt."

"And the bad news?"

"I don't know if you've noticed, but I'm not a big fan of antagonizing people who carry guns and swear a lot."

"Now that you mention it, I think I have noticed that. You'd be tougher on the nuns?"

"As a general rule, anyone whose first name is 'Sister' better not mess with me."

There was no eyewitness to the murder of Danny Diaz.

That in itself is certainly not unusual. Murderers generally like to commit them when no one is watching. Pretty much the only people they are okay with witnessing the act are the victims, who generally don't talk much about it.

It's also not very important. Eyewitness testimony can be unreliable and subject to impeachment by brilliant cross-examiners like yours truly. Forensic evidence is generally much more significant, and much more reliable in court. I have never yet gotten a strand of DNA to tearfully break down on the stand and admit that it lied, or even that it might be mistaken.

One of the key things for the prosecution to prove is that the defendant had the ability to commit the crime, with a central aspect being proximity. That is why Laurie and I have come back to Diaz's neighborhood to interview Stanley Wilson.

Wilson was in the house diagonally across the street from Diaz's, and he gave a statement to the police in which he said he heard gunfire, then went outside to investigate. He said that he saw Pete leaving the Diaz house, with the door open behind him. He said that Pete went to his car, which was parked in front of the house, but Pete did not drive away. Within a few minutes, the area was swarming with police cars.

Laurie said that when she called Wilson, he actually seemed eager to talk to us. That in itself is pretty unusual; prosecution witnesses generally are wary of defense counsel, often because the prosecutors tell them to be. Either Richard never had that conversation with him, or for whatever reason, he's choosing to ignore it.

Wilson greets us with a big smile at the door and invites us in. The house is well kept, though the furniture is old and worn. Knickknacks and plastic flowers don't do much to warm up the room, but it's clear the effort has been made.

I ask him if he minds if we record the conversation, telling him that it keeps me from having to take notes, which I find a major pain. He seems understanding and says "no problem," and I then get him to repeat the permission once Laurie turns on the recorder.

"How long have you lived here, Mr. Wilson?" Laurie asks.

"Oh, I don't. This is my girlfriend's place."

"But you were staying here the night of the murder?" I ask.

"Yeah, you know how it is."

I have no idea what he's talking about, and not inclined to ask. "Was your girlfriend home that night at the time you heard the shots?"

"Nah, she had the night shift; she's a nurse at the hospital."

"So what were you doing when you heard them?" Laurie asks.

"I was sacked out. They woke me up."

"Where were you sleeping?"

"In bed . . . in the bedroom."

I ask him where the bedroom is, and he says that it is upstairs, toward the back of the house.

I don't see an air conditioner in the window, so I say, "Must be hot up there."

He smiles. "You got that right. That's why when I sleep, it's just me and nothing else, you know? Cooler that way."

We take him through the events of that night, and he pretty much sticks to the script that he had given the police. When he's finished, I ask, "So you heard the shots and went right outside to see what was going on?"

"Sure. I figured somebody might be hurt, or in trouble."

"You could tell they were gunshots, and not a car backfiring or something?" I ask. I have to admit, I've never heard an actual car backfiring; it may just be a myth, or a movie conceit.

"Hey, I know a gunshot when I hear it."

"You weren't afraid?" Laurie asks.

He smiles proudly. "No way."

We thank Wilson for his time and leave. We have plenty we can use against him in cross-examination, but at its core his testimony is accurate. Pete did leave Diaz's house that night, with the door open behind him, and go to his car.

The question is when, and that is the only question that matters.

"When is my stepmom coming back?"

As a lawyer, I ask a lot of questions, and almost as many are asked of me, but this one immediately goes to the top of my most hated questions list.

Laurie is at the market, and Ricky and I are having breakfast. We're having Frosted Flakes; I have found that I can use Ricky as cover to eat sugary stuff that Laurie generally considers unhealthy. The question has come out of left field; I had been talking to Ricky about baseball.

I don't have any idea when or if his stepmother might be coming back, or how I should respond, so I lamely say, "I'm not sure, Ricky."

"Where is she?" he asks, demonstrating that his ability to ask an awful question wasn't a one-shot fluke.

"I don't know yet, but people are looking for her." I'm going to have to do the grocery shopping from now on; I can't have Laurie leaving me like this.

"Daddy said we were going to see her."

"He did?"

"Yup."

"When did he say that?"

"The same day I came here. Can I have more cereal?"

His changing the subject to cereal is a mixed blessing. It may well get me off this conversational hook, but it makes it harder for me to get information. I decide to back off for now, and I pour him the cereal. I also make a mental note to look into what is happening regarding the search for his mother.

Hike comes over, and it is a sign of how uncomfortable the conversation with Ricky has been that I'd rather talk to Hike. I give Ricky some more cereal, and he takes it into the den to eat it in front of the television. I know it's not the best thing to do, but he sees me eat while watching baseball all the time, so it's hard for me not to allow him the same privilege.

"I've got bad news" is how Hike starts the conversation. Actually, it's how he starts pretty much every conversation; it's his default position. He believes that the absence of bad news is a sign that terrible news is right around the corner.

"What might that be?"

"Wallace has filed drug charges against Pete."

This was so thoroughly expected as to not be news at all. Wallace needs the drug evidence to build his motive case, since Diaz informed on him for drug dealing. Without the charge, the mere presence of drugs in Pete's house might not have been admissible, since it in no way proves that he committed the murder. Adding the drug charge takes the decision out of the judge's hands.

"Has he turned over discovery yet?"

Hike nods. "Yeah. It's only the drugs found in the house. No customers, nothing showing a way he might've gotten the stuff, nothing like that."

"Good. Our position is that it was planted there at some point after Pete was arrested. Let's find out when the house was locked down by the police."

"Will do."

Once Hike leaves, I settle down to read the lists that both Pete and Phillips prepared for me, detailing all the possible enemies that Pete might have, based on past and present cases. Marcus and

Laurie have been checking out each of them, and they've prepared reports on each case for me to go over as well.

There are a few new reports, but basically I'm rereading documents for the third time. That is standard procedure for me when preparing a case, and I do it for a couple of reasons. For one thing, I need to know all the facts of a case completely cold, so that I can call upon that knowledge in the moment in court.

There are only a few situations that are not on both lists, and one of them on Pete's list strikes me this time as worth a special look. It's actually the death of a prominent businessman, apparently of natural causes. It interests me because it was not classified as suspicious by the police or coroner, and therefore should not have required Pete's continued attention.

The other reason it stands out is that the victim was wealthy, and the people that set Pete up spent considerable resources to do so. It's a thin strand to make that connection, but we don't have many thicker strands to go by.

By this time Laurie is already in bed reading, and I am sitting in the den, having been going over the casework all day. In my view, that is not the natural order of things, so I head for the bedroom. To my horror, she has fallen asleep while reading. That leaves me with two options: waking her up while pretending I was not trying to, or letting her sleep.

I delay the decision, and head to Ricky's room to make sure he's okay. He's also asleep, which is no great surprise, and Sebastian has crawled into his unpacked suitcase, which Ricky must have brought over to give Sebastian a comfortable place to sleep.

It's adorable. Not Tara-adorable, but right up there.

It actually reminds me of how I was when I was a kid. We had a dog named Terry, a Lab mix that Tara is sort of named after. It's a cliché to say a dog is a best friend, but Terry was my best friend, and we were devoted to each other.

That's how Ricky is with Sebastian.

If I were keeping score, I would chalk one up for Ricky.

But then I see Sebastian lying in the suitcase again, and I realize that it's more than just adorable.

Much more.

"Laurie, I need to ask you something."

She's asleep, so I'm touching her arm as I talk.

She wakes up, and I see it takes her a second or two to gather her bearings. She's in bed, I'm coming to bed, and I'm waking her up. This is not exactly breaking new ground. "If it's what I think you're going to ask me, the answer is no. No chance. Not a prayer."

"Is sex all you ever think about?" I ask. "What about love, and caring, and human connection, and friendship?"

"Those are things you've read about?"

"I saw them in a TV commercial; it might have been for a phone company. But this is really about something else. The night that Pete called us, and we went to Ricky's house, you went inside by yourself."

"Right."

"Where was Pete?"

"He was downstairs, talking to the forensics people."

"And where was Ricky?"

"At the neighbor's house," she says. "Remember, you went over there a few minutes later. What's going on?"

"When you and Pete went to the neighbors, Pete was carrying a suitcase."

"Right. That was Ricky's."

"Who packed it?" I ask.

"I don't know. I guess Ricky did." She thinks for a moment, remembering. "It must have been Ricky, or maybe Danny, because when Pete and I went up to his room to get his stuff, we were surprised that the suitcase was packed."

She just answered the key question, but I press the issue. "So Pete hadn't been involved in the packing, or told him to do it?"

"I wouldn't think so, not based on Pete's reaction." Then, "So they were already leaving."

"Right. When Ricky said his father told him they were 'going to see' his stepmother, I thought he meant that they would be seeing her at some point. Now I think he literally meant they were going to see her, probably that night."

"But we don't know where she is," Laurie points out. "And if she was in contact with Danny, and they had arranged in any manner to see each other, then she'd have to know by now that something happened to him."

I nod. "And it wouldn't be hard to find out what happened. Yet as far as I know no one has heard from her, and Ricky's sleeping down the hall in our house."

"So what are you thinking?"

"That Juanita Diaz is somehow involved in this. I have no idea how, but I don't buy that all of this, with Pete, and Juanita, and then the murder, wasn't somehow connected. I don't know which side she's on, but I'd bet anything she's a player."

"You think Danny was killed to prevent him from going to see her?"

"I doubt it. I think he was killed to put Pete out of commission, and a secondary reason might have been that Danny had become a loose end that needed to be tied. But I also think it's more likely that Danny was trying to get Ricky out of danger, rather than bringing him toward it."

"So what's the next step? Should we ask Ricky who packed the suitcase?"

"I don't think we'll have to. I'm going to see Pete tomorrow, and confirm that he didn't tell Ricky to pack the bag; otherwise it had to be Danny. Then I'll check on any progress finding Juanita; she might well be a key."

"You could call Pete now. I don't think he's getting much sleep these days, and he wouldn't mind your waking him anyway."

"No, if there's one thing that Sam has taught me, it's that you can't trust phones or email to be private. It can wait until the morning."

She nods. "Okay. You coming to bed?"

"You starting with the sex thing again? What are you, insatiable?"

"You're right," she says. "I'm sorry; I've got to learn to control myself."

"Hey, don't be so hard on yourself. Insatiability is a very underrated quality."

"I hadn't heard that," she says.

"That's why I'm here. To teach you and guide you."

"I have no idea why his suitcase was packed," Pete says. "I had forgotten that it was until you just reminded me."

"Danny told Ricky that they were going to see his mother."

"That night?"

"I think so, but I'm not sure." I need to be careful not to conflate the two, and make incorrect assumptions. That can lead to a lot of wasted time and effort down the road. "I can't fully make that connection yet."

"But did Ricky pack the bag that night?"

"I don't know that either; I don't want to give the kid the third degree. And I certainly don't want to remind him of that night. At some point we might have to bring in a therapist to ask him questions like that."

"Good . . . be careful with him," Pete says, starting to pace around the room. The house definitely has that "lived-in" look. Dishes are piling up in the sink, and mail is strewn around. I've been in Pete's house many times, and he usually keeps the place pretty neat. I think the confinement is already starting to get to him.

Pete pours himself a cup of coffee, and asks, "So what else have you come up with?"

"That's pretty much it."

"So let me make sure I understand this. On their side, they've got a boatload of evidence that I committed a murder and sold drugs, and on our side you've got a hunch that an eight-year-old was already packed? That's where we stand?"

"Pretty good, huh?"

"I may be starting to get worried," he says.

"The state of New Jersey wants to put you away for the rest of your life, you're stuck in the house wearing an ankle bracelet with a guard outside your door, your lawyer is getting nowhere, and you're just starting to get worried? You should have hit full-fledged panic days ago."

"Thanks."

"Tell me about William Hambler," I say. That was the rich, dead person that Pete had mentioned in his current case file.

"He's dead."

"How did he die?"

"Heart attack," he says. "No evidence of foul play."

"Yet as I recall, you're in the foul play business."

"I was."

He says it as banter, but I can tell it hurts. Pete is many things, but at the top of the list is the fact that he's a good, dedicated cop. The inescapable fact is that it has been stripped away from him in the worst way possible.

"And will be again," I say, with more hope than conviction. "Why were you investigating William Hambler's death?"

"Because his son Robbie believes he was murdered."

"But the coroner said a heart attack was the cause of death?"

"Yes," Pete says.

"Yet you believe Robbie could be right?"

"I do."

"Why did Robbie come to you, if the guy lived in Englewood Cliffs?"

"Because Robbie is a friend; I've known him for twenty years. We were in the army together."

Pete is too good a cop to believe something just because it was said by a friend, so it seems worth pursuing. But I haven't yet gotten out of him any logical reason for his suspicion. "You think I should talk to Robbie?" I ask.

He shrugs. "Can't hurt, although I doubt that it's connected to this case. But you should make your own judgment. I have other information I can give you as well, and I'll email it to you if that's easier. But start with Robbie."

"Time is at a premium, Pete, unless you want me to get a delay."

He shakes his head. "No. No delays."

"Then give me a reason why you believe Robbie when he says that his father was murdered, other than the fact that he's your friend and you trust his judgment."

"Because it's just possible his father may not have been the only one that was murdered."

These are the calls made from Diaz's cell phone," Sam says, showing me the list. "Here are the calls he received, and here are the calls he made and received from the landline in his house. He used the cell much more than the landline."

"Do you have the names attached to the phones he communicated with?"

"Some of them; I'm working on it."

I don't know if what I'm looking at will be helpful or not, but it certainly will give us something to do. "This is great, Sam, thanks."

"There's one more thing I can give you, if you want it."

"What's that?"

"Well, you know there's a GPS in every phone, right?"

I certainly do know that, and I say so. We used it on a past case to track down some people. "If we find any people on the list you give me that we want to locate, we might want to use that."

"What about Diaz's phone?" he asks.

"I would think the cops have it, but what good would it do us to know where it is now? Diaz isn't around to use it."

"The phone company keeps the records in their database," he says. "I know it's there for months, and my guess is it's much longer than that."

"Are you saying that you can tell me where Diaz's phone was any time in the past couple of months?"

He nods. "I just have to find it. But if it's in their computers, I'll find it."

"You get me that and I'll double your pay."

"You don't pay me anything."

"Then I'll triple it. Seriously, Sam, if I can trace Diaz's physical whereabouts in the weeks before his death, it could be very helpful."

"I'm on it."

Sam leaves, and I briefly ponder the implications of this. Nothing he gets me is admissible in court, because his hacking efforts are not legal. However, once I know what is there, I can subpoena the same records through proper channels, and then it becomes admissible.

However, this may or may not be true with the GPS records. The fact of the matter is that knowing that Diaz's phone was somewhere is not proof that Diaz was there. Someone else could have had his phone; I have no way to demonstrate otherwise. It would be up to the judge to determine if the jury can hear the information, and it's probably a coin flip one way or the other what the decision would be.

But whether or not it can be used in court, the investigative value could be great, and we will try to take every advantage of it. If Danny Diaz knew his killers, and I increasingly believe that he did, then this may lead us to them.

But for now, all I can do is focus on those who knew Danny Diaz. To that end, I head down to Arturo's Body Shop on Market Street in Paterson. It's where Danny worked, alongside the man Laurie has determined was his best friend, Louis Cimino.

I had called ahead, and Cimino seemed quite willing to talk to me. That was something of a surprise, since a close friend of the victim might generally be disinclined to help the person defending the accused killer. That didn't mean Cimino was likely to try and help me, but talking was all I cared about at the moment.

Often it takes many probing questions to draw people out, and then there are those like Louis Cimino. I can't finish a question before he grabs on to it and commences a soliloquy.

"Me and Danny, we were buddies, you know? I still look over at his station every day, and I can't believe he's not there. Like I think any second he'll show up with a cup of coffee, like nothin' happened."

"In the weeks before he died, was he acting—"

Cimino nods vigorously as if he knows where I'm going, even though I could have finished the question with "acting in *Romeo and Juliet* in Shakespeare in the Park?"

"Weird, yeah," he says. "Really weird. It wasn't Danny at all; I told him he was like an alien. Juanita not being there, that was the problem. I wanted to tell him, 'you're better off, man,' but he wouldn't have listened."

"Better off?"

"Yeah, she was fooling around, almost from the time they got married. He never had no idea, and I wasn't gonna tell him. He'd have punched me out."

"Who was she fooling around with?"

He shrugs. "No one special; one-night deals, you know? But she didn't really want to be married, and she didn't want no kid. Never did; she shouldn't have gotten married in the first place. And I guess she finally couldn't take it no more. She told Danny she couldn't breathe. What kind of bullshit is that? Can't breathe? You open your mouth and you breathe. Give me a break."

"So her leaving made him act weird?"

"At first. He kept talking about wanting her back, hoping she'd come back. But then one day, maybe two weeks before he died, not another word out of him. I mean nothing; he just went cold, you know? Like he was scared of something. Missed two days of work; Danny never missed work."

"And you don't know why?" I asked.

"Nah, he wouldn't talk about it. And then all of a sudden he was dead, you know? Used to work right over there, and now he's dead. I still can't believe it."

"Who do you think killed him?"

"I don't know, but if I find out, that guy is gonna be in deep shit. I just want five minutes in a room with him."

I decide to ask the question straight out, in order to determine if I might want to call him as a witness. "You think it was Pete Stanton, the cop they arrested?"

Cimino shakes his head. "No chance. That cop was good to them, and Danny used to tell me how much he loved the kid. You don't love a kid like that, and then kill his father."

"I'm getting some internal pressure about Diaz's son," Richard Wallace says.

"What kind of pressure?" I ask. The next time Wallace calls me with good news will be the first.

"There are those who don't think he should be living with you."

I had worried about this possibility. Sometimes I think that my worrying about something means it will automatically come true. Maybe I should worry about winning the lottery.

"Why the hell not?" I ask, pretending I don't know.

"Because he was in the house when his father was killed. There is a possibility that he will be a witness at trial. We generally don't like to put up our prosecution witnesses at the defense attorney's house."

"Makes sense. Let's take the kid and dump him into the system. Better yet, let's put him in solitary confinement."

"Come on, Andy."

"No, Richard, this is bullshit. We are not talking about trial tactics here, we're talking about a little boy who lost his parents. He likes it at our house; he likes Laurie, and Tara, and he doesn't even think I'm an asshole. He's gotten comfortable, and he's not leaving. This I will take to the Supreme Court."

Wallace is quiet for a few moments. I know I haven't intimidated him, and I also know that he has no desire to take Ricky out of our house. Finally, he says, "So give me something."

"Give you something? Like what?"

"We might want to talk to him . . . if so a trained therapist will do it. You'd get a transcript of the conversation."

"Fair enough." That can't be what he meant by my giving him something.

"So give me your word that if, while he is at your house, he says anything relevant about the case, you will turn it over to me."

"You think we're spending the time grilling him?"

"No. But kids say things. Can I report back that I have your word?"

"You can. And just to show good faith, I'll tell you something that he already said. Just came out with it; he wasn't answering a question."

"What is it?"

"He said that his father told him they were going to see his stepmother." I have no problem telling Richard this. It in no way helps him, and I was going to call him about finding Juanita Diaz anyway.

"What does that have to do with his murder?" Richard asks.

"Probably nothing, but I'm not sure about that. Which reminds me, how is the search going for Juanita Diaz?"

"I'll have to check; it's a police matter. But I haven't heard anything about any progress."

"Maybe some of the internal pressure should be directed toward finding his stepmother, rather than making him homeless."

"I'll see what I can do. Meanwhile, do we have a deal?"

"We do. Will that make this problem go away?"

"I can't make any promises, but I've been around long enough that I know how to exert some internal pressure myself."

Richard gets off the phone, leaving me to reflect on a very good deal for our side. I'm happy to share anything that Ricky says, unless of course he says something damaging to Pete. It's pretty hard to imagine myself turning that kind of information over, but I don't feel bad about it, since Richard knows that as well as I do.

Integrity, especially mine, has its limits.

I walk into the kitchen, where Ricky is sitting on the floor in the corner. He's got a pencil in his hand, and there's a large book on his lap. Tara and Sebastian are on the floor with him, each with their head resting on one of his knees.

He looks comfortable, and happy, and he's not leaving until he has someplace better to go.

"Can you help me?" he asks.

"Sure. What do you need? Another dog?"

He laughs. "Noooo. I'm doing a crossword puzzle book. Edna gave it to me."

"That's a shocker," I say.

"Sit down next to Tara," he says, indicating an open space on the floor.

"Down there? You'll need a crane to get me back up."

I have never been comfortable sitting on the floor. It's hard, and there's no back, and no place to hang your legs. Floors are actually the reason they invented chairs. Yet some people seem quite fine doing it.

But I crouch down and assume the very uncomfortable position. "So what's the problem?" I ask, noticing that he is eagerly writing something in the book.

"Never mind," he says, "I got it."

"So I should get up?"

"Okay."

I work my way back to a standing position, not the easiest thing to do. Then, "Hey, next time I take Tara and Sebastian to the park, you want to come? There's a whole bunch of people with dogs there."

He lights up. "Yeah!"

"Great . . . that's a plan. We'll have fun."

If you're a big shot in need of a root canal, you call Dr. Robbie Hambler.

His office is on Central Park South in Manhattan, and if you think that your "canals" are worth three times as much as anyone else's, but you want to get rid of the root, then Robbie's your guy. At least that is what Pete told me, and there is nothing about the office, or its location, to make me think otherwise.

I'm afraid of a lot of stuff—snakes, bugs, mice, guns, Laurie, Marcus, you name it—but for some reason I've never been afraid of dentists. Unless, of course, I'm in the chair, and they have a drill in their hand.

But Robbie is waiting for me in his private office, with no drills or needles in sight. Pete had called and told him what I wanted to talk about, so I didn't need to do much in the way of a preamble.

"Why do you think your father was murdered?"

"He was the picture of health. He ran marathons, never sick a day in his life, and had a complete physical six weeks before he died. They found nothing wrong."

"Heart attacks happen, very often without warning."

He nods, but frowning as if he is talking to a dope. "Of course they do. They can be unpredictable."

"Right."

"But he predicted this one," he says.

"Tell me about that."

"My father owned gas stations; he bought one about twenty years ago, and slowly was able to expand by buying more. About seven years ago, it became advantageous to merge with his chief competitor, a man named Lawrence Winters. Their businesses were of equal size, and so they were equal partners."

"How big a business are we talking about?"

"Last year they did a billion one in sales."

"That's a lot of gas."

"Yes it is. During the past year, or at least a year ago is when my father first mentioned it to me, he came to believe that there were serious problems with Winters. He was acting erratically, possibly drugs, possibly not. But he was uncharacteristically detached from work, often not showing up for meetings without explanation. He also often talked about people he knew, friends he had, making them sound like they were dangerous people." He continues, "But that was only part of it; my father came to believe that he was stealing from their company."

"Did your father confront him?"

He nods. "He did, and Winters denied it. So my father offered to buy him out. This was just three months ago."

"But Winters refused?"

"Yes, and he professed to be outraged. They had a huge fight about it, and my father told him that he would be bringing in outside auditors to check the company books. Soon after that, he and I had a conversation that I will never forget. He told me that Winters might be capable of dangerous things, and that he was going to look into hiring private security. But that if anything should happen to him, it was Winters who would be behind it."

"Did he hire the security?"

"He never got the chance."

"So what happens to the company now?"

"There is an automatic buyout triggered, partially funded by life insurance that the partners held. The rest comes from the company; my mother will be a very rich woman. But of course she was already a very rich woman."

"You're a smart guy," I say, "so I'm sure you see the problem here."

He nods. "I do. No matter what threats might have been made, the death appears to be of natural causes."

"Right."

"I understand all that, but I don't buy it. The coincidence is too great, and there has never been a heart attack in my family. My father's parents lived into their nineties. When someone tells you that they are afraid they are going to be killed, and then they die days later, it is not something you can just let go. At least I can't."

At this point I understand where he is coming from, but I don't think he is correct. Of course, Pete claims to have more information, which I will certainly consider. But I'm not about to tell Robbie about other possibly related deaths, at least not at this point.

"In your situation, I would feel the same way," I say.

"So now let me ask you a question," he says. "Pete's in jail for a murder that there is no way he committed. And you're defending him."

"What's your question?"

"What the hell does that have to do with my father?"

They should have killed the cop.

He knew he wasn't second guessing, not Monday-morning quarterbacking. Alex Parker told his people back then; he told them they should kill the cop.

They were worried that his sudden death would get fellow cops to pick up his investigation, and might see his unexpected demise as part of a pattern. But they weren't giving Alex enough credit for his abilities; he would have done it in a way that no one would have realized what had taken place.

There was no doubt they had to get rid of the cop. He was getting too close, even if he didn't realize it. But he needed to be dead, and instead they had gotten cute. They used Diaz, who knew too much anyway, and his wife, who fell into their laps. The plan was complicated, but Alex had executed it perfectly, as he was paid to do.

Nevertheless, they seemed to be back at square one. The lawyer, Carpenter, was obviously picking up on the investigation, and he had the cop to provide a road map. So in that sense they brought on the worst of both worlds.

Not that it couldn't be managed. It would take Carpenter a very long time to get close to them, much longer than the trial would take. After that he would probably drop it, but even if he didn't, it was unlikely he could ever prove anything.

And if need be, Carpenter would have to die.

He would tell his people that, and this time he would be believed. So he'd kill the lawyer, and they'd move on. And it wouldn't be by slipping him a pill. Parker was tired of that; he wanted to go back to his roots, kill the way he had always killed.

And killing was his specialty.

It's a perfect day for the park.

Which is probably why the entire city of Paterson seems to be here. But Eastside Park is a pretty big place, and for every person, there's a hell of a lot of open grass.

This is Tara's favorite place on Earth, and she seems to take pleasure in showing Sebastian her favorite sniffing spots. We've been here way more times than I can count, and she has never once done anything but wag her tail and smile happily.

If Tara were to die, Eastside Park is where I would spread her ashes. But since she is going to live forever, there will never be ashes to spread. Enough said about that.

If Ricky had a tail, he'd be wagging it as well. The park has tennis courts, and baseball fields, and a small zoo, and a few playground rides for kids. It's nothing special as parks go, but Ricky reacts as if it were Disneyland.

I have a brief moment where I think it would be nice to take him to the actual Disneyland, but it passes quickly. From what I've seen of it, people smile way too much there; it would get on my nerves.

We head down to the lower level, where I show him Dead Man's Curve, a steep winding hill that we used to go down on our bikes in the summer and sleds in the winter. Then we meet up with a group of people, mostly women, who come with their dogs almost every day.

I introduce Ricky and Sebastian, and everyone spends a few moments greeting Ricky warmly and petting Sebastian. When it's finally time to leave, Ricky says, "Do we have to go?"

I nod. "Sorry, but I have to do some work. But we can come back, if you want."

"I want to," he says.

It's on the way home that he drops the bomb. It comes from nowhere, in the middle of a conversation about dogs.

"My dad is dead," he says. It's not a question, but rather a statement of fact.

I don't know what to say; my instinct is to be vague and noncommittal, but Laurie's therapist friend said that honesty is absolutely crucial.

I take a deep breath. "Yes, Ricky, he is. I'm very sorry about that."

"So he's not coming back?"

"No, I'm afraid not."

"That's not fair." He says it calmly, as if he is simply stating a fact, which I guess he is.

"No, it's not fair. It's not fair at all."

We walk a little more, and then he asks, "Do you have a father?"

"Not anymore."

I'm holding Tara's leash with my right hand, and I put my left hand on Ricky's shoulder, and we walk the rest of the way home, just like that.

Danny Diaz made 641 calls in the last two months of his life.

And that was just from his cell phone; he made another 247 from his home phone. He received 227 calls on the cell, and 109 at home.

And of course, he might have made some calls from work, or even from a pay phone, if he could find any.

The point is, we have a huge job on our hands to find something significant in this mass of information that Sam has provided. And he hasn't even given us the GPS data yet.

Sam has done an amazing job. He has attempted, mostly with success, to assign a name or place to the phones that Diaz called and that he received calls from. But just having those names doesn't solve the problem. In virtually all cases we don't recognize the names; they could be, and mostly like are, benign in nature.

Then there are businesses that he called. Was he calling to order something, to complain about bad service, to ask a question, to apply for a job? Or was there someone at that business that would be significant to us if we knew who it was? Even Sam couldn't tell us who Diaz actually spoke to on each of these calls.

And to complicate matters a bit more, there are a few numbers that Sam couldn't get names for. Were they perhaps phones purchased without a contract, to use and dispose of? Or is the fact that they did not have names attached in itself suspicious, and might therefore make them priorities for us?

Last but not least, maybe there's no one that Danny talked to on the phone that we have any reason to give a damn about.

But all these numbers have to be regarded as leads of some significance, and require our checking them out. Our group is already strained. This kind of investigating is not Marcus or Willie's forte, and Sam is tied up working on the GPS data, which is crucial.

Hike has been working on the more traditional aspects of Pete's defense, our trying to rebut the prosecution's case without pointing to any other suspects. That leaves Laurie and me, and we already have a lot on our plate.

"What about Pete?" Laurie asks.

"What about him?"

"He can run down this stuff as well as we can, probably much better. He's a trained detective, he's got access to a phone, and way too much time on his hands. And if there's anybody that he thinks needs to be checked out in person, one of us can do it."

It makes such perfect sense that I'm not surprised I didn't think of it. But I ask Edna to make copies of all the lists, so I can bring them to Pete and fill him in on what he has to do. My guess is he'll be thrilled at the chance to actually do something concrete to aid in his own defense.

The phone rings, and when I hear Laurie say, "Hello, Richard," I experience a sense of dread. Wallace doesn't call with good news, and the calls have been getting progressively worse. This time he's probably alerting me to evidence that Pete has been identified as second in command of the Yemen chapter of al-Qaeda.

"Break it to me gently," I say, when I pick up the phone.

"No bad news this time. Just a report on the search for Juanita Diaz."

"Good. What have they found out?"

"Not a hell of a lot. There was one sighting that they considered credible in Spring Valley, someone said they saw her a couple of weeks ago, but there's no sign of her there now."

"That's it?" I ask.

"For now. Andy, you need to understand that this isn't a high priority for the police. She's not considered integral to the investigation, and she's not even really considered a missing person. There is ample evidence she left on her own free will."

"She's the stepmother of a little boy who needs her."

"Well, she doesn't seem to see the urgency in that," he says, with more than a little bit of truth. "I'll let you know if I hear any more," he says. "But I'm not really in the loop on it. There barely is a loop to be in on."

"Okay. Thanks, Richard."

I update Laurie on the conversation with Richard, of course doing so out of earshot of Ricky. I have mixed emotions about the situation regarding Juanita. While I generally think it's a good thing for mothers and sons to be together, even stepmothers, I'm not sure that's true in this case. If Juanita does not want to be with Ricky, he just might be better off without her in the long run.

But it should come as no surprise that I have a more selfish interest in the matter. There is a decent chance that Juanita is somewhat involved in what happened to her husband, particularly since they seem to have been going to see her the night of the murder. At the very least, she might have some information, or an educated guess, about who might be his killer.

I head over to Pete's and bring him up to date. As Laurie predicted, he is very pleased to get on the phone and trace down as many of these numbers as he can. He's also worried that there might be a tap on his phone, but knows someone that can make sure that's not the case, or disable it if the tap exists.

He doubts that Juanita holds much of a key to his own situation; in his eyes it was simply a case of a bad marriage gone worse. If she and her family were planning to reconcile around the time of the murder, then that is fine, but unlikely to have anything to do with her husband's death.

I also tell Pete about my meeting with Robbie Hambler, and he asks what I think about it.

"Not a high priority," I say. "But if you really have other deaths that you think tie in, then I want to pursue it. Hambler's death involves big money, and it took big money to set you up, so that alone makes it worth following up on."

"Okay. I'll get the information out of my file and email it to you. There are a couple of deaths I was looking into that were similar, also of wealthy people. One in particular was very interesting to me. And there is a state police detective that I talked to about it."

"Why?"

"He called me, because he had information that I was looking into one of the deaths."

"The one you said was interesting?"

"Actually, yes. It was out of my jurisdiction, but he didn't care about that. The deceased was a wealthy woman, and he was looking into it as well. He wanted to make sure I didn't do anything that would compromise what he was doing. It's common practice. I'll send you his name and number as well, but I doubt it will come to anything."

Pete is far more interested in Sam's information, and he starts looking at it while we're talking. After a couple of minutes, he looks up at me. "Have you gone through these?"

"No," I say, "I just got them. We'll need to split them up among you, Laurie, and me."

"Well, we might want to start with these." He points to some numbers on one of the back pages. "These were the calls on the day that Danny died."

There are nine calls made either to or from three numbers on that day; all were made using Danny's home landline. Two of the numbers are listed as being in Spring Valley, New York, one seems to be a hotel named the Oakmont Gardens, and the other is listed in the name of Carla Alvarez.

The name listed on two other calls, both received by Danny, is Juanita Diaz.

Daniel Mathis simply could not take it anymore.

Ever since the horrifying discovery that the euthanasia pills were missing, he had not experienced a peaceful night's sleep. He had never bought into Blackman's rationalizations that there might be a benign reason for their disappearance, or that perhaps they would not be as deadly to humans as to animals.

Mathis knew with certainty that the pills were stolen; the fact that the records of his work were also gone certainly proved that. And he was just as sure that they would kill anyone who ingested one.

For a long time he pored over newspapers, checking the obituaries to see if any deaths could be connected to his work. But it proved impossible; there was simply no way to know.

Heart attacks are the listed cause of death for more than a million Americans each year. Only seventeen pills were stolen, yet Mathis imagined that each and every death was the result of his work.

He finally came to the conclusion that he had to go to the authorities. It no longer mattered what the repercussions would be, business and personal, though he recognized that they could be severe.

The fact that he had delayed coming forward for months made matters far worse. How would he explain why he waited? Could he be culpable for any deaths that had happened in the interim?

These were the kind of questions he had no good answer for, but they didn't matter.

He could no longer sit back, which meant he had no alternative but to come forward.

But even with all that, he couldn't make himself pull the trigger. His fear of going to jail as a result of his admission was intense. He was even afraid of going to a lawyer, since that would in his estimation start the ball rolling, and he would be unable to pull back.

Daniel had become friendly with a coworker, a young woman named Sharon Dalton. Their relationship grew to something more, and even though she left the company, they saw more and more of each other.

Finally, he confided the situation to her, and her view was a clear one. He needed to come forward; there was too much at stake not to, and the longer he waited the worse it would become, both for him and for the people that might be victimized by the missing pills.

Her conviction gave Daniel the courage and resolve that he needed. He informed his CEO, Mitchell Blackman, of his decision, and was surprised when he didn't get any pushback. Blackman expressed similar feelings to Daniel's; his conscience was tormenting him as well. They would come forward together, individually as well as representing the company, and let the chips fall where they may.

The relief that Daniel felt was palpable. Blackman had surprised him, but it was a very pleasant surprise. He knew that Blackman had far more to lose, and not just his preeminent position within the company. Daniel was single without any close family; Blackman had a wife and two teenage children.

But while misery loves company, so does anxiety, and just having someone alongside him felt very supportive and comforting. They would go to the FBI the next morning, and unburden themselves.

Daniel left the office that evening, heading home and not knowing if he'd ever be back, or what might lie in front of him.

He was never seen or heard from again.

Carla Alvarez said she has been friends with Juanita Diaz since grammar school.

They both grew up on Jerome Avenue, in the Bronx, and they have remained friends ever since. They refer to each other as "my sister from another mother."

Once we saw Carla's name on the call list, Laurie called her and asked if she'd been in touch with Juanita, and Carla's response was that she is very worried about her friend.

That response alone was enough to get Laurie and me up here to a diner on Route 45 in Spring Valley. Carla works as a cashier at a department store nearby, and she said that she could talk to us during her lunch hour.

We drive up the Palisades Interstate Parkway, the road that parallels the Hudson River on the New Jersey side. Of course, it gets a little complicated, since halfway up you enter New York State, even though you're still on the Jersey side.

It is a sign of New York's regional, obnoxious dominance that it refuses to stay on its own damn side of the river.

When we get to the diner, there is a Hispanic woman who seems to be around Juanita Diaz's age sitting alone in a booth. We take a shot and go over to her, and sure enough, it is Carla Alvarez.

"Thanks for seeing us," Laurie says. "We won't take a lot of your time."

"No, it's okay. I was going to call the police."

"Why?" I asked.

"Because I am worried about Juanita. She is my best friend."

"Why are you worried?"

"I don't know where she is. I cannot reach her for weeks. And her poor husband . . ." She doesn't finish the sentence, but if she did it would have reflected on Danny's murder.

Laurie's turn. "Where did you see her last?"

"She was at my house; she came to stay with me when she left home."

"Why did she leave home?" I ask.

"She and Danny, they were having trouble in their marriage. She needed time to think, and to be with someone who understood her. So she came to me. If I were in that position, I would go to her."

"How long did she stay with you?"

Carla thinks for a moment. "A week, maybe more. She talked to Danny a couple of times, and she seemed to feel better. So she was going to go back home."

"But she didn't?"

"I don't know; I don't think so. I got home from work, and there was a note from Juanita. She said that something had happened to Danny, and that she was going home. But I called Danny, and he told me that he had not heard from her, and that nothing was wrong with him."

"What happened next?" Laurie asks.

"I didn't hear from anyone for two days. I called Juanita on her cell phone a few times, but it was turned off. So I called Danny again, but this time he was different."

"What do you mean?"

"He told me that Juanita didn't want to speak to me, and that I should stop bothering them. That was crazy, you know? I did nothing wrong, and Juanita would never say anything like that."

Carla is obviously upset, and there is no doubt in my mind that she is telling the truth as she knows it. "Do you have any idea why Danny would say that to you?"

She shakes her head. "No. Danny and I, we were always friendly. We both had Juanita, you know? I kept calling Juanita, but no answer. I didn't call Danny anymore, and then I saw on the TV what happened to him. So terrible. . . ."

Laurie asks if Juanita seemed to be worried about anything other than her marriage, or if she indicated anything at all about she or Danny being in any other kind of trouble.

"No," Carla says. "And if there was anything, she would have told me. Me and Juanita, we tell each other everything." She continues, with more than a trace of sadness, "And now she tells me nothing. That is why I'm so worried. That is not Juanita."

We ask Carla to please call us if she hears from Juanita, and she agrees. "Should I call the police and tell them what I've told you?"

I think about this for a moment. It's unlikely her story will motivate anyone to do anything. The fact that Juanita Diaz hasn't called her friend is not by itself ominous news. But it certainly can't hurt to do so, and it has no potential to damage Pete's case. "If you feel comfortable with that, then of course," I say.

Laurie and I head over to the Oakmont Gardens, which is now no longer a hotel, but rather has been converted to mini-apartments. They are rented long term, and based on the look of them, must be rather inexpensive. The grounds are poorly kept, with litter strewn fairly liberally on the grass.

The manager of the place is Edward Rozelle, and when we tell him we are there to ask questions rather than rent an apartment, he adopts an attitude that is simultaneously wary and obnoxious. My first reaction is to dislike him, and I suspect that over time he wouldn't grow on me. "Our customers expect total privacy," he says.

I nod. "I'm sure they do. Is this one of your residents?" I show him a picture of Juanita. There is a slight reaction, but I can't tell what it means.

"I'm not at liberty to say."

"It must be comforting for your residents to have you protect them so diligently. But moving right along, have you seen her? She was staying in room 221; she made a phone call from that room."

"I really can't comment on that."

"Makes sense," I say. "So let's try a different subject. What are you doing on Thursday and Friday?"

"What do you mean?"

"Well, if you don't answer these very reasonable questions, I'll present you with a subpoena, and a federal marshal will escort you to a two-day deposition, which will feel like root canal without novocaine. Sound good?"

I am, as per usual, lying through my teeth. I don't have the power to subpoena him, and I have as much chance of getting a federal marshal to help as I have of bringing in Marshal Dillon, or declaring martial law, or being named grand marshal of the Rose Bowl Parade.

Fortunately, Rozelle is not aware that I am full of shit, and he folds like an accordion. Laurie, who is totally aware that I am in fact full of shit, manages a slight eye roll with a smile, a maneuver she's perfected over the years.

"You guys always have to get your way, huh?" Rozelle asks. "Don't you ever talk to the cops?"

I have no idea what he's babbling about, so I say, "We're talking to you now."

He nods. "Yeah, she was here. With a guy."

"Did you talk to her?"

"Nah, she was in the car, and he brought her into the room. I didn't see her again."

"How long were they here?" Laurie asks.

"Almost two weeks. I saw him coming and going a couple of times, but not her. What's the story with her?"

"I'm sorry," I say. "Did I give you the impression that we were going to share information? Forgive me if I did. Do you have housekeepers that clean those rooms?"

"What do you think this is, the Hilton?"

"Is that a no?" I ask.

"Yeah. That's a no. People clean their own rooms, until they leave."

We question Rozelle a while longer, and actually manage to get a little information, which may or may not prove helpful. The guy with Juanita paid in cash, twenties, which Rozelle no longer has. He signed his name Wally Reese on the check-in sheet, but did not have to provide identification to prove that was his real name.

Rozelle says the car he was driving was silver colored, and he thinks it was a Toyota Corolla, but he isn't sure. He did not get the license plate number.

"Has anyone else stayed in that apartment since they left?" Laurie asks.

"No, we got a bunch of vacancies."

"Go figure," I say. "Make sure no one goes in there before tomorrow. We need to get forensics people in here." I know Pete has people he can call on to retrieve fingerprints, and I want them in there as soon as possible.

"You're going to get prints, or maybe DNA?" Rozelle asks, apparently somewhat impressed by the concept. "Any chance you'll tell me what's going on?"

"Zero."

We're making progress in the search for Juanita Diaz.

Unfortunately, my job is not to find Juanita Diaz; it's to defend Pete Stanton. That's not working out quite so well.

I've put Hike in charge of the traditional defense aspects of the investigation, meaning interviewing prosecution witnesses, analyzing the evidence, recruiting our own experts, etc. He has been updating me on all of it, and he's done a nice job.

The problem is that while we may score points in that area, it will not carry the day for us. If it is ultimately a jury's choice between the prosecution's evidence, and our refutation of that evidence, we will come in second place. A very distant second place.

I've been skirting the edges, spending my time finding out about rich people having surprise heart attacks, and a wife who left her husband and son. What I really need to know is who the hell wanted Danny Diaz dead, and why.

Sam moves that ball forward a giant step by coming over with the first of the GPS records of where Diaz's cell phone has been in the past couple of months. The locations are listed by coordinates, which of course mean absolutely nothing to me. But Sam has started the large, tedious task of assigning actual locations to the coordinates, and is about ten percent finished with that process.

"I thought you might want to get these now, because of this one," he says, pointing to an entry on the list.

I immediately know why he focused on this particular one. It is an address in the Riverside section of Paterson, which is the territory of Dominic Petrone and his family. There are many law-abiding, peaceful citizens in this area, but I'm betting that Diaz was not visiting one of them.

"Did you check who lives at the address?" I ask, although knowing Sam as I do, I have no doubt that he did so.

He nods. "Yup. The house is owned by Gina Russo, wife of Joseph."

This is good and bad news. The bad news is that Russo is number two in the family to Petrone himself, which means he's probably ordered beatings or killings more times than I've ordered beer. I am uncomfortable being on the same planet with Russo, to say nothing of having to deal with him. I have no idea why the house is in his wife's name, and it doesn't seem like a priority for me to find out.

The good news is that I have an in with Russo. When Willie Miller was in prison, Russo was an inmate there as well. Three prisoners, clearly paid for their efforts, were on a mission to kill Russo in the exercise area, and they had makeshift knives to help them in the process.

Willie, who had never so much as exchanged hellos with Russo, happened to be there as it was going down. Willie's the kind of guy to instinctively take the side of the "one" in any "three-on-one" encounter, particularly when the three have weapons.

Willie himself is a walking weapon, and using his karate skills, he kicked the three assailants all the way to the hospital. The only thing worse than killing a high-level Petrone family member is failing to kill one, and the three assailants all mysteriously died within a month of being released from the prison hospital.

Russo was understandably grateful to Willie, and offered his services whenever needed. Willie has never quite understood Russo's attitude; he just never considered what he did to be that big a deal. In fact, Willie told me that the fight was the most fun he had in his seven years in prison.

We took advantage of Russo's gratitude to Willie once before on a case, and now it's time to do so again.

I call Willie and tell him, "I need to meet with Joseph Russo."

"You got it," he says, with casual certainty.

"Just like that?"

"Just like that," he says. "I'll call him now."

"Mention how we're good friends, you and I, and that he shouldn't kill me."

"You got it," he says again, so matter-of-factly that I'm afraid he'll really repeat what I said to Russo.

Ten minutes later, Willie calls back. "He asked what you wanted to see him about."

"What did you tell him?"

"That I didn't know."

"What did he say?"

"Come on over."

Willie wants to go with me, as does Laurie. I say yes to Willie but no to Laurie. I don't see Russo as the type to open up to women. And if he insults Laurie, I sure as hell don't want to have to challenge him to a duel.

The real question is whether or not to bring Marcus. My instinctive reaction is to have him there for protection, but when Marcus is around there is always the chance that things will get out of control. My goal is not to antagonize; it is to get information. Besides, Willie's relationship with Russo will hopefully provide me at least a thin blanket of protection. So Marcus is out.

Willie is going to pick me up, and a few minutes before he is due to arrive, Hike shows up to go over some elements of our potential defense.

"I can't do it now," I say. "I'm going to a meeting. Hey, maybe you should come along."

"Who are you meeting with?"

"Joseph Russo."

"As in Joseph Russo, Joseph Russo?"

"The very one," I say. "You want to meet him?"

"What have I ever done to make you think I'm an idiot?" Hike asks. "I'll wait for you here with Edna and Ricky, in case you happen to survive the meeting."

I know Michael Corleone lived in that huge family compound.

And I know it was surrounded by walls, so fortified that even Kay couldn't go out shopping without Tom Hagen's permission. And I know that they had that amazing house on Lake Tahoe with those glass windows looking out at the snow. And I know their part of the lake was so secluded they could shoot Fredo while he was in a canoe, out in the open, without worrying that anybody would see it.

But that has not been my experience. I don't hang out with too many crime kingpins, but I've been to a couple of their houses. I've even been to Dominic Petrone's. And it is nothing like Michael Corleone's.

Petrone lives in a regular neighborhood, nice but certainly not ostentatious, and you would never know which house among the group is his. There are no walls, no gated entrance. He always has a couple of his people on the main floor, but I think the main protection is the knowledge that no one would be dumb enough to go after Dominic Petrone.

It surprises me, but more than that, it gives me some insight. I've sometimes wondered why these people do the things they do, and the only answers I ever come up with are money and power.

But when I come to this neighborhood, I feel that power must be by far the dominant motive.

Petrone is in effect the head of a huge company, but he doesn't have a fancy car, or a private jet, or a yacht, or most of the trappings that CEOs of large corporations have. I know he makes a fortune, but I think the money is just another aspect of the power. It's also a way to keep score.

Joseph Russo's house is very similar to Petrone's. I know, because I've been there before, and when Willie and I arrive this time, my first impression is that he hasn't done much with the place in the last couple of years.

Willie knocks on the front door of Russo's house, and it is opened almost instantly. A very large person says, "Miller?" and Willie answers "Yeah." We men of danger speak very few words.

Once we're inside, we see a second large person. The second guy comes over and frisks me, which is one of my least favorite things. They don't frisk Willie, which must be on specific instructions from Russo. The fact that they consider me more dangerous than Willie is sort of flattering.

We're led into the den, where Russo is waiting. The TV is on, and I note for posterity that he is watching the Food Network. This comes as no surprise; Russo is about my height, and probably outweighs Willie and I put together.

Russo sees Willie, smiles, and says, "My man." He comes over and they embrace, for longer than I would expect. I'm thinking of asking them if they want to be alone, when they disengage and Russo turns toward me.

"Speak," he says.

"I'm investigating the Danny Diaz murder," I say.

"Tell me something I don't know."

"Danny was here, in this house, three days before he died."

"You think I don't know that?" He throws a glance at Willie, which seems to say, "Why do you hang around with this dope?" Willie just shrugs in return, probably wondering the same thing.

Actually, while Russo obviously knew that Danny was here, until now I couldn't be sure of it. I only knew that his phone was here, and although it was likely that he was carrying it, it wasn't definite. Now it is.

"Why was he here?"

Russo thinks for a moment, as if weighing his answer, but I suspect he knew why we were coming over, and knew exactly what he would be willing to say. Finally, "He worked for me."

"Not for years."

"That don't change nothing. Like Willie here, he was one of my guys."

"So he was here for help?"

He nods. "Like you."

"So help me find his killer," I say.

"If I knew where he was, he'd be dead already."

I know that Russo means that sincerely; he's a scary guy that radiates danger. As someone who was scared of the cookie monster until I was seventeen, it's intimidating to me.

What is really scary is knowing that at some point, I might wind up implying to the jury that Russo and his people might be guilty of the Diaz murder. The fact that Diaz worked for and hung around with such dangerous people can be seen as creating other suspects besides Pete.

But that is for another time, and hopefully in another galaxy, far, far away. "What did Danny want you to do?" I ask.

"To find a guy."

"What was the guy's name?" Russo is not exactly the talkative type, and only answers the exact question he is asked, as briefly as possible. It'll serve him well if he's ever called before a Senate Committee, like Michael Corleone.

"Diaz didn't know the name, or much about the guy. Which makes him harder to find, you know?"

"Why did Diaz want to find him?"

Russo laughs a short laugh. "You don't know nothing, do you?"

"Not so far, so tell me, please. Why did Danny Diaz want to find him?"

"Because the guy had Diaz's wife."

"What does that mean? He kidnapped her? Or she went with him willingly?"

Russo can't stifle a frown at what he sees as my latest stupid question. In fact, I doubt he is even trying to stifle it. "If she wanted to be with the guy, Diaz wouldn't have come to me."

"What did you tell him?"

"That I didn't know the guy, but that if Diaz found him, I should be the first call he should make."

"Did he say why this guy had his wife?"

"No, just that he was leaning on Diaz. I didn't care why; I don't like my people getting leaned on."

"If you find him, will you call me?" I ask.

He nods. "Right after I kill him."

Edward Rozelle was worried by the lawyer coming to see him.

He didn't know what happened to that woman, the one Carpenter referred to as Juanita Diaz, and he didn't want to know. But the guy who brought her to the apartment, the one who used the name Wally Reese, was a scary guy. And Alex Parker was even scarier. And so were the cops.

Rozelle didn't want to get involved; he was well paid for providing the apartment, and he hoped that would be the end of it. But his desire to remain out of it suddenly conflicted with his desire to make more money. He now had information that he knew Parker would pay for.

So he called him on the number that Parker had given him, and the man answered on the first ring. "This is Edward Rozelle," he said. "From the apartment."

"I know who you are."

"A lawyer named Carpenter came to see me. He was asking about the two people who stayed here. Said the woman's name was Juanita Diaz."

"What did you tell him?"

"Nothing. I said I didn't know what they were talking about."

"What else?"

"Nothing. He tried to threaten me, but I didn't say anything. I just thought you'd like to know that he was here; you said you were interested in more information."

"Do you know how they came to find you?"

"Yeah. They said a phone call was made from room 221."

"Did they ask the man's name, or who he was?"

"Yessir. Told them I had no idea."

"How about the car?"

Rozelle jumped at the chance to answer this question. "I told them it was a silver Toyota." Since the car was actually a black Honda, Rozelle saw this deception as a way to further please Parker.

Parker saw it a bit differently. Rozelle had said he told Carpenter nothing; claimed to the attorney that he didn't even know who he was talking about. Then describing the car, even if inaccurately, proved that his previous statements were a lie.

Rozelle would die for the error.

"You did well," Parker lied. He then said truthfully, "You will get what you deserve."

Once off the call, Parker didn't bother to reflect on what he had always known to be an essential truth: it was never a good idea to count on other people. But sometimes there just was no choice; one person could not be in two places at once.

It wasn't Rozelle who was the problem; he knew nothing and would eventually be easily disposed of. The issue that Parker needed to address was Wally Reese, the man he had hired to deal with Juanita Diaz. He did not know if Reese had used his real name with Rozelle, but he was stupid enough to have done so. And if that were the case, Rozelle would probably have been cowardly enough to share it with Carpenter.

Just about the only good news in all this was that he was supposed to meet with Reese that very night. They were meeting in a strip mall parking lot in Mt. Ivy, about ten minutes from Spring Valley. The place would be deserted at that hour; the stores would have long since closed.

Reese was there first; he was anxious to report in and get his money. When Parker arrived, he wasted no time with pleasantries. "Where is the woman?" he asked.

"Where nobody will ever find her."

"So you did exactly what I asked?"

"Yup. Everything right to the letter."

"All phone calls to her husband were made from her cell phone?"

Reese hesitated. There had been one time when cell service at the apartment was weak, and he had let her use the apartment phone. He regretted doing so, but assumed Parker would never find out. How could Parker have known that?

"Yeah," he said, with an obvious hesitation. "All calls were from the cell phone."

"You're sure?" Parker asked.

"I'm sure."

"You'd bet your life on it?"

"Hey man, I told you she used the cell phone, okay? How about giving me my money, and letting me get out of here?"

"You already bet your life on it," Parker said, the gun by then in his hand. "And you already lost."

A state of bewilderment has become my home state.

Of course, I would prefer it if I knew exactly what I was doing, and how to do it. But I'm able to find the positive in a situation like this, one in which I have no idea what is going on.

It instills a sense of discipline in me. I don't know enough to know what is important and what isn't, so I treat everything as if it is crucial. Not to do so would mean that I might gloss over something that is vital to our case.

I think we're on to something with the Juanita Diaz angle. Based on his meeting with Joseph Russo, Danny Diaz seemed to think his wife was being held against her will. That may or may not have been true; he could have been led to believe that, and she could have played a role in the deception.

But one thing seems very likely: whatever situation she was in, it was being used to apply pressure to Danny. And there seems to be a strong probability that it had something to do with his murder, and likely his false identification of Pete as a drug dealer.

Of course, none of this is admissible or even relevant in court, not at this stage. Not only couldn't we get any of it in, but Richard and the jury would laugh us out of the courtroom if we did.

What the hell is the difference whether Diaz informed on Pete because he was under pressure? It doesn't mean what he said isn't true. And the prosecution would claim that whether it was true or not, it wouldn't lessen Pete's anger, or desire for revenge.

But not knowing what really happened with Juanita Diaz is motivation for me to keep looking at everything else, including Pete's suspicions about the apparent heart attack death of William Hambler. Pete believed that there were other, similar deaths, and I plan to look into them as well. But first I'm going to follow up on Hambler.

It's an excuse to see Janet Carlson, the coroner in Passaic County. Janet looks very much like Laurie, which is to say she is the best-looking coroner in the history of coroners. I know lawyers who try to depose her on their cases even when nobody involved died.

I had called and told her I wanted to discuss the Hambler case with her, and she said, "I didn't know that Hambler would be considered a case."

But she agreed to meet with me, and when I show up she has the file open and is rereading her notes to remind her of the facts. When she finishes, she looks up and says, "Okay, I give up. Why are you interested in this?"

"I think he might have been murdered."

"Think again."

"You're sure?"

"Andy, the guy had a heart attack."

"But what caused the heart attack?"

"You want my professional opinion?"

"Yes."

"A bad heart."

This is getting frustrating. "Work with me here, Janet. Is there any way a heart attack can appear to be a natural event, but actually be induced? This guy was apparently in excellent physical condition."

She looks like she is going to answer quickly, but then pauses and opens the file again. She reads for a minute or so, and then says, "Mmmm."

"Now you're talking," I say.

"There are a couple ways that heart attacks can be induced, though I am certainly not saying that it happened here. One might be an electric shock to the system, but it would have to be a severe event, and the result could not be guaranteed. Plus there might be other, noticeable effects, possibly burn marks."

"What else?"

"Well, there are certain compounds that occur naturally in the body, but when ingested in combination can cause a sudden cardiac arrest."

"What kind of compounds?"

"There's a bunch of them—potassium, chlorine, calcium . . . it depends on the combination and the concentration."

"Would you be able to detect them in an autopsy?"

"In those kinds of levels? Unlikely, unless the autopsy were done very quickly."

"How fast was this one done?"

"Twenty hours. It was a busy time, and this did not appear to be a suspicious death."

"So that's enough time for those kinds of compounds to break down?"

"Way more than enough. In certain cases an hour is more than enough."

"And it wouldn't leave a trace?"

She looks at the file again. "Certain compounds are elevated in the test results, but they could be elevated naturally. It would take a suspicious mind to read anything into it."

"Then we caught a break, because I happen to have a suspicious mind," I say.

She laughs. "I've become aware of that over the years. You want to fill me in on what is going on?"

"I'm trying to figure out who set Pete Stanton up. I have reason to believe that if Hambler was murdered, then the killer is the man I'm looking for."

She turns completely serious. "If I can help Pete in any way, don't hesitate. I know you won't, but I want to reemphasize it. Do. Not. Hesitate."

"Thanks, Janet. I appreciate that, and so will Pete. But I . . . actually, there might be something you could do."

"Name it."

"There's at least two other cases, like Hambler's, that I need to look into. If I give you the details, could you call your counterparts in those jurisdictions and get copies of the autopsy results? Maybe compare them to Hambler's?

"No problem at all. Just get me the names and locations."

"Will do."

Can I watch with you?"

I look up from the couch and see that Ricky has entered the den. Actually, it would more accurately be described as Ricky and his entourage, since Tara and Sebastian follow him around pretty much twenty-four/seven.

I've got the Mets game on, but in truth I'm not really watching it. I'm reading through case notes and discovery documents, and the game is on mostly as background noise.

"Sure," I say. "You like baseball?"

He shrugs. "It's okay."

"Who do you root for?"

"Who do you root for?" is his response.

"I like the Mets," I say.

He nods. "Me too." Then he sits down and asks, "What's the score?"

"Mets are ahead of the Cubs two to one."

"Chicago Cubs?"

"Very good," I say, and he brightens at the compliment.

I put the file down, and we watch the game together. He doesn't know many of the rules, but he's aware of the basic concepts. He's got a lot of questions and seems sincerely interested in learning. If given enough time, I could mold him into a sports degenerate in my own image.

The Cubs tie the game and it goes into extra innings. In the bottom of the tenth, the Cubs have the bases loaded and two out. The next batter hits one toward the gap in left center, and it seems certain to end the game. But miracle of miracles, the Mets center fielder makes a diving catch to end the inning.

Ricky and I jump up, screaming, and we slap each other a high five. I'm not a big fan of high fives, but I like this one, even though his height causes the high five to be relatively low.

Laurie hears the noise and comes down the stairs quickly and enters the den. She sees what is going on, and her face does something between smiling and crying. I'm not sure what the expression means exactly, but I know I've never done it.

"Careful what you say, Ricky. There are women folk in the room."

She smiles. "Is this club for men only?"

"No, you can stay," Ricky says, then turns to me. "Can Laurie stay?"

"Okay," I say. "She can stay, if she watches the game."

"Will you watch the game?" Ricky asks.

"I'll do better than that. I'll go make some popcorn."

"All right!" Ricky yells. I think if given a choice between popcorn and watching the eleventh inning, he'd opt for the popcorn.

The game goes fourteen innings, but I'm the only one who has to watch the Cubs score the game winner on an error by the Mets's second baseman. By then Laurie is sound asleep on the couch next to me, and Ricky is out cold as well, sleeping across the two of us, his head resting in Laurie's lap. Tara and Sebastian lie at our feet, also gone to the world. When I turn the television off, the only sound that can be heard is Sebastian's snoring.

The last thing I want to do is disturb the tranquility of this setting, so I reach over and start reading the case documents again. I'm doing this for about twenty minutes when the phone rings. The noise is jarring in the silence, but neither Laurie, Ricky, nor the two dogs so much as stir, even when I jostle them to get up to get the phone.

"Mr. Carpenter? My name is Jonathon Castro. I represent Carson Reynolds."

It takes a moment for me to make the connection, even though it was just this morning that I called Carson Reynolds's office and said that I wanted to meet with him. Reynolds's wife Katherine was the death that Pete said had most interested him, and that the state cop had called him about.

I had to leave a message when I called, and was deliberately vague, simply saying that I was an attorney and my business with him was very important and very personal.

I have had some very high profile cases recently, and certainly would have been surprised if Reynolds had not heard of me. Apparently he had, which is why he took the message seriously enough to have his lawyer call me back.

"Yes, Mr. Castro, thanks for calling. I would like to meet with your client."

"In reference to what?"

"It's a personal matter."

"So I understand," he says. "Fortunately, I am empowered to discuss Mr. Reynolds's personal matters."

"Then consider yourself invited to the meeting," I say.

"Mr. Reynolds is in mourning; he has lost his wife."

"I am aware of that. Our meeting will be brief and hopefully painless, and should not interfere with the mourning process." I find I often dislike people the moment I meet them, but in Castro's case, he's on my nerves and we haven't even met yet.

"I'm afraid I—"

Based on the way that sentence started, it seems like a good time to interrupt. "Look, Mr. Castro, I'm a serious guy, and I'm not interested in bothering Mr. Reynolds. But I need to speak with him about a matter currently before the court. I can ask the judge to intervene, but that will make the process far more intrusive and time consuming for Mr. Reynolds."

I'm bluffing; I wouldn't have a prayer of getting a judge to intervene. It's the kind of bluff that almost always works, even with a lawyer like Castro. He's probably a corporate attorney, and therefore relatively unfamiliar with the comparatively slimy world that he believes we criminal attorneys inhabit.

Besides, Castro could not possibly know why I need to speak to Reynolds. He probably did the research and learned that my only current client is Pete Stanton, but the connection between Reynolds and Pete's case is so thin as to be invisible.

"Very well, I am relying on your professionalism," Castro says, which in and of itself proves he doesn't have a clue. "Mr. Reynolds will see you tomorrow morning at ten a.m. at his home in Alpine. You will have fifteen minutes to state your business."

"Super; I'm a really fast business-stater," I say, and I write down the address he gives me. "See you tomorrow."

I hang up and take Tara and Sebastian for their nightly walk. When we get back, Laurie and Ricky are no longer in the den. I go upstairs, look into Ricky's room, and see Laurie tucking him into bed.

She kisses him lightly on the head, then tiptoes out of the room toward me, still standing in the doorway. I get a kiss on the lips, and a very big hug. The full body kind, which is a personal favorite of mine.

"Thank you, Andy," she says.

When you get thanked like that for watching a Mets game, life is good.

Where was Daniel Mathis?

Sharon Dalton had been unable to think about anything else.

It had been a week since she had the conversation with Daniel about going to the authorities and reporting the theft of the pills from his office. He had seemed relieved, as if the decision to do so had already begun to remove a heavy burden. She had been proud of him, and said she would be there to support him.

But that was the last she heard from him. He was supposed to call her the next day to update her on what happened, but she waited for a call that never came. She tried him on both his phones, but he never answered.

By the third day, she was very worried. This was completely uncharacteristic of the Daniel she had come to know. She could have imagined him having second thoughts about coming forward, but she could not imagine him cutting off from her like this.

She went to his apartment and cajoled the superintendent into letting her in by saying that she was worried for his safety. And in fact she was; after all, at the core of the issue were drugs that could be used to quickly and painlessly commit suicide. Could he have been that desperate?

But Daniel was not there, either alive or dead. His bed was made, and everything was neat and orderly. There was no sign that anything was wrong, but there was absolutely no sign of Daniel.

Since Sharon had previously worked at Blaine Pharmaceuticals, she knew the people Daniel worked with. She called a few of them and learned that Daniel had not been to work either.

Then she called a friend in HR, who said that Daniel had been behaving strangely, that he had seemed withdrawn and anxious in his last weeks at the company. This came as no surprise to Sharon, since she knew what he was worried about.

The HR person said they were assuming that Daniel had quit, but had been unable to reach him to confirm it. They certainly did not consider him to be a missing person, and at that point felt that it would have been a significant overreaction to report the situation to law enforcement.

Sharon didn't think it was an overreaction at all, but she waited, for a couple of reasons. For one, she thought that law enforcement might not take her seriously. An adult away for three days was not exactly Amber Alert material.

Secondly, there was always the chance that Daniel had actually reported the situation to the authorities, and they had taken him into the system, perhaps in protective custody. It seemed unlikely, but Sharon was not exactly an expert in these kinds of matters.

But her biggest concern was that in talking to the FBI or police, she might be exposing Daniel to criminal liability. She had advised him to come forward, but it was his right not to. It was also his right to run, and to avoid contact with her and everyone else.

If she were to report the matter, she'd be taking those rights away from him, and it could rebound to his detriment. She just didn't see that as something she should be doing; it was his business and his alone, not hers.

But finally, after a week, she could wait no longer. She was worried, and felt her reporting him as missing was justified. If something had happened to him, then maybe the authorities could help. And if not, if he was just ignoring her completely, knowing how worried she was, then she'd be angry enough not to care what he thought.

She knew that his plan had been to go to the FBI; he felt the matter was beyond the scope of local police. So that is what she did: she physically went to the FBI offices in Newark and said that she needed to talk to an agent about what might literally be a matter of life and death.

She was pleasantly surprised that they took her seriously enough that she was in a room with an agent within thirty minutes. His name was Special Agent Spencer Akers, and he listened attentively to everything she said, taking occasional notes.

After five minutes, she took it as a sign that he was interested that he called in another agent, and turned on a tape recorder. He repeated some of the earlier, untaped questions, so that they could be recorded. All in all, she spoke and answered questions for well over an hour.

Akers was noncommittal about where the matter would go from there, but promised that they would investigate what she had to say. He thanked her, and raised the possibility that they would be in touch with her again as the investigation progressed.

And that was the last she heard from him.

Fingerprints are not what they used to be.

At one time they were the definitive way to learn if someone was in a particular place. They are unique, and their presence positively connected a person to a room, or object, or weapon.

Now we leave our indelible fingerprints everywhere, and they pretty much have nothing to do with fingers.

Obviously there is DNA; it is almost impossible to spend any time in a place without our genetic makeup remaining after we're gone. Investigators have had the use of the technology to identify DNA for quite a while now, but it is hard to comprehend how many criminals could have been convicted, as well as convicted people exonerated, in the years before it existed.

But that is far from all the tools investigators have at their disposal. There are cameras everywhere, public and private, that seem to document our every move. It seems like nothing happens without being captured on film, and it has become a fantasy to expect privacy or anonymity.

If we write an email, or a tweet, it is permanent. If we visit a website, the world of law enforcement, to say nothing of the world of advertising, knows we have been there, what we did once we were there, and how long we spent there.

And then there are the ubiquitous GPS devices, in rental cars, in our own cars, and most notably in our cell phones. We implant chips in our dogs to make sure they can be found, and then we carry devices around in our own pockets and in the process inadvertently let phone companies track our own movements, or at least that of our phones.

We're attempting to make good use of the GPS in Diaz's phone; Sam is still assigning addresses to the list of coordinates, and we'll try to retrace his movements in his last days as best we can.

But for now, a phone call from Pete brings me back to the good old days. "We've got the prints," he says. "The guy used his real name. Wally Reese."

Pete had asked a friend, a forensics cop named Kathleen Flory, for a favor. Flory was to check for prints in room 221 of the Oakmont Gardens, where we believe Juanita Diaz was held. Wally Reese is the name he wrote on the register, but I had assumed it was a fake.

It was not; Reese was apparently unconcerned about being caught, and Flory reported that his prints were all over the room. That means he is either stupid or wasn't doing anything illegal, which in turn would mean that Juanita Diaz was there voluntarily.

I am hoping for stupid.

"Great," I say. "Can you have someone run his record?"

"I already have, and that's where the news gets less great."

"How so?"

"Reese was arrested three times for assault and attempted murder. Convicted twice, served six years, got out two years ago. He lived in Hackensack."

That's all interesting and helpful, but what I instantly notice is Pete's choice of tense. "Lived?" I ask.

"Lived. His body was found yesterday in a ditch off Route 80."

"Let me guess," I say. "It wasn't a car accident."

"Not unless the other driver got so pissed that he put a bullet in Reese's head. Everything is a goddamn dead end."

I had seen something about it on the news, but they hadn't

named the victim. "In a way it's good news, though probably not for Reese."

"How is this good news?" Pete asks.

"We were chasing the angle of Diaz's wife without really knowing if it had anything to do with his murder. Now we know; there are no coincidences that huge."

"So?"

"So it means we're making progress. It's even possible that Reese died because of our progress; we were getting close to him, so maybe someone got worried."

"You think Diaz's wife is alive?" he asks.

"I don't." What strikes me in the moment is that Pete thinks of Juanita as Diaz's wife, while I think of her as Ricky's stepmother. It is quite likely that Ricky has permanently and violently lost two parents in a very short time. It is, in a word, awful.

"I don't either," he says.

We seem to have exhausted that depressing topic, so I move on. "You doing okay?"

He shrugs. "Yeah. Okay. Starting to get a little scared. You?"

"I'm a little scared as well. But in my case that's a good thing."

"How is that?"

"It keeps me alert . . . on edge. Bill Russell used to get so nervous and scared before every game that he threw up in the locker room, and he is probably the greatest winner of all time."

"Did Michael Jordan throw up?" he asks. "Did Larry Bird? Joe Montana? Willie Mays?"

"I think you might be missing the point."

"You gonna throw up in court?" he asks.

"I'm going to do whatever it takes to win."

Call waiting cuts in, interrupting a conversation that was badly in need of an interruption. I tell Pete to hold on and I answer it. It's Hike, so I tell him to hold on as well, and then it's back to Pete.

"It's Hike," I say, and since I'm not in the mood for another depressing conversation right now, I add, "You want to talk to him?"

"No chance. I'd rather plead guilty."

I hang up with Pete, and switch over. "What's up, Hike?"

"Sam finished assigning addresses to the coordinates on Diaz's phone GPS; he brought the last week over a few minutes ago."

"Good."

"I looked at the day Diaz died, and there's something interesting there."

"What's that?"

"Well, that morning, he was at Pete's house."

"Was Danny Diaz at your house the morning he died?"

Pete thinks about it for a moment. "I don't think Danny has been to my house in years. Not since he stayed here."

"He stayed with you?"

"Just for a couple of weeks, when he first got out of prison. The whole family did; they were getting ready to move into their own place. Why?"

"The GPS on his phone says he was here that day."

"Well, I suppose it's possible, because I wasn't. I was working that day. But I strongly doubt it."

"When he stayed here, did he have a key?"

"Of course. He was a guest, and he was a friend."

"Did he return the key?"

"I don't remember. Why?"

"Did you put the drugs in your house?"

"You know I didn't," he says.

"Well someone did. And there was no evidence of a break-in. Which there wouldn't be if someone entered with a key."

"Damn. None of this makes sense, Andy. Danny was a good guy."

"He may have been a good guy under unbearable pressure," I say.

"Or maybe someone else had his phone."

"One sure way to find out." I pick the phone back up and call Richard Wallace, and it only takes him a couple of minutes to come to the phone.

I dispense with the pleasantries, since I basically find pleasantries unpleasant, and get right to it. "Richard, we'd like to examine Diaz's cell phone."

"Fine," he says.

"Where is it?"

"Beats me. Hold on a second."

He's gone for much more than a second; it's closer to five minutes. Five minutes holding on a call is a long time, but at least there's no recording that keeps cutting in to tell me how important my call is to them, or saying that the call volume is higher than expected. Since some places always claim the call volume is higher than expected, they might want to adjust their expectation level.

Finally, "Sorry about that, Andy. But we don't have it; it wasn't in the inventoried items."

"Oh. Okay, no big deal. If you find it, let me know."

"You're full of shit, Counselor," he says. Richard knows me well enough to know that I wouldn't call if it weren't important, but that I want to pretend it isn't.

"Watch your language," I say. "And don't call me counselor. Don't you think I have feelings?"

He laughs. "Not that I've noticed."

I'm about to banter right back at him, when I realize something and end the call.

I ask Pete, "You know that text you got from Diaz that evening asking you to come over to his house?"

"What about it?"

"I don't think he sent it."

"Who did?"

"The person who was here that day, planting the drugs in your house. The same person who was responsible for the kidnapping of Juanita Diaz. The same person who killed Danny Diaz, just before you arrived, knowing that it would therefore look like you killed him."

We talk about the implications of this. We still don't know nearly enough, and the trial date is coming at us like a freight train, but we know more than we did yesterday, and a lot more than the day before that.

Having said that, I still think I'm going to try throwing up in court. It worked for Russell.

Carson Reynolds knows where his next meal is coming from.

Most likely it will be prepared by his private chef, served in his private dining room, on fancy china with the family crest engraved on it. Or it might be prepared by the flight attendant on his private plane, while jetting to the islands, or the "Continent." Based on his house, he certainly can afford either option.

I already knew that Reynolds would not be living in a shack; he runs a midsize private equity fund in Manhattan. Their approach is to buy controlling interest in companies, change management where necessary, build up the business, and then sell it at a profit. Last year he made sixty-one million dollars, and last year was not a particularly good one for him.

It's a one-story home, and from the outside appears to go on forever. I expect a butler to come to the door, and I would have much preferred that to what I get, which is a lawyer. Jonathon Castro is tall for a lawyer. In fact, he's pretty tall for a basketball player. He's probably six eight, and doesn't have an inch of fat apparent under his very expensive suit. Considering he's got to be sixty years old, that's pretty impressive.

"Come in, Mr. Carpenter. I'll ask Mr. Reynolds to join us, at which point your fifteen minutes can begin."

"Should we synchronize our watches?"

If he cares one way or the other about the sarcasm, he hides it well. "That won't be necessary," he says. "My watch will suffice."

I'm led down the hall into a den, and through the glass wall to the outside I can see that the house is shaped like a half circle, and in the center is a sensational swimming pool. Just beyond that is a clay tennis court.

There are fresh flowers in both the foyer and den, and that potpourri stuff in bowls everywhere. I have never in my life bought potpourri, or been in a potpourri store, if they have such stores.

He leaves and comes back with Carson Reynolds, who seems to be about the same age as Castro. Perhaps they went to high school together, and Castro climbed onto the money tree back then.

My guess is that Reynolds is a lot wider than he was in those days, and my other guess is that he and his lawyer do not use the same personal trainer. Reynolds could accurately be described as short, fat, and bald, the exact opposite of Castro.

"I'm sorry for your loss, Mr. Reynolds," I say, ever gracious.

"Thank you. It was sudden, and a true nightmare." He picks up a picture of himself and his late wife from the table, and seems to wistfully reflect on happier times. Unless he's already forgotten what she looked like, he's doing this for my benefit.

In the photo, they seem to be on an island vacation, and based on his age in the picture, it must have been taken recently. His wife was a very good-looking woman, about the same age as her husband. There are no pictures of children or other family members anywhere.

"I can only imagine," I say.

Castro looks at his watch, probably wondering why I'm using up my fifteen minutes on comments of no substance.

"I'll tell you why I wanted to talk to you, Mr. Reynolds."

"Please do."

"Did your wife have any enemies?"

He laughs a short, derisive laugh. "Katherine? Don't be ridiculous. Jonathon, what is this about?"

Castro, not pleased that his boss seems not to be pleased, turns to the source of the displeasure, me. "Mr. Carpenter, what kind of a question is that?"

"I am simply trying to determine if Mr. Reynolds believes his wife's death might not have been of natural causes."

"That is ridiculous, and probably even beneath you," Reynolds says. If he thinks that question was beneath me, he hasn't checked me out very well. He continues. "She died of a sudden heart attack. It was confirmed by an autopsy. Is there anything else?"

I shrug. Since I now don't believe him, I'm not going to get much more from listening to him. "No, that's pretty much it." I turn to Castro. "I think I'll use up a few of my minutes by going to the bathroom, and I'll still have six or seven minutes to give back." Back to Reynolds, "Do you mind?"

"It's down the hall." He's probably already making mental plans to have the bathroom fumigated after I use it.

"Thanks." I walk down the hall, which puts me out of their sight line. There's a bathroom on the left, but I pass right by it and go down to another one much farther down, which is off of what appears to be the master bedroom. If it isn't, the actual master bedroom must be the size of Madison Square Garden.

I don't have to use the bathroom at all, so once I close the door behind me, I instead use a minute or two to take inventory. Then I leave the bathroom and walk back down the hall to the den, where the two men are waiting for me. I stop at the door and say, "Thanks. I can't remember when I've enjoyed myself this much."

Castro gets up and follows me to the front door. "Your reputation is an accurate one, Mr. Carpenter."

"You trying to get on my good side?"

"Hardly."

On the way home, I call Sam Willis. "Great job on the phone lists," I say.

"Thanks. What else you got for me?" Sam desperately wants to be a detective.

"There's a guy named Carson Reynolds. Lives in Alpine and runs a private equity fund in New York."

"What about him?" he asks.

"Can you get his phone numbers?"

"That's an insulting question. Of course I can get his phone numbers."

"Good. Get them, and a list of all the calls he's made in the last couple of months. Then compare them to the list of Diaz calls."

"You want to know if Diaz called him? Because I don't remember seeing Reynolds's name on the list."

"You can check, but I doubt that Diaz called him. What I want to know is if any of the numbers on the called or received lists appear on both Diaz's phone and Reynolds's."

"What about calls made to and from Reynolds's company?" he asks.

"Can you check those?"

"Sure, but there will be a lot of them, so it will take a while. And of course, one of his employees could have made any of the calls."

"It's worth a try anyway," I say.

"Okay, I'm on it."

"Fast, please. Very fast."

Reynolds was lying. I'm seventy percent positive."

Laurie smiles. "Seventy percent positive?"

"Yes," I say. "I'm also somewhat sure, and mostly certain."

"You might want to avoid those terms in your summation to the jury. But why do you think he was lying?"

"Because when I said I thought his wife might have been murdered, he got pissed off."

"Seems like a natural reaction to me," she says.

"Of course it is. But the thing is, that was his only reaction. If it were me, I'd be angry also. But I'd also want to know why he asked the question. I'm an attorney, often involved in murder cases. His lawyer would have done some research on me; they would know I'm a reasonably serious guy."

"Reasonably," Laurie says.

"Right. So he wouldn't even be curious why I thought his beloved wife might have been murdered? It doesn't make sense."

"That's it?" she said. "The guy is in mourning; maybe his reactions aren't what they would be if he were not under that stress."

"It may not be as much stress as you think," I say. "I checked out his master bathroom while I was there."

"Excuse me?"

"Hey, when you gotta go, you gotta go. Anyway, there were

three kinds of shampoo in the shower. One was just regular stuff. Another was for colored hair, and another was some kind of conditioning thing for split ends."

"So?"

"So he's mostly bald; his ends split a long time ago. And his dear, departed wife had gray hair; I saw her in a picture in his den."

"So you think he has rebounded quickly from his loss?"

"I do. I think he's a fast rebounder. And his rebound-ee is named Susan Baird. There was a prescription bottle for a thyroid drug in the medicine cabinet with her name on it."

"You looked in their medicine cabinet? This may be a new low for you, Andy."

"You think looking in a medicine cabinet is a new low for me?" I ask. "Reynolds said pretty much the same thing; he thought a question I asked was beneath me. Do you people not know me at all?"

"Perhaps not."

"Anyway, I'm going to check out Susan Baird, and I'll bet I find out she has colored hair, split ends, and a screwed-up thyroid. And I'll further bet she loves potpourri."

"Potpourri?"

I nod. "The place reeked of it."

"Of course, he could have been fooling around with Susan Baird without having murdered his wife. Or Susan could be his daughter, and Baird is her married name. And he could have a thing for potpourri."

I nod. "All very true. Which is why I am only seventy percent positive."

The phone rings and Laurie answers it. She spends a couple of minutes chatting with the caller, and then hands me the phone. "Janet Carlson," she says.

I take the phone, and it turns out that while Janet chitchats with Laurie, she has no inclination to do so with me. "I checked the other two autopsies, Reynolds and Zimmerman. And I spoke with the doctors who did them," she says.

"And?"

"Well, of course both doctors listed the cause of death as natural heart attacks, and they see no reason to doubt their conclusions."

"What's your view?" I ask.

"Taken individually, I see no reason to doubt them either, but I did find some consistencies that are worth noting. Certain of the compounds that we talked about are elevated in each case, in a similar pattern."

"So what does it mean?"

"I want to be careful about how I state this," she says. "I am slightly suspicious, but only because of what you've told me. Had I not spoken with you, and just examined the results, I would not have raised any red flags."

"On the remote chance that I can get any of this admitted, will you testify to it in court?"

"Who's the prosecutor?"

"Richard Wallace."

"Andy, you'd be better off if you couldn't get it admitted. With what we have here, Richard would laugh me off the stand."

I have no doubt that she's right, but at this point it's moot, since I couldn't begin to establish enough relevance to our case to get a judge to allow it.

When I get off the phone, I tell Laurie what she said. "She thinks I'm nuts."

"So do I," Laurie says. "But that's never stopped you before."

"I've got a hunch there's something there. Pete had the same hunch, and he hunches much better than I do."

"You got anything better?"

"No," I say. "I don't."

"Then let's hope your hunch is right."

Everything is elusive, and nothing connects.

I know these things are real; I know it in a place and a way that I have learned not to question.

But it is one of the imperfections of life that Andy Carpenter is not in complete charge. I can't be the judge, and I sure can't be the jury. I can't say, "Andy, you're right. Pete, take the ankle bracelet off, you're a free man." I wish I could. If I had the choice, I would rather be a dictator than the quarterback of the Giants.

In the world that I inhabit, I have to go much further than convincing myself that something is true. I have to convince others, twelve others to be exact, and to do so I have to make sense out of it. I have to create a truth and a logic that other people can see, and right now I'm not close to that.

Part of the problem is that the things I see don't have any relation to each other, not even in my mind. I believe that Juanita Diaz probably left Danny and Ricky willingly, the result of a troubled marriage. But I believe more strongly that after that decision she was kidnapped and held prisoner in that dump, the Oakmont Gardens. The purpose was to pressure Danny to turn on Pete.

I also think that Carson Reynolds was lying, and that his wife, and Robbie Hambler's father, and maybe this guy Zimmerman, and who knows how many others, were probably murdered. I'm not as certain of this as I am about Juanita Diaz, but it's close.

But these two things might well have nothing to do with each other. In fact, they probably don't. The Juanita Diaz piece is the essential one: it explains why Danny was under such pressure, and why he would lie about Pete. What it doesn't include is a reason why the bad guys would be after Pete in the first place.

The "Hambler-Reynolds" piece has no connection to Diaz at all, but connects to Pete. Pete was investigating those deaths, the killers became afraid he was getting too close, so they wanted to remove him from the picture. That's the theory, at least, but it presents some major obstacles.

The first one would be proving that these were murders at all. The medical and forensic evidence simply isn't there, and what is there leads to the opposite conclusion. The fact that Robbie thinks his father was killed, or that Reynolds was having an affair and was unconcerned about my view that his wife was murdered, just doesn't cut it as proof to anyone.

But even if we got through that problem, the tie to Pete is remote at best. Pete does not think he was close to breaking the case, so why would they have been so afraid of him as to hatch and execute this complicated plan?

Pete mentioned that there was a New Jersey state police detective who had contacted him about the Reynolds case, so he is my logical next step. Maybe he has already solved the case and tied it up in a neat bow for me to present to the jury. Then they can unwrap it in court, everybody can nod in agreement, and Pete can go free.

The detective's name is Lieutenant Simon Coble, and he works out of the Englewood station. I call him and leave a message, simply my name, that I'm an attorney, and I want to talk to him. He doesn't call back, so I leave a second message, then a third. Perhaps he is unfamiliar with the Andy Carpenter legend.

My fourth message says that it's about Pete Stanton and Carson Reynolds, since the Reynolds case is the one he had called Pete about. This seems to do the trick, and Coble calls me back fifteen minutes later.

He sounds like a man who is really busy, or wants me to think he's really busy. He's rushed to the point of being breathless; I wonder if he might be talking to me while on a treadmill.

"Carpenter? What's this about?"

"I'm defending Pete Stanton."

"Did he do it?"

"No."

"I hope that's not defense attorney bullshit," he says. "He seemed like a good guy."

"It's not, and he is."

"So what do you want from me?"

"To help me prove it."

He seems reluctant to get involved, but finally agrees to meet with me, if I can come down right now. He'll give me fifteen minutes, which seems to be the standard amount of time that people have for Andy Carpenter.

Englewood is just twenty minutes from Paterson; it's adjacent to Fort Lee, which means it's right by the George Washington Bridge, but there is an accident on Route 4, so it takes me forty-five minutes. I'm concerned that Coble won't be available when I get there.

But he is. He's much younger than he sounded, maybe thirty-two or thirty-three. "You're late. Your fifteen minutes were up a half hour ago," he says.

"Traffic."

He nods. "Big surprise. Talk to me."

"There are at least three deaths that were recorded as having been from natural causes, in each case a heart attack. I know you are familiar with Katherine Reynolds, and I know you spoke to Captain Stanton—Pete—about her."

"He turned his cases over to you?"

The tone is a tad derisive, which is one of my least favorite tones, at least when directed at me. But I can't afford to antagonize Coble just yet. "No, it's my feeling that this can aid in his defense."

This brings on a smirk, not one of my preferred facial expressions. "How is that?"

"Can we start at the beginning? Why did you contact Pete?"

"Katherine Reynolds's niece reported some concern about the circumstances of her death. I investigated and came to the conclusion that her concern was unfounded, that she died of natural causes. Then I found out that Stanton was investigating as well."

"How did you find that out?"

"Local cops. He went to them first to keep them in the loop, since he was out of his jurisdiction. It's courtesy. Anyway, Stanton came in, we had a nice talk, I thought he was wrong, he thought I was wrong, and we said goodbye."

"What made you conclude that Katherine Reynolds was not murdered?"

"Because there was no evidence that she was. When the coroner tells me that someone died of a heart attack, I tend to believe that the person died of a heart attack, unless there is evidence that the coroner is wrong. You're familiar with the concept of evidence, right, Counselor?"

"Vaguely. I've also seen cases where the evidence exists, but it takes a competent cop to investigate and find it."

"You're saying I'm not competent?" he asks.

"No way. You did all you could; you called the coroner. That must have been exhausting."

He smiles. "I think your fifteen minutes are up."

I return the smile. "Time flies when you're having fun."

Ricky and I are watching cartoons, and Laurie is making pancakes.

I'm not sure where Wally and the Beav are, but they're missing out on a typical American morning with the typical American family. And truth be told, I'm starting to get into the cartoons. And if more truth be told, I'm also starting to get into hanging out with Ricky.

Interrupting this idyllic moment is Sam Willis ringing the doorbell, which is a lot better than Eddie Haskell, or Hike Lynch.

The fact that Sam didn't call is an indication he has something that he considers significant to tell me. "Andy, you're going to want to hear this."

"I hope it's good news," I say.

"That's for you to figure out. I just report the facts."

I take Sam into the kitchen where Laurie is, out of earshot of Ricky, although Ricky is so engrossed in the cartoons I don't think he would notice a bomb going off.

"Sam's got big news," I say to Laurie, which causes her to put down her spatula.

"I've been doing two things," Sam says. "Finishing up on Diaz's phone, assigning names and addresses to the numbers I couldn't get easily, and trying to match up calls from Reynolds's phones with Diaz's.

"There's one cell phone that Diaz called twice, and he received two calls from that number as well. It's a Vegas cell number, in the name of Glenn Kennedy."

"Did you track him down?"

"I tried, but had no success. That's because there is no Glenn Kennedy. The address and social security number the phone company had on file are fakes."

"That is, in fact, interesting," I say. People only fake their identity when they have something to hide. Hopefully what this guy has to hide relates to our case.

"I haven't gotten to the key part yet."

"Please tell me the same phone number is on Reynolds's call list as well," I say.

"Bingo."

This is big news, and well worth interrupting cartoons for, although I recorded them anyway. It immediately gives us the connection we never had between the mysterious heart attack deaths and Danny Diaz.

"There's more," Sam says.

"More? Sam, you are the gift that keeps on giving. Laurie, give this man a pancake. But first let's hear it."

"Reynolds called that number twice the day you met with him. Once before you got there, and once right after you left."

"We need to find out who this guy is," Laurie says, and in the process speaks my thoughts aloud.

"How do we do that?" I ask Sam.

"I have no idea," he says, and it is the first sentence he's uttered since he came over that I don't like. "I got all the information that the phone company has, and it's all bogus."

"He has to pay his phone bill, right? Can you get a look at the checks he used? Or learn the account it was drawn on?"

"Come on, Andy. Who do you think you're dealing with? He paid by postal money order. He put down a thousand dollars, which gave him a large credit, and they just keep taking from that credit.

This guy did not want his identity known, and he did a good job concealing it."

"And this number is a cell phone?"

"Yeah."

"Well, since you can tell me where Diaz's phone has been, can you do the same with this one?"

Sam breaks into a big smile. "You know, I don't see why not."

The trial is like a train bearing down on us, and we're sitting in lounge chairs on the tracks drinking piña coladas with those little umbrellas in them.

At least that's what it feels like. We've learned a great deal about Juanita and Danny Diaz, and about the murders that we believe are somehow being committed. But we haven't learned enough, and for the last week it feels like we've been running in place.

It took Sam longer than usual to get the GPS data on the cell phone that both Danny and Reynolds called. There was a technical reason that it was difficult, and Sam told me what it was, but like all technical sentences, I couldn't translate it into normal language.

But he finally came up with it, so that we know where that cell phone has been for the last three months. And one entry is nothing short of stunning. That phone was also in Pete's house, at the same time that Diaz's phone was there. Either there was a family circle meeting there that day, or the guy we're looking for had both phones.

Unfortunately, we still don't know who that mystery guy is, or why Danny and Reynolds had individually been in contact with his phone. But I'd bet anything I know why he was in Pete's house: he was there to place the drugs.

At the moment the phone is in a large apartment building in

Hackensack, very close to Route 80. Unfortunately, there are 142 apartments in that building, all with the same GPS coordinates. So it is impossible to tell whose apartment the phone is in.

And that phone has been in the building, unused, for the last week. It's frustrating; for a mobile phone, this one is not particularly mobile.

Sam begged me to be able to go "out to the streets," as he put it, and I agreed. He didn't have to beg too hard, since I had no one else to do it, but I did admonish him four times to be extra careful and not take chances. In similar circumstances a while back, Sam almost got himself killed, and would never have survived except for the rather forceful intervention of one Marcus Clark.

Sam is performing two simultaneous functions for us. Through his computer, he is tied into the phone company GPS system, so he will know if the cell phone leaves the building, and he could follow it. We'd be less concerned about where it goes; what we want to know is who is carrying it.

Sam is also tracing the places where the phone has been, and trying to match those places in some manner to Diaz or Reynolds. It's not easy: first he has to get the address, then learn exactly what the place is, and then try to make a connection. It is tedious, difficult, and very frustrating work.

As for myself, I've been reduced to going over every detail of the case as preparation for trial. Pretty much the only breaks I take are to hang out with Ricky, Tara, and Sebastian. Ricky's presence doesn't even seem so unusual anymore, and he may even be starting to like me. Having said that, it seems like I'm just about the only male he's ever met he doesn't call "uncle."

Pete has been growing increasingly anxious, and with good reason. I've been updating him regularly as I do with all my clients, but I get into more detail with him than the others. That's because he understands the process, and can place the things he hears into the proper perspective.

I think that as much as he hates being a prisoner in his own house, he might be regretting having insisted on a trial as soon as possible. But that boat has sailed; there is no longer any chance for delay.

Laurie, Ricky, and I are having dinner, which represents another positive that Ricky has brought to the house. Because of his presence, Laurie has relaxed her nutritional standards somewhat. Tonight we're having hot dogs, something she would ordinarily not give me if I were starving on a deserted island. Although, in fairness, I'm not even sure that deserted islands have hot dogs.

I've been slipping Ricky food ideas for him to suggest to Laurie, and tonight we're literally enjoying the fruits of that approach. We're having apple pie topped with vanilla ice cream, one of my all-time favorites.

Ricky actually winked and smiled proudly at me when Laurie brought the pie out. The kid is so conniving and manipulative; it's hard to believe he's not actually my son.

I'm just polishing off my second piece when Sam calls. None of his calls since he started watching the apartment house have brought any good news, but I live in hope.

"I've got something for you," he says.

"The phone is moving?"

"Nope. Stuck in place. This is something else."

"What is it?"

"One of the places the phone has been was a company called Blaine Pharmaceuticals; their headquarters are in Paramus."

"I think I've heard of it," I say.

"I thought so, too, so I Googled it and found out why. One of their research scientists, a guy named Daniel Mathis, was reported missing about three weeks ago. Vanished without a trace."

"Right," I say, because I vaguely remember it. I think I passed by the story on the way to the sports page. "What does that do for us?"

"The phone was there."

"Are you sure?"

"Of course I'm sure," he says. "And once again, that's not the best part."

I'm starting to enjoy my conversations with Sam a lot. "I am looking forward to hearing the best part."

"The day it was there is the day Mathis disappeared."

I read everything I can find about Daniel Mathis and his disappearance.

It was front-page news a few weeks ago, but the media seemed to get bored of it quickly. If Mathis were a young, good-looking woman, or an adorable toddler, the media would have been falling all over themselves to prolong the story. But instead he is an ordinary-looking guy who did research in veterinary medicine, so he was not invited into the ranks of hot media tickets.

Even from the sparse reports, there is one thing in particular that interests me a great deal. First of all, the FBI was immediately identified as the lead agency in the investigation. That would not happen in the normal course of events. They would only come in if invited by local authorities, or it they had reason to believe the missing person was kidnapped across state lines, or if he was of particular import to public safety.

There is no obvious reason why any of this should have been the case, at least not as quickly as it seems to have happened. The earliest reports mentioned the FBI, and Special Agent Spencer Akers in particular. They were clearly involved from day one, and I'd like to know why.

He apparently was reported missing by one Sharon Dalton, a former colleague at Blaine who was identified as Mathis's girlfriend. She was interviewed by a couple of media outlets, but basically had nothing to say, other than she was worried about Daniel, and asked anyone with information to please contact the FBI.

Based on my persuasive powers with women, I decided it was best to have Laurie call Ms. Dalton and get her to talk to me. My failure with women over the phone dates back to high school, and has pretty much continued unabated ever since.

Laurie works her magic, and together we drive to Sharon Dalton's Ridgewood home, since she has agreed to see us right away. "I was surprised how easy it was," Laurie says. "There's something going on there . . . some undercurrent."

"Like what?"

"I'm not sure, but I expect we'll find out soon enough."

We are only in her house for thirty seconds before I, and I'm sure Laurie, pick up on what Laurie was talking about. The undercurrent is anger: Sharon Dalton is angry at something, or someone, and it's not us.

We start to ask her questions about Mathis's disappearance, and she answers them, albeit not providing much significant information. I'm surprised that she is not asking us why we are there or want to know these things, but I'm fine with her not doing so.

"He just went missing. He did not tell anyone where he was going, or why. One day he was here, the next day he wasn't," she says.

"And you have no idea where he could be?"

She shakes her head. "But he didn't leave voluntarily. No way Daniel would do something like this."

"And you have no idea what circumstances could have led him to leave . . . involuntarily?" Laurie asks.

Dalton hesitates a moment before answering. My sense is that she wants to tell us something, is close to doing so, but can't quite get there. "No," she says.

"So you reported it to the FBI?"

"Yes."

"Why not the local police?"

Another hesitation; there is definitely something there. "I don't know; I just thought of them first."

"What agent did you speak with? Was it the Spencer Akers that was mentioned in the media reports?" I've had some involvement with the bureau over the years, at least enough for them to hate me. In the process I've gotten to know a few of the agents, but Akers is not one of them.

"Right . . . Spencer Akers," she says. "He called himself a 'Special Agent.'"

"They all think they're special. What did he say?"

She frowns. "He just took the information; asked me questions. That's all. Then he told me I might be hearing from them."

"And have you?"

"Not a word," she says, and Laurie and I exchange brief looks. Sharon Dalton's anger is with the FBI for not keeping her in the loop about her boyfriend's disappearance. "I feel like nothing is happening; I'm totally in the dark."

There is much more to this story, and Sharon Dalton knows it. I believe she wants to say it, if I can just find a way to draw it out of her. I feel like Tom Cruise trying to get Jack Nicholson to admit he ordered the Code Red. She wants me on that wall . . . she needs me on that wall.

"That's been my experience with them," I say, shamelessly goading her. "The fact that you might be worried about your friend, that doesn't really enter into their thinking."

She nods. "They tell me not to say anything, and then they say nothing at all." Then, suddenly, she switches gears and asks, "Why are you interested in this?"

I could lie, but I decide to take a shot; in the moment the potential reward seems greater than the risk. "I believe that Daniel's disappearance may relate in some way to a case I am investigating, involving some mysterious deaths," I say. "I have no reason to believe he is himself a victim, nor do I think he's done anything wrong."

A light seems to go on, and she says, "You're a lawyer."

"Right," I say. Laurie had told her that when she called her, but I guess it hadn't registered.

"Then let me ask you something. If the FBI tells me not to say something, but I'm the one who told them, do I have to do as they say?"

"It would be a very rare case that they can prohibit you from talking about something that you did not receive as classified information."

"So I can talk about it?" she asks.

"I can't answer that with certainty unless I know what it is, but it is very likely that you can say it. This is information you came upon yourself?"

"Yes. Daniel told me."

"All I can do is promise you that if you tell us, and I feel that it places you in any legal jeopardy, then I will tell you so, and we will treat what you said in total confidence."

She thinks for a few moments, weighing her options. I want to shake her by the shoulders and scream at her to just tell us the damn thing already, but I have a hunch that might not be the best approach.

Finally, she nods. "Okay, here goes. Daniel was working on a new drug for animals, but not a drug to make them better. It was a carefully controlled study; he worked directly with his boss, Mitchell Blackman, on it."

I instantly know where she is going, but I want her to say it. I can tell that Laurie wants her to say it.

But she has more to say first. "After the study was over, the remaining pills were stolen from Daniel's office. He wanted to go to the police, but Mr. Blackman told him not to, that it would be bad for the company.

"Finally, Daniel couldn't take it anymore, and he decided to report it. Before he could do so, he disappeared."

"What kind of a drug was it?" Laurie asks. We both know the

answer that is coming, but we just wait for Sharon to drop the bomb.

"He was working on a drug to stop the animal's suffering. A euthanasia drug."

Kaboom.

"You did nothing wrong by telling this to us. You don't have to fear the FBI."

I'm telling her the truth, but my goal is not just to ease her mind, though that is part of it. She may someday be in a position to tell it from the witness stand, so I want her to fully understand she is not doing anything illegal.

I believe that she has told us everything she knows, and it fits like a glove with our case. She talked about the stolen pills, the fact that Daniel described them as a natural compound, and that he believed they could induce instantly fatal heart attacks in humans, as they do in animals. It is rare that pieces of a puzzle fit so perfectly together, but that is what has happened here.

As Laurie and I are heading home, my legal mind is speaking to me, and my investigative mind tries to get it to shut up. This is all fascinating and compelling stuff that we've uncovered, but there is no way we are close to getting the judge to admit it at trial. We have to show relevance to the murder of Danny Diaz, and we're just not there.

But I can't listen to my legal mind yet; I need to follow this wherever it goes, and worry about the legal implications later. It's the only way I can function.

But I come to the conclusion that my next step should satisfy both of my competing minds. I need to get actual law enforcement involved, or at least more involved than they are already. For one thing, they have resources that, if properly applied, can get a lot further, a lot faster, than I can.

Just as important is the credibility they can bring to the matter in the eyes of the judge. My talking about these things can sound like wildly speculative defense attorney ramblings. If I can get a cop to say the same things, it carries far more weight.

For the moment at least, I'm not going to the FBI. They are already allegedly investigating, though they may have dropped it a while ago. In any event, they seem to be getting nowhere, and wouldn't tell me about it even if they were making progress. It feels like going to them in this case would be like descending into a black hole.

The logical choice would seem to be Lieutenant Simon Coble. As a state police officer, he has jurisdiction in all areas of New Jersey. He also is already familiar with the case. A niece of Katherine Reynolds had come to him with a fear that her aunt had been murdered. He said that he investigated and found that her fears were unfounded, and later talked to Pete when he learned that Pete was investigating as well.

"You again?" Coble asks when he hears my voice and name on the phone.

Such disdain might hurt a lesser man, but I am undeterred. "You remembered," I say. "I'm deeply touched."

"What do you want now?"

"I have some information that might cause you to reopen your investigation, as rigorous as it was." He had said that he called the coroner, got the report, and then dropped the case.

"Let me guess. You want to meet again."

"You got it."

He sighs. "All right. You've got fifteen more minutes."

I head to Englewood to see Coble, and am brought right in to his office. I get right to the point. "Katherine Reynolds's niece was right when she said that her aunt was murdered."

"I believe that was your point last time," he says. "And I believe I mentioned the need for evidence."

I nod. "And since I hang on your every word, I took that to heart. So I brought some evidence with me."

"What is it?"

"It's a name. Daniel Mathis. He is a researcher and chemist in veterinary medicine at Blaine Pharmaceuticals. And he is what we in the legal world call a missing person."

I think I see a reaction from Coble, but I'm not sure. "What does this Mathis have to do with Katherine Reynolds?"

I proceed to tell him about the drug Mathis was developing, the theft, and his disappearance just before going to the FBI. Then I mention the FBI investigation, without using Sharon Dalton's name.

"You're sure the bureau is on this?" he asks. The competitive feeling that local and state cops have toward the FBI is pretty universal.

"Positive, although I don't know what kind of progress they might be making. I thought maybe you'd want to jump in and beat them to it, since it was your case to start."

I've definitely got his interest. "Assuming everything you've said is true, and I'm far from convinced it is, how does this tie in to Reynolds?"

"Carson Reynolds has had phone contact with a man who I am certain is responsible for Daniel Mathis's disappearance."

"Does this man have a name?" he asks.

"I'm sure he does; I just don't know it. Yet. Perhaps you can help in that regard. I think I know where he lives—it's in Hackensack—and when I'm sure I'll share it with you."

"How do you know Reynolds was in contact with this unknown man?"

"That you'll have to take on faith, but it's ironclad." I'm not about to tell him about Sam's phone and GPS work.

"And what makes you certain that this unknown man caused Mathis to disappear?"

"We're into another faith, but ironclad, situation here."

"So I should trust you? Because of our long, close, personal relationship?"

He's making sense, but getting on my nerves in the process. "That's the point, Lieutenant. You shouldn't trust me. You should hear what I'm saying and set out to prove me right or wrong. If I'm right, you can be a hero. If I'm wrong, no harm, no foul."

"Fair enough," he says. "I'll look into it."

"Good. Look into it really fast."

"Why?"

"Pete Stanton's trial starts tomorrow."

"So?"

"So you're my star witness."

I leave Coble's office and am on the way home when I get the call I have been waiting for. It's from Sam, and he says, "I got him, Andy. The phone is on the move, and I'm following the guy now."

"Where are you?"

"At the Coach House Diner on Route 4."

"You're in the parking lot?"

"No, I'm in the diner; I'm at a table. The guy is maybe twenty feet from me as I'm talking to you."

"Do not approach him," I say.

"I don't need to. I got his license plate, and his picture. He doesn't suspect a thing; we got him whenever we want him."

I spend a moment trying to decide what to do. We get nothing by confronting him; first we need to check him out and learn all that we can about him. Sam is right that we can get him any time we want to, now that we know what he looks like and where he lives, and soon we'll have his name.

I instruct Sam to leave the diner and head home. He seems disappointed, but he agrees.

Things are looking up.

Jury selection is always a crapshoot. This time it's worse.

Jury consultants have created an entire industry; they give statistics and use psychographics and all kinds of data to tell the lawyer who is the perfect juror to pick. And sometimes they're right, and sometimes they're wrong.

Just like me.

So I don't use them; I go by logic and gut instinct. But in this case logic is not very logical, because I am representing a very unique defendant.

Usually the defense looks for people who might mistrust the government and police, who don't accept at face value that the defendant is guilty merely because the system says so. We want free thinkers, who are willing to look at both sides of an issue, and not worry about power or pressure.

The prosecution wants jurors who show great respect and deference to law enforcement. Such people, though aware of the "innocent until proven guilty" ground rules, consciously or unconsciously adopt the reverse rule, and challenge the defense to prove innocence, rather than put the burden on the prosecution to prove guilt.

But Pete as the defendant muddies the water. Do I still want people distrustful of the police, since I'm defending a cop? Or do

I want people who are prone to favor the police? Will it be Pete they're favoring? Or the cops who arrested him?

So I basically put all of that aside and do what I usually do, which is choose people I feel like I want to talk to, especially since I'll be talking to them a great deal. I instinctively feel that if I want to talk to them, then they'll want to listen to me. It's worked pretty well for me so far.

It takes us only one day to pick the jury. There are seven men, five women, eight whites, three African Americans, and one Hispanic. Richard looked at me in surprise when I accepted the Hispanic woman, since the victim was Hispanic. I just really liked her, and think she will be fair.

Pete is completely attentive throughout the proceedings, but he doesn't interfere or even offer his opinion. It must be very strange for him to be on the opposite side of this; it's probably the first time in his life that he's rooting for an acquittal.

I head home to meet Sam; he's coming over to update me and Laurie on what he's learned about our mystery man. When I walk in, Sam and Laurie are talking in the den. I can hear Ricky playing with some toys in his room; Ricky's room now looks like the local Toys "R" Us, and I have to confess that I have bought a bunch of them.

"We've got a problem" is the first thing that Sam says to me when I walk in.

"Just so you'll know," I say, "when it comes to an opening conversational line, I prefer, 'Andy, I've got great news.' "

"It's not all bad," Laurie says. "Most of it is good. Sam has done great work."

"Start with the good."

"We've got his name: it's Alex Parker. And I've got a picture of him."

He hands me the photo; I've never seen the guy before. He's sitting in a booth at the diner, eating. He's probably in his thirties, looks very large and solidly built, and apparently likes club sandwiches.

"Now the bad."

"He's gone, and the phone is dead."

"What do you mean?"

"It's off the grid. Shut down."

"Turned off?"

"If it is, it's the first time. But I think it's more than that."

"Why?"

"Because I also noticed that his car was gone from the apartment building parking lot, so I asked the superintendent about him. He said the guy left and wasn't coming back."

"Did he have a lease?" I ask.

"No, it was a week-to-week rental, and he didn't renew. He's out of there."

"Could he have seen you at the diner, Sam? Saw you taking his picture? Maybe it spooked him."

"No chance, Andy . . . I swear."

On balance Laurie is right: it's still good news. We've got Alex Parker's name and photograph. It's much easier to find someone when you know who you're looking for. Of course, it's even easier if you know where they're staying, but you can't have everything.

I call Lieutenant Coble and say, "The guy we're looking for is named Alex Parker."

"How do you know that?"

"I'm a brilliant investigator," I say.

"Yeah, right. You know anything else about him?"

"No, but I will very soon. And I've got his picture. I'll email it to you."

Coble gives me his email address, and then says, "When you know more, I want to hear it."

I hang up, and think about where we are. I don't know why Parker suddenly took off, but hopefully it won't matter in the long run.

We'll get him.

The defense will tell you that Pete Stanton has had a fine career," Richard says to the jury. "Well, this may surprise you, but I'm going to stipulate to that. He has had a fine career, at least until now. And he has enjoyed a good reputation, and a series of promotions."

He walks over to the jury box. "But here's the thing: we are not here to give out a lifetime achievement award. No one, not a police officer or anyone else, earns immunity points to protect them and allow them to commit crimes. And certainly not crimes of this magnitude.

"I take no pleasure in this. I, like everyone else, considered Peter Stanton to be a fine cop. And he probably was. But somewhere along the line, things have gone terribly wrong. Because fine cops don't deal drugs, and they don't commit murder.

"Peter Stanton did both of those things, and we will prove it."

I can feel Pete tense up next to me. In my experience, except for the waiting for and reading of the verdict, this is the toughest time for a defendant. You hear the state saying all these terrible things about you, and you think there is no way anyone will believe otherwise.

"We don't have evidence of his crimes. We have *overwhelming* evidence of his crimes. And you will hear all of it; you will hear about the drugs, and about the cold-blooded murder.

"Danny Diaz did not deserve to die. He deserved our thanks, because he tried to make this world a better place by telling the truth. And his reward was two bullets through the heart.

"So don't let a biography be a substitute for evidence, and logic, and truth. And the truth is that Peter Stanton is a criminal, and cannot be allowed to get away with his crimes."

Judge Matthews asks me if I would like to wait until after lunch to give my opening statement, and I decline. There is no way I'm going to let the jury sit through lunch having heard only Richard's point of view. They're going to hear both sides, hungry or not.

"They're isn't much that Mr. Wallace and I will agree on throughout the course of this trial. Believe me, there will be two sides to every story, his and mine. But remarkably, we can start off with something we are in complete agreement on.

"He is right when he says that Pete Stanton has had an outstanding career, and that he has been promoted with remarkable regularity for his fine work, and that his reputation has always been outstanding among his peers, and the public he has sworn to protect. I certainly cannot quarrel with any of that.

"But, respectfully, here is where he is wrong. While Pete Stanton's biography is not proof of his innocence, it *is* proof of his character. People do not respect him because they know his résumé; they respect him because they know the man.

"Each of you know people you respect, whose character you would never question. Would you believe that person did something terrible, just because someone leveled an accusation? Of course not.

"But please understand that I am not telling you to find Pete Stanton not guilty because of what he has done in his life, or because of what people think of him. All I am asking is that you take all of that into consideration, and because of it hold the prosecution to a high standard.

"Make them prove their case," I say, and then pause a moment, before repeating, "Make them prove their case.

"They will not be able to do so, and that is because Pete Stanton did not commit these terrible acts. He isn't a criminal; he brings criminals to justice. You do not have to protect society from Pete Stanton; he has spent his life protecting us.

"Listen to the facts, and then let him go back to his life. Let him go back to what he does best. Let him continue to be the finest police officer I have ever known.

"Thank you."

I go back to the table and put my hands on Pete's shoulder. Hike gives me a slight nod, his way of saying that I did a good job. I hope so, because I believe every word I said.

As soon as Judge Matthews adjourns for lunch, I head to the diner down the street to meet Lieutenant Stan Phillips. He told me that if I needed help, he was completely available, so I'm calling on him now.

It's to his credit that he's willing to meet with me in public. It takes courage for a member of the department to obviously be supporting Pete at this point, but Phillips does not seem worried about that at all. I've never thought much of him before, and we've obviously had our run-ins, but maybe I should reassess.

"How's the trial going?" he asks.

"All we've had are opening statements. The bad stuff starts after lunch."

"They got a case?" he asks.

I nod. "A strong one."

"So how can I help?"

I take a copy of the Parker photograph out of my briefcase and put it on the table. "This is Alex Parker. He is the guy that I believe murdered Danny Diaz, and set Pete up."

"What makes you think so?"

Again, I am not going to sandbag Sam. "I can't say, but it's legit."

He considers this for a moment, and then nods. "So you want to know what we have on him?"

"Exactly."

He holds up the photo. "Can I keep this?"

"Of course."

He stands up, apparently not planning to have lunch, which is just as well, because I have another meeting. "Let's see what we can find out about Alex Parker," he says.

A half hour later, right on schedule, Willie Miller walks in. "What's going on?" he says.

"I need you to go back to your friend Russo," I say.

He nods. "No problem. What for?"

I give him another copy of the Parker photo, and tell him the name. "Tell him that this is Alex Parker, and he's the guy that hit Diaz. I need him found."

"That's it?" Willie asks.

"No, there's one more thing that is absolutely crucial. If Russo finds Parker, I want him. He is not to have him killed. Tell him you need this as a personal favor."

"Russo wants him dead pretty bad," Willie says.

"Tell him he can get to him in prison, but first I need him alive."

"Okay."

"Will he listen to you?"

Willie thinks for a moment. "If I tell him it's a personal favor? Yeah, he'll listen; he thinks he owes me."

"He does owe you," I point out. "You saved his life."

He shrugs. "It was no big deal; I enjoyed it. You would have done the same thing."

"You think I would have jumped into a prison fight and taken on three guys with knives to save a mobster I never met?"

"No?"

"Willie, I've got to be honest with you, I have trouble picturing it."

At strong safety, number twenty-four, George Selby."

That was how the stadium announcer at the University of Maryland introduced him on November 21, 1993. Selby had two interceptions that day, returning one for a touchdown in a four-point Maryland win over Virginia Tech.

George thinks back upon those days, and especially that game, but not as often as he used to, and only when he is sober. And the memory of the interceptions, and the crowd reaction, is not what is most clear in his mind.

What dominates is what happened on the next-to-last play, when Virginia Tech was driving to try and salvage a win. A linebacker made the tackle, and Selby was simply standing near the pile when an offensive tackle took his leg out. It destroyed his right knee, tearing the MCL and ACL ligaments. Knee surgeries are much better today than in Selby's day, and the injury effectively ended his chance of making it in the NFL.

Plenty of people have similar disappointments, and most of them come back and create productive lives for themselves outside of football. Not George Selby. He left school, bounced around unsuccessfully in a few jobs, and found drugs and alcohol.

He didn't lose his family and his money, because he had no family and money to lose. So his spiral downward wasn't long and deep, but it certainly reached the bottom. For the last four years, Selby has been homeless, living in shelters when the weather is bad, and on the street when it's good. He's been eating where and when he can, mostly at soup kitchens or from handouts.

This particular night was clear and not too hot; the July temperature actually got down to seventy-one degrees. Selby, therefore, was sleeping beneath a trestle on Market Street in Paterson, under a blanket with all of his worldly possessions in a duffel bag behind him. The duffel said UNIVERSITY OF MARYLAND on it, truly his only remaining physical attachment to the glory days.

At two o'clock in the morning, Selby was awakened by a leg nudging him. He was used to being hassled, but it hadn't happened in a while, and almost never at that hour of the morning.

"Get up," said the voice, sounding so authoritative that Selby figured it had to be a cop.

"Aw, come on, man. Why are you hassling me? Go hassle someone else."

Selby had no idea that the man had considered hassling six other people in various locations, but had settled on him instead.

"I said get up."

"Who am I hurting?" Selby asked, still not having opened his eyes fully to look at this intruder.

"How tall are you?" Alex Parker asked.

It was such a strange question that Selby started to turn to look toward the voice. "Six three."

"Get up."

Selby, now fully awake, saw that it was not a cop at all. It was a stranger, a guy as big as himself, and he was carrying a gun.

"Hey, what are you doing? I ain't got nothing."

"You'd be surprised," said Alex Parker. "Time to go."

Richard is starting off by demonstrating opportunity.

He is beginning his case with testimony designed to show that Pete was present and physically able to commit the murder of Danny Diaz. That is why his first witness is Stanley Wilson, the man who came from across the street and identified Pete as coming out of the house just after the bullets were fired.

Wilson is dressed in a suit and tie, beaming and looking like he's making his Broadway debut. Once he gives his name and confirms that he was across the street that night, Richard asks, "Is that where you live?"

"No, I was at my girlfriend's house. Her name is Rita, and she's sitting right back there." He points to an area near the rear of the courtroom.

Richard opts to not have Rita take a bow. Instead he brings Wilson back to the night in question, and asks what happened.

"Well, I heard these shots, so I ran downstairs to see what was going on."

"You could recognize them as gunshots?"

"Sure, I know that sound when I hear it. I own guns myself."

"How long did it take you to get downstairs?"

"Maybe a minute. Maybe less. I was really moving," he says, with obvious pride.

Wilson goes on to describe the events of that night much as he described them to Laurie and me. He heard the shots, came downstairs, and saw Pete leaving the house. Pete then went into his car, and sat there for a few minutes, before other cops arrived.

The story is straightforward, and while it's not eyewitness testimony in that Wilson isn't saying he saw Pete fire the shot, it is certainly very damaging if not impeached.

Enter Andy Carpenter, Impeacher in Chief. "Mr. Wilson, you testified that you were sleeping in the bedroom. Is that the one upstairs, in the back of the house?"

"Yup. Yes. That's the one."

"When you jumped up to go downstairs, did you turn the lights on in the bedroom?"

"Let me think . . . no, I was in a hurry."

"Were you wearing pajamas?"

"Nah, I told you. I don't wear nothing when I sleep."

"So did you get dressed before you came down?" I ask.

"Well, sure. I wasn't going to go outside like that."

I nod. "Probably just as well. What did you put on?"

"Not much. I was in a hurry."

I walk toward the wall, where Hike has placed two large, blown-up photographs mounted on Styrofoam. I ask the judge to admit them into evidence, and she does so without objection from Richard.

"Mr. Wilson, this is a police photograph taken twenty minutes after they arrived on the scene. Do you see yourself in this photograph?"

He points. "Sure. I'm right there."

"And behind you and to the right, is that the house you were sleeping in?"

"Yes."

I get him to agree that there are no lights on in the house, and the windows of the bedroom he was sleeping in are dark as well. "So you didn't turn the lights on before you left, correct?"

"Yeah, like I said, I was in a hurry."

I take the other Styrofoam mounted photograph and introduce that into evidence as well. "This is the same photograph, except the area where you are standing is magnified. But that's still you, right?"

"Yeah."

"What are you wearing in the photo?"

"A shirt, jeans, and sneakers."

"Socks?"

"Sure."

"Underwear?"

He laughs slightly, still amazingly not having a clue where I'm going. "Of course."

"So, just to be clear, tell me if this accurately sums up your testimony. You were sleeping. You heard gunshots, so you jumped out of bed, naked. You put on underwear, then proceeded to put on a shirt, which you buttoned completely, including the cuffs."

Finally, it dawns on him. "Hey—"

"I'm sorry, Mr. Wilson. Let me finish my question, please, and then you can talk as long as you like. You then put on jeans, zipped them up, buttoned them, and fastened your belt. Then you put on socks and sneakers, and as you can see in the photograph, tied the laces on both. And you did all of this in the dark.

"Then you came all the way downstairs and to the front of the house, and went outside. And you did all this in one minute. Is that your testimony?"

"I did it fast, that's all I know."

"How fast, Mr. Wilson. Ten minutes?"

"No, not that long. Five minutes."

"Five minutes to do all of that, just having woken up? To find your clothes, put them on the way you did, and come downstairs, all in the dark?"

"I think I could do it in less than five minutes."

"Care to prove it?" I ask.

"What do you mean?"

I turn to Judge Matthews. "Your Honor, my associate has brought with him clothing that is an exact match for what Mr. Wilson is wearing in that photograph." Hike holds up a bag to show her. "I would propose that Mr. Wilson go into anteroom four, which has no windows. We can make it completely dark in there, after which he can strip naked, lie down, and on signal, he can jump up and put the clothes on."

Richard is up, objecting. "Your Honor, this is ridiculous." The packed gallery is roaring with laughter.

Since I am not aware of "ridiculous" being a valid objection, I continue. "We can see how long it takes, not including the time he needed to run downstairs, go to the front of the house, and exit. In the dark."

"No way am I doing that," Wilson says.

I smile as condescending a smile as I can manage. "Of course not, because you know how long it would take you. Ten minutes would be conservative. You know how many cars can pull up and leave a street in ten minutes, Mr. Wilson?"

"Objection. Badgering," says Richard.

"Sustained." The judge is trying to regain control of the courtroom. "I believe you've made your point, Mr. Carpenter."

I nod. "I believe I have."

She excuses Wilson, and announces that we'll take a ten-minute recess. I smile. "Ten minutes? That's a really long time."

My dismantling of Stanley Wilson was more style than substance.

Which is not to say that it was not important, but rather that triumphs like that, by themselves, will not carry the day.

The style victory was significant, especially because of its timing. We showed the jury right at the top that they should not take whatever the prosecution witnesses say at face value. That is a major hurdle, because although the burden of proof is technically on the prosecution, the reality is that jurors have a tendency to believe them, unless they are shown a reason not to.

Substantively, the cross-examination was less valuable. Yes, Wilson was shown not to have gotten downstairs in one minute, and that is a positive for our case. But the truth is that whether it took one minute, or five, or ten, Pete was in fact on the scene, and was in the house.

Pete called in for backup, and reported the murder himself. Obviously, he had to have been in the house; he admitted it. We can't and won't deny it, so Wilson isn't necessary for Richard to place him there.

At the end of the day, we're going to have to point to someone else and say that he did it and that Pete didn't. If we can give the jury an alternative person to consider, then we'll have made a huge jump toward creating reasonable doubt.

That person is Alex Parker. The problem is that we don't know where he is or what is his motivation. We don't even know for sure what happened to Juanita Diaz. We have theories, but that's all they are.

Worse yet, much worse yet, is that even if we had these answers, we'd have to relate them directly to Danny Diaz's murder, in order to get the facts in front of the jury. That may be the highest hurdle of all.

I leave the courthouse and head home, and my arrival there is now the second night in a row that I've had what for me is a new experience. I've been working from home, so I literally haven't come home from work. The last two days I've been at the courthouse, so I've not been home all day.

It's a domestic scene right out of a 1950s sitcom. Laurie is in the kitchen cooking, Ricky is watching TV, and the two dogs come to greet me at the door. It makes me want to call out, "Honey, I'm home," but I don't in case Edna is here. I don't want her to think I'm talking to her.

This just seemed to happen. One day I was a swinging bachelor, except for the "swinging" part, and except for the "bachelor" part, and the next day I'm a patriarch. I won't say that I dislike it; it's more that it doesn't seem real, or natural. At least not yet.

I say hello to Ricky, and Laurie, and then take Tara and Sebastian for a ten-minute walk. I think Tara has loved having Ricky and Sebastian around. She hasn't mentioned it, but I can tell.

When I get back with the dogs, I go into the kitchen to talk to Laurie. With the case in full gear, and Ricky in the house, talking between just Laurie and me has been in short supply.

"He asked about his stepmother," Laurie says, softly.

"What did he ask?"

"If she was coming back."

"What did you say?" I ask.

"That I didn't know. But that he didn't have to worry; he will always be taken care of."

"She's not coming back."

She shakes her head. "You don't know that."

"Yes, I do."

"We have to protect him," Laurie says. "He's been through so much."

I know what women are thinking just about as often as the Jets win Super Bowls, but suddenly I completely understand what is in Laurie's mind, and it is borderline horrifying. If Juanita Diaz is in fact dead, and maybe even if she isn't, Laurie wants to adopt Ricky.

I cannot voice this; if I do so, it will become a topic to discuss, and debate, and I will come in second. We've talked about marriage a few times in the past, but neither of us ever considered it important. We've even talked about someday having children, with an emphasis on the "someday."

But certainly we've never considered having a child this fast, or this large.

This is absolutely a conversation I do not want to have now, and even though silence does not come naturally to me, I have got to keep my mouth shut.

"You want to adopt him," I say, amazed at the lack of control I have over my own mouth.

"I think it's something we should consider."

"We've talked about this. You said you weren't ready to have kids."

"I'm not ready to have 'kids,' " she says. "But I think I am ready to have this particular kid."

"But I'm not ready to be a father, Laurie. I'm not even ready to be an adult."

"Just think about it," she says. "That's all I ask."

"I'll make you a deal. I'll promise to think about it, if you promise not to think about it."

"The best I can do is promise not to talk about it," she says, and then ominously adds, "for now."

I just about fall down rushing to get out of the kitchen; the conversation with Laurie has shaken me up. I make a mental note to avoid the kitchen in the future.

While I was at court, Stan Phillips delivered the information he was able to get on Alex Parker. I go into the den to read about him.

After five minutes of reading about Alex Parker, I wish I was back in the kitchen.

Alex Parker was U.S. Army Special Forces. He might still be in the service, except for the fact that he killed two Afghan civilians outside a nightspot in Kabul.

Parker was not charged with a crime, since fellow soldiers testified that the two men approached Parker and threw the first punches. It must have been hard to imagine anyone in their right minds attacking Parker, but the army prosecutors could not make the case.

So Parker walked on the charges, and was invited to keep on walking right out of the army. Phillips has managed to get some records from Parker's army file—I have no idea how and I don't want to know—and they are sketchy. Many paragraphs are redacted, meaning that they were classified operations.

Reading between the lines, and the redactions, it is clear that Parker was a stealth operator, sent in to places to both blend in with the environment and cause violent havoc. One thing is for sure, anyone who knew Parker is in agreement that he is extremely dangerous, emphasis on "extremely."

The time he has spent since, as a civilian, is shrouded in some mystery. There were reports that he worked as a hit man for a Nevada crime family, but then other, just as speculative, reports that he had gone off on his own.

And then, nothing.

I call Lieutenant Coble; since my plan is to use him as a witness, I want him as current and informed as possible. This time he takes my call and doesn't even start off by insulting me or sounding annoyed, a marked improvement over our previous encounters.

"What have you got?" he asks.

I proceed to tell him about Parker's background with the Nevada crime family and how dangerous his military record makes him appear. "This is our guy," I say.

"Let me know if you locate him," he says.

"You'll arrest him?"

"Of course not; we've got nothing on him, a judge would laugh at us. But I'll bring him in for questioning and see what shakes out."

That's better than I thought, so I promise to keep him advised.

Next, I call Willie Miller and ask him to convey to Joseph Russo the possibility that Parker worked for a Nevada crime family. I figure maybe they all know each other from crime conventions or mobster book clubs or something, and he might be able to get information.

Willie tells me that he already told Russo about Parker, and that Russo said he would see what he could do about finding him. He also promised not to kill him, but rather to deliver him to us, although he wasn't pleased about it, since he wants revenge for Diaz.

After reading about Parker, maybe killing him isn't such a bad idea.

I spend the rest of the night reading through all of my files on the case so that I will be prepared for court tomorrow. I try not to think about deadly Special Forces operatives turned bad, or child adoptions. I'm only partially successful, but I force myself to continue, because tomorrow is a big day.

Actually, pretty much every day of a trial is a big day.

Richard's case is going to kick into gear tomorrow. It's actually both my favorite and least favorite time of any trial. The reason it's my least favorite is fairly obvious: one witness after another is going to come on the stand and, in a carefully rehearsed manner, give information that, if taken at anywhere close to face value, will assert that Pete Stanton is a cold-blooded killer.

But I also look forward to it, because cross-examining these witnesses gives me the opportunity to be on the attack. Presenting my own case feels passive and defensive; I'm the one putting the witnesses up, I know what they're going to say, and then the other side tries to bring them down. Cross-examination is much more fun than direct testimony.

Of course, the risks are great. If I can't challenge what a witness is saying, and in the process get the witness to back off or appear incorrect, then the incriminating testimony becomes accepted fact by the jury. My only chance then is to introduce rebuttal witnesses much later in the trial, and it can often be too little, too late.

I'm feeling the pressure.

The tip came in the form of an anonymous phone call at eleven p.m.

It had been routed to Lieutenant Coble's office, because he was in charge of the investigation and had put out the word that he was searching for Alex Parker.

Coble was at home at the time, but the message was relayed to him. Cognizant of how rare it was that tips actually amounted to anything, he directed that an officer on duty drive by the house in question, which was in a fairly rural area near Montvale.

The officer did as instructed, and saw a car parked in the driveway of the house. The license plate and description of the car matched what Coble had included in the information packet, and what he had received from Sam's reconnaissance of Parker at the diner.

In an instant, the unconfirmed tip had turned into apparent gold. Coble was again called at home, and he requested backup. He would meet four other officers at the barracks in thirty minutes, and together they would go out to the house and bring Parker in for questioning.

Since Carpenter had emphasized how dangerous Parker was, and since the military records Coble obtained had confirmed it, he was going to be extra cautious. Using a detailed description of the house and the grounds around it, Coble devised a plan. They would completely surround the house at prearranged locations, and then approach.

There was one light on in the interior of the house, which was how it had appeared when the drive-by took place. The car remained where it had been as well.

One major advantage for the cops was the seclusion of the house. There would not be any curious onlookers or neighbors, and with no outside interference, they could advance to the house with less chance of being detected.

Once the team was in place, Coble and another officer went to the front door. They were surprised to discover that it was ajar, and their knocking opened it a little more.

Nobody answered, so they knocked again, opening it even further, which was fine with Coble. There was still no answer or sign of life, and without a search warrant, they would not have been able to enter . . . had they not seen the blood.

It was spattered in the corridor just beyond the door. Coble and the other officer just looked at each other, understanding what the other was thinking. This was obviously evidence of a crime, which removed the restriction on entering.

Coble conveyed what was happening to the other officers. They had to proceed as if someone dangerous were inside, so they entered the house from all sides simultaneously, guns drawn. Coble went through the front, and immediately saw the source of the blood.

There was a body lying at a grotesque angle near the stairwell. The victim had been savagely beaten around the head and shoulders, obviously with the blood-covered baseball bat that was on the floor beside him.

Coble looked down at the body. "Hello, Mr. Parker."

For Richard, placing Pete at the scene of the drug crime is easy.

Since the illegal drugs were found in Pete's house, it is fairly credible for the prosecution to claim that Pete had access to them.

But Richard still needs someone to testify that the drugs were in fact there, and he has logically chosen Lieutenant Patrick Bagwell of the Paterson Police Department. Bagwell was one of two leaders of the team that investigated Pete, and he executed the search warrant on Pete's house, in the process finding the heroin. And while I did not know his name at the time, Bagwell is the guy who arrested Pete at Charlie's.

Bagwell is here simply to testify about the drugs; his partner will be on later to talk about other aspects of the investigation. Richard takes him through the process of entering Pete's house and commencing the search.

"Was the defendant at home?" Richard asks.

"No. He had been taken into custody the day before."

With Richard leading the way, Bagwell describes finding the drugs, hidden in a suitcase in a guestroom closet.

"You knew immediately it was heroin?" Richard asks.

"I was quite certain, but obviously we had it tested after we got it back to the lab. It was high-quality heroin."

"Can you estimate the street value of it?"

Bagwell nods. "Definitely in excess of a hundred thousand dollars."

"In your experience, is it possible that this was for one person's recreational use?"

"That is not possible for any human that I am aware of."

Bagwell's people did not find anything else incriminating in the house, and Richard is quite willing to have him say that. The effect is to make himself and Bagwell look reasonable and unbiased; they are simply reporting the facts, good and bad.

Once again I am limited in how much I can accomplish on cross-examination. The facts are the facts; the drugs were there and I'm not going to be able to change that. I have no reason to believe that Bagwell is lying, or that the police planted them. They had no reason to have a vendetta against Pete; he was a valued partner to them for a very long time.

"Were you surprised when you found the drugs?" I ask.

He frowns. "Nothing surprises me anymore."

"Really? You don't have expectations going into something?"

"I try not to. I just take the facts as they present themselves."

"That's very impressive. But you take experiences into account, don't you? For example, if you were approaching someone you knew had attacked people violently in the past, you might expect more danger than if, say, you were approaching Judge Matthews?"

There is laughter from the gallery, but not so much as a smile from the judge. "Of course I take experience into account."

"Thank you. So based on your fifteen years' experience of friendship and partnership with Pete Stanton, were you surprised to discover that he had all these illegal drugs in his house? Or did you always suspect him all these years, but never said anything to anyone or tried to prove it?"

He's stuck, so he says, "I was surprised. Yes. But I was also surprised that he committed a murder."

"Thank you for that. I was afraid I'd have to drag that out of you as well."

Richard objects and the judge sustains; business as usual.

I continue, "The closet where you found the drugs, was it locked?"

"No."

"Did it have a lock on it? One that required a key?"

"Yes."

"In your search, did you find a set of keys in the house?" I know from the search warrant list that he did.

"Yes."

"Was one of them for the closet?"

"Yes."

"So your position is that Captain Stanton hid the drugs, but while he could have also locked them away, he chose not to?"

"I don't know what was going through his mind," he says.

"Prior to this, did you consider him a smart cop, and a good investigator?"

He could duck this, but doesn't. "I did."

"Thank you. So you took this package of surprising drugs back to the lab, and the forensics people went over it?"

"Yes, of course."

"And Captain Stanton's fingerprints were all over the package?"

"No."

I of course know all this from the discovery, so I go into my best surprise-feigning reaction. "Really? Whose prints were on the bag?"

"No one's. It was wiped clean."

"But as a detective, you do think someone brought them to that closet, right? I mean, they couldn't have been beamed there or anything, could they?"

"Obviously someone brought them there. Maybe he wore gloves."

"In the summer, Lieutenant Bagwell?"

He ignores that. "The drugs are illegal," he says. "It is natural for people to not want their fingerprints on them."

"So your hypothesis is that Captain Stanton wiped his fingerprints from a bag of drugs in his own house? He figured that if the drugs were found in his own closet where he lives, his fingerprints would be the problem?"

He has no good answer for that, so rather than beat that horse any more, I move on. "Now that you had this surprising bag of drugs, you assumed that because there was so much of it, Captain Stanton must be dealing. You testified that he couldn't be using all of that himself. Correct?"

"Correct."

"So did you consult with the detectives in your department whose expertise is in the drug trade?"

"I did."

"Did they give you any information at all, based on their experiences in the local drug world, that confirms Captain Stanton's involvement in this?"

"No."

"Nothing, Lieutenant Bagwell? Not even a hint of anything?"

"No."

"So, as a trained detective, how do you analyze this? Do you think he took his police salary, bought a hundred thousand dollars worth of drugs, and just put them away, thinking he'd someday sell it if he needed the money?"

"I have no idea."

"Is heroin like wine? Does it get better with age? For example, does a dealer say, 'I've got a wonderful 1991 bag of junk; that was a terrific year for poppies?' "

Richard objects, and this time Judge Matthews sustains and admonishes me. I'm fine with that, since I'm almost finished.

"Lieutenant Bagwell, you found the drugs hidden in a guestroom closet in Captain Stanton's house. As you sit here, do you know with absolute certainty who put them there?"

"I don't. But no break-in was ever reported at that location, nor were there any signs of one."

"If I told you that someone other than Captain Stanton had a key to the house, and placed those drugs there, could you tell me with certainty that I was wrong?"

Again, he could duck, but doesn't. "No, not with certainty, no."

"No further questions."

My good feeling about the cross-examination lasts about four minutes after court is recessed.

That's how long it takes me to go out into the corridor and return the phone call from Lieutenant Coble. He left a message on my cell phone that he needed to speak to me on a matter of considerable importance.

He says, "Coble," when he picks up the phone. So I say, "Carpenter." We've got quite a conversation going.

Then it takes a turn for the worse. "Parker is dead," he says.

"When? How?" I'm asking those questions, but there is no answer that will make this anything other than a disaster.

"In a cabin near Montvale. We got a tip he was there, but somebody else found out about it before us. They used his head for a piñata."

"You're sure it was him?" I ask.

"Who do you think you're dealing with, Barney Fife? Fingerprints match his army records."

"Any suspects?" I ask, though I already have one.

"Not at this moment."

I get off the phone, effectively ending one of the most depressing conversations I've had in a very long while.

I call Willie, who is at the Tara Foundation adopting out dogs, which is where I wish I was right now. "Parker is dead," I say. "Someone bashed in his head.."

"That can't be good," he says. Willie is a master of understatement.

"Couldn't be worse," I say. "I want to know if your friend Russo had it done." I am at the moment mentally kicking myself for bringing Russo into this at all, and thinking Willie could control him.

"Andy, he told me he wouldn't, so he didn't."

"Willie, I know he's your friend, but he's a murderer and a thief. He's been a criminal his entire life. You think he would draw the line at lying?"

Willie agrees to call him, while still vouching for his honor. I need to take some time to process where this leaves us. Parker was the key link between Reynolds and the mysterious deaths on the one hand, and Danny Diaz and Pete on the other.

We didn't have him, but we were trying to get him very badly. So badly that it probably caused me to blow it by enlisting Russo's help. Now that he is out of the picture, we are back to . . . is there a square before one?

Much as I'd like to leave and think this through, or leave and put my head in a gas oven, I've got to get back into court. Richard's next witness is Sergeant Candice Woo, who was Diaz's contact in the department in his role as low-level informer.

She testifies on direct examination about her relationship with Danny and his actions as an informant. "He didn't provide much information," she says. "Until recently with Pete . . . Captain Stanton."

"What did he say about Captain Stanton?"

"That he was dealing drugs. Danny couldn't stand drugs, so even though he owed Captain Stanton, he couldn't stand by and let this happen."

"Did he express any other concerns?" Richard asks.

"Yes, he was afraid for his safety if Captain Stanton found out that he was informing on him."

I start my cross by asking, "Sergeant Woo, you knew Danny Diaz well?"

"Fairly well," she says.

"And you knew Captain Stanton well? You had years of dealing with him? Saw him almost every day?" I know that to be the case; Pete told me he has actually had dinner a number of times with Candice and her husband, Brian.

"Yes."

"Did you know what their relationship with each other was like?"

She nods again. "I knew quite a bit about it, yes."

"Please describe what you believed to be true about their relationship."

"They seemed very close," Sergeant Woo says. "Captain Stanton took a liking to him, and actually had a lot to do with his not getting a longer sentence. He vouched for his character; said he would help him turn his life around."

"And did he?"

"Yes. And he also took a strong liking to Diaz's son. Took him to ball games, that kind of thing."

"If you know, did the Diaz family ever stay at Captain Stanton's house?"

"Yes. When he first got out of prison, he needed a place to stay. Captain Stanton was on vacation, so he let them use his house. I believe they stayed there another week after he returned."

"So Danny Diaz would have had a key to Captain Stanton's house?"

"I would assume so."

"Do you know if he returned it?" I ask.

Sergeant Woo shakes her head. "I'm sorry, I have no idea."

"Thank you. No further questions."

"We need to talk," I say to Pete when court is adjourned.

"Uh-oh" is his appropriate response, since "needing" to talk rarely results in fun conversations. I probably shouldn't have characterized it that way, although the news I have for him is not good at all.

"I've arranged for us to go into the anteroom."

As if on cue, the bailiff comes over, and we exchange nods, which tells me that he knows where he is bringing Pete.

I've been updating Pete every step of the way, more than I generally do with most clients. So once we're settled in the room, I come right to the point. "Parker is dead."

I can see him stiffen slightly as he absorbs the blow; finding Parker was his main hope, as it was mine. "How?"

"Got his head crushed in. I'm checking, but my guess is Russo's people got to him, and reneged on our deal."

"This is not good at all," Pete says. "What are you going to do?"

I realize in the moment that, while I have been diligent in keeping Pete aware of the various goings-on, I haven't been picking his brain as much as I should. Investigating is what he does, and does well.

So I throw the question back at him. "What would you do?"

He thinks for at least forty-five seconds before answering. "The focus has to be on Reynolds."

I was thinking the same thing, but mainly because I had no other possibilities. I'm interested in Pete's rationale. "Why Reynolds?" I ask.

"Because all of this started when I began investigating him. When I was looking at Hambler and the others, nobody paid attention."

"The problem for me is I have no authority. No subpoena power, nothing. Reynolds can just shrug me off."

"You can use Coble."

In the moment I make a decision: if we're going to go down, we're going to go down using the biggest guns we can find. "Coble is not getting it done," I say. "I'm going to the bureau. And if I get nowhere with them, which is probably what will happen, then I'm going public."

"Okay," he says, in a tone that makes me question whether he is onboard with that strategy.

"What do you think?" I ask. I don't need Pete's approval; these are my calls and I'm going to make them. But I am interested in his input.

"When this is over, however it ends, I want you to forget I ever said this. But I trust you, and I'm comfortable with whatever decision you make."

"Wow," I say. "I can't even tell Vince you said that?"

"Especially not Vince."

We talk a bit more about the case, and just before I'm going to leave, I say, "Laurie told me that if Juanita Diaz is really dead, or otherwise not coming back, she wants us to adopt Ricky."

"I love Laurie," Pete says.

"Yeah, me too."

"So what are you going to do?"

"I don't know," I say, because I don't. "I'm not sure I'm ready to be a father, and I feel like I shouldn't do it just because Laurie wants me to."

"Then do it because I want you to. No kidding, you'd be a great father," he says.

"That's two nice things you've said to me in one conversation."

He nods. "I've been cooped up way too long."

I head home, and Laurie is there playing a video game with Ricky, where they stand in front of the television and move their arms, holding a joystick, which in turn controls what is happening on the television. They're actually playing virtual tennis. I swear, if they had these things when I was a kid, I would have never left the house.

I join in the game, but it's way beyond me, and Ricky beats me, six-one.

"You got lucky," I tell him.

He practically sneers at me, with a derisive laugh thrown in for good measure. "Lucky?"

"How was he lucky?" Laurie asks, once again taking his side.

"I sprained my joystick."

Finally, I manage to get Laurie out of the room, so I can discuss with her what happened in court, and most importantly what happened to Parker.

She knows all about Parker. "Willie called," she says. "He spoke to Russo, who says he had nothing to do with it, but wishes he had."

"Do you believe him?" I ask.

"Probably," she says. "Because Russo told Willie that this means it's not over, that somebody has to be above Parker. He said that Parker wasn't the type to make plans; he simply and sometimes literally executed them. So Russo wants to find and deal with whoever is above Parker."

"I'm going to go to the FBI with this; Sharon Dalton spoke to an agent named Spencer Akers," I say. "So, can you call Cindy?"

"Again? I think this time you should call her, Andy."

Cindy Spodek is an FBI agent I met on a case a while back who has since become friends with Laurie and me. Of course, Laurie speaks to her frequently, as a real friend might. I only call her when I need a favor, a fact she has pointed out to me with some frequency.

Cindy is currently located in the Boston office, where she is second in command. But since it's after hours, I try her at home, and she answers.

"Cindy? Andy Carpenter. . . . How the hell are you?"

"Let me guess, you need a favor," she says.

"You know, usually when I ask someone how they are, they say, 'fine, thanks,' or something like that."

"Fine, thanks," she says. "What do you need, Andy?"

"Actually, I'm calling because I found out today that we have a mutual friend."

"Who's that?"

"Spencer Akers."

"Who is Spencer Akers?" she asks.

"It's amazing that you ask that, because I asked the same thing. 'Who is Spencer Akers?' " Laurie is literally groaning as she listens to this conversation.

"Andy, what the hell are you talking about?"

"Spencer Akers. He's an agent in the local bureau office here."

"You're making even less sense than usual," she says. "Let me speak to Laurie."

I hand the phone to Laurie. "She wants to talk to you."

"I think it's more that she doesn't want to talk to you," Laurie says, taking the phone.

Laurie explains the situation to Cindy in clear, concise terms, an approach I never considered. Then she directly asks her if she can contact Spencer Akers and arrange a meeting with him. Then she says, "Thanks, Cindy," and hangs up.

"So?" I ask.

"So she said all you had to do was say you need a favor that could help Pete." Cindy knows Pete well, and they like and respect each other.

"Will she set it up?"

"She's going to contact this Akers guy and will call you back."

I'm expecting her to get to it tomorrow, but she calls back fifteen minutes later. I'm smart enough to let Laurie answer the phone, and Cindy gives her the news that Akers will meet with me after court tomorrow, at the bureau office in Newark.

"I know how to make things happen," I say to Laurie after they hang up. "Now, any chance you'll call Hike for me?"

"Zero."

"Fair enough." I pick up the phone to call Hike and tell him I want him to ask the judge to issue subpoenas for all the phone and GPS records that Sam has already collected on Diaz, Alex Parker, and Reynolds. We're going to need them, and the only way we can use them is if we can show we obtained them legally. Hike says he'll do it first thing in the morning, before court starts tomorrow.

Next I call Sam. "I need you to get me all you can possibly find about Carson Reynolds. I want to know everything there is to know about him."

"You mean biography, or financials? You want his credit card bills?"

"I want everything."

"Business also?"

"Everything, Sam. I want you to give this guy a cyber rectal exam."

He laughs. "With pleasure," he says, and hangs up.

Today was a bad day because of the death of Alex Parker, but for some reason I'm feeling okay.

Taking the offensive sometimes does that for me.

I meet with Pete before the court day begins, to apprise him of developments.

When I finally get into court, Hike is there and waiting for me.

"Judge approved the subpoenas," he says. "Phone companies will have thirty-six hours to comply."

"Just like that?" I ask.

He smiles. "Not quite. She called Richard in, who proceeded to go nuts. Said no relevance was established, that he never heard of Reynolds and Parker, that it was a fishing expedition, blah, blah, blah."

"What did you say?"

"That if he never heard of these people, how would he know we were fishing?"

"Beautiful."

"So the judge approved it subject to our demonstrating relevance later in the trial. Which I assume you'll be able to do?"

I shrug. "That's the plan."

Just then Richard comes over to me. "You want to tell me what's going on?" he asks.

"Not particularly."

"You are aware that you are a pain in the ass?"

I smile. "It's part of my charm."

Judge Matthews takes her seat on the bench, and Richard calls

Dr. Donna Palmieri, a professor of forensics at the John Jay College of Criminal Justice. Dr. Palmieri examined the bullets and shell casings in the Diaz shooting.

Her testimony, while dry as dirt, sounds authoritative; the lady knows what she is talking about. She describes the very distinctive characteristics of the material she analyzed, and then Richard asks if she has seen those characteristics before.

"Yes," she says. "The same weapon was used a year earlier, in the murder of Carla Kendall."

"You're certain of that?" Richard asks.

"I am."

"Was the weapon ever found in that case?"

"No, sir."

"And do you know what police officer was first on the scene, and ultimately conducted the investigation?"

"Yes," she says, pointing to the defense table. "Captain Stanton."

I could object, but her testimony has been relatively straightforward, and this gives me something to go after her with in cross-examination.

"Dr. Palmieri, you mentioned that the gun was used in the Carla Kendall case. How much work did you do on that case?"

"I didn't work on it."

I feign surprise. "Really? Then how did you know the same gun was used?"

"I was given the ballistics records by Mr. Wallace."

"When?"

"Last week."

"I see. But you knew other things about that case. For example, you knew that Captain Stanton was first on the scene, and conducted the investigation. When did you learn that?"

"Mr. Wallace told me that last week."

"Is there anything you said in your direct testimony that Mr. Wallace didn't coach you to say?"

Richard is out of his chair and objecting, but this time I'm in the right. "Your Honor, the witness passed on information that she was given by the prosecutor; they were things she did not know independently. That is the classic definition of coaching. Bill Belichick has less control over this team than Mr. Wallace does over his."

"That last remark was uncalled for, Mr. Carpenter."

"Sorry, Your Honor," I lie. I'm playing for the jury, of course, and Richard, as mad as he is, will ultimately know that.

The judge overrules Richard's objection, which allows me to have a little more fun with this. I don't get far, but there's really nothing to get. The gun was used in both killings, and we'll just have to deal with that.

Next witness up for Richard is Sergeant Cathy Conley, one of the department's fingerprint technicians. Richard takes much more time with her than he should, in my humble opinion.

Conley lets him guide her through all of the places in Diaz's house where Pete's fingerprints were found. They were in the bathroom, the kitchen, the den, and the area near the front door where the shooting took place. I'm not sure what he is aiming for, except to possibly demonstrate that Pete and Diaz knew each other well.

This, in the cross-examination business, is low-hanging fruit. "Sergeant Conley, based on the fingerprints, can you tell me when Captain Stanton was there?"

"I cannot."

"Could it have been the night of the murder?"

"That is certainly possible."

"Could it have been a month ago, or longer?"

"Yes."

"Can you leave fingerprints when you wear gloves?" I ask.

"No."

"If I may ask a personal question, do you have friends that you visit on occasion?"

"Of course," she says.

"Have you ever murdered any of them?"

"Certainly not."

"Of course not; they're your friends. But bear with me for a second, and imagine you did go over to one of your friends' house, for the purpose of murdering that friend. Do you think that while you were there, you would go to the bathroom, the kitchen, and other rooms, leaving your fingerprints everywhere?"

"I can't imagine myself in that situation."

"But as a trained police officer, you would know how fingerprints work, right? You'd know that if you were inclined to commit a crime, leaving fingerprints behind could be a problem, correct?"

"Yes."

"Trained police officers would know that, wouldn't they?"

"Certainly."

"Now, supposing you didn't care about that, and you left your fingerprints everywhere, and then shot your friend. Would you put gloves on to do it?"

"I don't know."

"If you had brought gloves with you, wouldn't it have made sense to put them on before you started leaving prints everywhere?"

"I suppose so," she says.

"As do I. No further questions."

During a trial, time ranks just below evidence as the most valued commodity.

There is simply never enough of it, and I find myself doing so much reacting that it's hard to find a moment to actually think.

One of the things I force myself to do, often sacrificing sleep in the process, is to read and reread all of the documents associated with the case. It is important for me to know every detail cold, so that I can react instantly and instinctively in court.

But beyond that, I find that in repeatedly going over documents, new things emerge, sometimes critical, that I have simply missed in previous readings. I'm not sure what that says about my power of concentration, but it's something I've had to learn to live with, and adjust to.

Hike and Sam have made it somewhat easier for me. They somehow managed to copy all the documents onto my iPad. This way I can use any free time productively, without having to carry around a box filled with paper.

It comes in especially handy at times like this, while I'm sitting in the reception area at the FBI offices, waiting to be called in to see Agent Spencer Akers. I'm reading through the information Sam prepared on Carson Reynolds. This is actually the first time I've done so, since he just prepared it last night and this morning.

Reynolds's biography seems relatively uneventful, at least for my purposes. He went to Tufts, then got his MBA at the University of Virginia. He began his career on Wall Street and worked his way up to where he now heads up a private equity fund.

Reynolds and his late wife are philanthropists, having donated millions through a foundation they themselves set up. They did not have any children, and in fact Katherine Reynolds had no family at all. Her parents and younger sister were killed in a car crash when she was eighteen years old. She was at college at the time. Carson Reynolds does not have any siblings either.

There is nothing here to indicate that Carson Reynolds is a murderer; there is also nothing here to indicate I'd want to have a beer and watch a football game with him. He seems upstanding and boring, although I suppose his mistress must see a side of him that I don't. Actually, that's a side I don't ever want to see.

Sam titles every document he gives me with the words "Investigative Dossier, prepared by Samuel Willis." He thinks he's James Bond, but he does great work.

There's a second section, entitled "Investigative Dossier, Section B, by Samuel Willis," which gives the background on Reynolds's company. They take controlling financial interest in companies, put their own people in, and then improve the balance sheet until the companies can be sold off at a profit.

I'm reading it quickly when a young woman comes out to tell me that Agent Akers is ready to see me. I close the iPad cover and stand up, then realize what it was that I just read. I say, "One second," and open the cover again to reread the key part.

It's a section that lists the companies in which Reynolds Equity has a controlling interest. Most of them I've never heard of, but number six on the list is one that I've become familiar with just recently.

Blaine Pharmaceuticals.

Workplace of Daniel Mathis, the missing chemist who created the euthanasia drug for animals. And the location where Alex Parker's phone, presumably in the possession of Alex Parker, was identified as being on the day that Mathis went missing.

The pieces that would not connect are starting to connect.

I apologize to the young woman and then follow her in to see Agent Akers, who looks like he's in his early thirties. After we say hello, he says, "So my boss says to take Agent Spodek seriously, and Agent Spodek says to take you seriously. So here we are."

"You received a visit a while back from Sharon Dalton, reporting one Daniel Mathis as missing."

He doesn't respond, so I say, "Have you made any progress in finding him?"

He smiles. "We don't comment on an ongoing investigation."

"I've got a hunch you're not taking me seriously."

He smiles again. "Why don't we start by you telling me why you're here?"

"I'm here to make a deal with you. I will give you some information, most of which you probably do not already know. If you investigate the case and crack it, you will be a star within the bureau."

"And in return?" he asks.

"You act quickly, you give me information as you get it, and you apply pressure where it needs to be applied."

"I should tell you to leave now," he says.

"No you shouldn't, for two reasons. First, because you'd have to answer to your boss when this explodes in your face. And second, because the deal costs you nothing, and has the potential to make you a hero." I smile. "And I say that as someone who is to be taken seriously, and as someone who may call upon you only to make a phone call."

"Okay," he says. "Sight unseen this is hard to agree to, but the quick action and exchange of information I can live with. The application of pressure I can't agree to until I know who and why."

It's a reasonable position for him to take, and I say so. Then, "Start with updating me on the status of the Mathis missing persons investigation."

"There is no status," he says. "We sent out a bulletin, he's still missing, and there has not been a single report that he has been spotted anywhere. I don't have the slightest idea where he is."

"He's dead," I say.

"You know that?"

"I haven't seen the body, but I know it. He's one of an ever-increasing group of dead people."

I lay out every piece of information I have about the situation. It's a long spiel, and he doesn't say a word or ask a question throughout. It's a fairly compelling presentation, and as I speak it, I'm surprising myself with how much we actually have learned. Of course, what is most important to me, which is making it relevant enough to Pete's case to be admissible, is where we are weakest. But that is not Akers's concern, nor should it be.

When I'm finished, he says, "That's quite a story."

"And I just learned another piece a few minutes ago. One of Reynolds's companies is Blaine Pharmaceuticals."

"How do you know all this information about where the cell phones have been?"

"That doesn't matter; just accept it as true. And by tomorrow evening I'll have the documents to prove it anyway."

"So bottom line, what do we have here?" he asks.

"A murder-for-hire business, for only the wealthiest customers. With no risk, because no one has any idea that the deaths are murders."

"How much money are we talking about?"

"Well, take Reynolds as an example. He's worth 500 million dollars. If he were to get a divorce, it would cost him 250 million. You think he'd pay five to keep 250?"

"Yeah," says Agent Akers. "I think a lot of people would."

"But I think Reynolds may have been paying the money to himself, or maybe his partners. I think he's the source."

"You could be right," Akers says.

"So we have a deal?"

He nods. "I believe we do."

"Good. And to get the ball rolling, I need you to make that phone call."

It's crucial that we mount an attack on Reynolds, and there's very little time.

Richard's case will be coming to a close in a couple of days, and if I can't find a way to get my theory admitted, the defense case will last about twenty minutes, including intermission.

But at the moment I'm stuck in court, trying to pierce holes in witnesses, who as a group are trying to imprison Pete for the rest of his life.

The court day starts off on a relatively high note, as a woman named Jane Michael shows up to comply with the subpoena Hike sent out. Ms. Michael works at the phone company, and she is delivering the requested documents twelve hours ahead of schedule.

Even though the material is part of the defense case, Judge Matthews holds a brief session with the jury not present. To vouch for the legitimacy of the documents, Ms. Michael would technically have to come back when we start our case to testify.

In order to prevent that inconvenience, Judge Matthews asks Richard if he will stipulate to that legitimacy, therefore preventing Michael from having to return.

"We will so stipulate, Your Honor," Richard says, preventing an unnecessary hassle.

"Very well. Ms. Michael, you are free to go. Thank you."

With the phone records admitted, Richard and his team will

go over them and digest them. Diaz's records will make sense to him, and he will understand why we wanted them. He will take particular note of Diaz's phone being in Pete's house the day of the murder.

But Parker's phone records, and those of Reynolds, will make absolutely no sense to him. He might even think we're leading him on a wild-goose chase, though the truth is the goose isn't wild at all; this particular goose represents our entire case.

The reason for all the phone records won't be a mystery to Richard for long; at some point in the near future I'm going to have to reveal everything to both him and the judge, in an effort to get it admitted. Richard will object and we will fight it out. If we lose, then we lose the case; that much is certain.

Richard's first witness today is an important one. Sergeant Daniel Sproles is going to testify that he found a pair of gloves in Pete's car—not a particularly heroic act, but one that has large implications.

Richard doesn't beat around the bush, or drag this one out. He brings Sproles to the night of the murder immediately, and asks him if he saw Pete's car that night.

"I did," Sproles says. "It was right out in front of the house."

"Was the defendant in the car?"

"Not when I saw it."

"When did the car leave that street?"

"I assume when Pete . . . Captain Stanton . . . left."

"When did you next see the car?" Richard asks.

"About twenty-four hours later. We impounded it when we made the arrest, pursuant to a search warrant."

Richard gets around to asking about the gloves, and Sproles says that they were hidden under the passenger's seat in Pete's car. I object to the use of the word "hidden," and the judge sustains. Big deal.

"Were the gloves tested for gunpowder residue?" Richard asks.

"Yes. The results were positive."

"Is there any way to tell when the gloves received that residue?"

"Not precisely," says Sproles. "But based on the tests, it was recent, within the previous week or maybe two."

Richard introduces the gloves as evidence, and holds them up for the jury to see. "Do you see many people wearing gloves like this in the summer?" he asks, and I object before Sproles can answer.

Judge Matthews sustains, but the point is made. Even so, Richard drives it home. "Are these police-issued gloves?"

"I've never seen any like them in the department, no," says Sproles.

"Are there gloves issued for target practice in winter?"

"Yes."

"But not like these?"

"That is correct," Sproles says.

Richard turns the witness over to me, and I ask, "Sergeant Sproles, when were the gloves placed in that car?"

"I couldn't say."

"Speculate with me for a moment. Can you think of a reason why someone would wear gloves in the summer to fire a weapon?"

"Well, just speculating, I would assume it was to keep residue off the shooter's hands, or to avoid leaving fingerprints."

I nod. "Makes sense. Does residue wash off?"

"Sure. Careful washing would get rid of it."

"If you had residue on your hands, and you had twenty-four hours, could you wash it off?"

"Yes, certainly."

"Were Captain Stanton's hands tested for gun residue?"

"No, I don't believe so. Too much time had passed since the shooting when he was arrested."

"Twenty-four hours?" I ask.

"Yes."

"Why wasn't he tested at the scene?"

"I don't believe he was a suspect at that point," Sproles says.

"So if he could have just used his bare hands to fire the weapon, and then washed the residue off, then why use the gloves?"

Richard objects, but since the witness has already agreed to speculate, the judge lets him answer. "I really couldn't say."

"And since we're still speculating," I say, "if the idea was to avoid the presence of residue, why not get rid of the gloves?"

"I don't know."

"Do you know Captain Stanton?"

He nods. "Yes."

"Have you always considered him a smart cop?"

Another nod. "I have."

"Then why would he do something so stupid?"

This time the judge sustains Richard's objection, and the witness doesn't have to answer. Which is okay, because the jury should know the answer on their own.

We have to find a vulnerable spot in Reynolds's armor, and I'm hoping that I have. Sharon Dalton told me that Daniel Mathis worked closely with the company CEO, Mitchell Blackman, on the study involving the euthanasia pills. It was Blackman, according to Sharon, who initially dissuaded Daniel from reporting the theft of the pills to the police, warning that it would be bad for the company.

Blackman was installed as CEO of Blaine when Reynolds's company took control, and I'm hoping that Reynolds was pulling the strings on him regarding Mathis. If so, maybe Blackman can be shaken.

I had requested that Agent Akers call Blackman and tell him that the FBI wants to interview him regarding the Daniel Mathis disappearance, and "other related issues." I check my phone during the lunch recess, and there's a message from Akers saying that he made the call.

Next I place a call to Blackman, and in an effort to get past his assistant, I say that I need to speak with him urgently, "about his meeting with the FBI." This does the trick, and he picks up the phone.

"Mr. Blackman, I know you received a call from Agent Akers of the FBI," I say. "I know why he is calling, and it goes much further than Daniel Mathis."

"I don't know what you are talking about."

"Then you need to have a conversation with me about this to find out, because you need to play this just right, or you could find yourself in serious difficulty."

It doesn't take much more cajoling to get him to meet with me after court adjourns for the day. It's a meeting I'm looking forward to, because he sounds scared already.

"Mr. Blackman," I say, "I would strongly advise you not to consult with Reynolds on this. He is the reason the FBI is after you; he is not your friend. If you talk to him, I can't help you."

He agrees, but I'm not sure if he'll call Reynolds or not. My hope is that he'll wait to see what I have to say.

I catch a break when Richard says that his next witness got food poisoning that morning. The judge asks me if I will agree to an early adjournment; if not she'll make Richard call a different witness.

I'm fine with getting out of here early, and when I agree, Richard thinks I'm being gracious. I'm trying to remember the last time I was gracious, but I can't think back that far.

I head home to discuss the latest developments with Laurie. She thinks that Marcus should go with me to meet with Blackman. "A lot of people have died, Andy. Diaz, Parker, Reese, Juanita Diaz, and probably Mathis. If you're viewed as a threat, and Blackman is involved, they could want you out of the way."

I ordinarily want Marcus around whenever there is a chance that someone might inflict pain on me; I've even considered bringing him to the dentist. But in this case I'm afraid having Marcus there will send the wrong message. Besides, since I have made it obvious to Blackman that I know the FBI is involved, he'd have to assume it's a two-way street, and that the FBI would be aware of my own involvement.

That gives me some immunity, at least at this point. "Killing me would cause them problems," I say. I don't like sentences that come out of my mouth with the phrase "Killing me" in them, and I'm starting to change my mind as Laurie responds.

"Killing you would cause you some problems as well," she points out.

I decide to bring Marcus along, but have him wait in the reception area. I will set my cell to text message him, so that all I have to do is press Send if I need him.

It's only a twenty-minute ride to Blackman's office at Blaine Pharmaceuticals, but that's the equivalent of four hours in "Marcus minutes." Even after all this time, being alone with Marcus makes me extremely uncomfortable, and it's fair to say that the time does not exactly fly by when we are in a car together.

We're there at six-thirty, and the place is basically empty; people do not seem to work overtime here at Blaine. Blackman actually comes out to the modern reception area himself to greet me. I introduce him to Marcus, who gives him the Marcus stare. Based on Blackman's face when he sees Marcus, I think he might confess right here in the lobby.

When we get back to his office, I get right to it. "I'm going to be straight with you," I say, a sure tipoff that I have no intention of being close to straight with him. "What you do in the next twenty-four hours will determine whether you spend the rest of your life in prison."

"I've done nothing wrong."

"You sound like an inmate already," I say. "Here's what the FBI knows. They know that people are dying from the pills that Daniel Mathis created. They know that those pills were stolen, and they know that you prevented Mathis from reporting that theft."

"That's not true," he says. "I—"

"I've got to be honest with you," I say. "You're starting to bore me. I'm not telling you what the FBI thinks. I'm telling you what they know. So if you're just going to keep with the bullshit denials, we can stop talking now."

He thinks for a moment, then, "Go on."

"What they don't know, but what I do know, is that Reynolds put you up to it. But you need to say that, and say it fast, because if you try and protect Reynolds, even one time, even for a moment, then you're part of the conspiracy, and part of the cover-up. And then you'll spend the next forty years talking to your wife through a glass window, if she bothers to show up at all."

"I didn't know why the pills were stolen, or who took them. I still don't."

"Fascinating, but that's not enough," I say. "You have to give them Reynolds."

"What is your role in this?"

"I have a client who will go to jail if the truth does not come out. So I'm going to see that it does, one way or the other. If you're smart, it will be through you."

"I need to think about this," he says.

"You better think quick. The FBI is going to move on you tomorrow. You're a hell of a lot better off if you go to them."

"I understand," he says. "I understand."

He said it twice, I suppose in an effort to make me think that I really believe him. Which I really do. Which I really do.

I leave and go back to the lobby, where Marcus is waiting for me. I say. "It's set up. . . . So you're on him twenty-four/seven, okay?"

"Yunh," says Marcus, and I couldn't have said it any better.

Blackman has a few choices now, none of which will be appealing to him.

He can take me at face value and tell the FBI everything he knows. I doubt that will happen, because the last time someone took me at face value, there were pay phones on every corner and people were buying encyclopedias.

He can do nothing, and hope it will all go away. This would be predicated on his seeing me as an outsider, with my own agenda, that he has no reason to further. I don't think this is likely; he is no doubt a smart guy, and I suspect one who has been a pawn in this whole thing. One way or the other, he's got to make a move.

His third option is the most likely. He'll probably turn to Reynolds, both to find out what he knows about this, and to receive advice on what to do. Whether or not he ultimately takes that advice, chances are he'll want to hear it.

If he chooses door number three, I think it likely that he will be killed. The conspirators have shown an inclination to eliminate those with knowledge of their operation. Laurie was right when she suggested Marcus should come with me because I was in danger: people who know what is going on are in fact dying.

I could have warned him about this, but I didn't because I need him to make his own decision. That's the only way I can place his role in the conspiracy. And he certainly should be aware by now of whom he is dealing with in Reynolds.

But I'm still feeling a little guilty that there is a chance I've set Blackman up to be killed, so I've taken steps to prevent it from actually happening. Marcus is going to watch him and intervene if he is in danger. Marcus is a really good intervener.

So I put Blackman in danger, and now I'm saving him. Andy Carpenter has the power to giveth life, and taketh life away.

Marcus has instructions to keep me informed if anything happens, or appears about to happen. Of course, I won't get the message immediately if it happens while court is in session, but there's nothing I can do about that.

Richard surprises me before court by announcing that he will be concluding his case this morning. Since he had told Judge Matthews and me that it would likely go a day or two longer, and since today is Friday, she tells me that if I would like, I can delay starting the defense case until Monday. My preference would be to start it in January, but I don't have that option, so I tell her that Monday it is.

Richard points out that he has not received a defense witness list as yet, and I respond by admitting that the defense case is a work in progress.

I have decided not to preview my case to the judge to determine admissibility. I'm going to go ahead as if there is no question but that our information is relevant, and only defend it when challenged. But it will, of course, be challenged.

In the process of doing that I will be springing a surprise on Richard, not the nicest way I can handle it. But he's a big boy, and his life will go on. If I don't win, then Pete's life as he knows it is over.

So basically, I have no interest in being nice.

Richard burns through two quick witnesses, both lab technicians who testify to the collection methods and test results regarding the search warrant, drugs, gloves, etc. I let them basically go unchallenged; I wouldn't damage them anyway, and they are fairly harmless to our case.

Richard's last witness is Chief Franklin Carnow, Pete's immediate boss in the department. Carnow is six foot four, 220 pounds, and looks like central casting's version of a police chief. He's even got a cleft that makes Kirk and Michael Douglas look flat-chinned.

Chief Carnow is a good witness for Richard to end with, because of what he has to say, but more importantly because of who he is. Carnow is widely respected for his toughness, honesty, and integrity, and he is rumored to be the frontrunner in next year's mayoral election. At forty-two years old, he has a long time to work his way up the political ladder.

"Did Captain Stanton report directly to you?" Richard asks.

"Yes, sir."

"And what did you think of him?"

"I've always held him in the highest regard, personally and professionally." Carnow looks right at Pete as he says this.

"You still do?"

"I'm waiting until all the facts are in."

Richard's letting Carnow praise Pete is a smart move; it makes the negative things he is going to say more credible, since he obviously has no interest in sandbagging Pete.

"Did you meet with Captain Stanton the day that Danny Diaz was murdered?" Richard asks.

"Yes, sir."

"What was the purpose of that meeting?"

"To tell him that Mr. Diaz had provided the department with information that implicated Captain Stanton in some kind of illegal activity. That I wanted him to be aware of this, and that he should cooperate with an internal affairs investigation that was to begin."

"What was his reaction?"

"As you might expect, he was very upset."

"Angry?"

Carnow seems to hesitate, as if reluctant to go further. He is inadvertently making it worse for Pete by doing this. "I would describe him as angry, yes. And bewildered."

"Did you have any advice for him?"

"I said that he should not have contact with Mr. Diaz in any fashion, at least until this was resolved, and probably after that."

"And what did he say?"

"He said nothing."

"Were you concerned that he would not take your advice?"

Another hesitation, then, "I was . . . yes."

My cross is a brief one. "Chief, what did Mr. Diaz say when you called to warn him, after your meeting with Captain Stanton?"

"I did not call him."

I once again feign surprise, this time with a slight double take and head turn. It's a move I have perfected over time. "So you just assigned security to him, and figured they would protect him?"

"I did not assign any security to him."

"You mean even after seeing how angry Captain Stanton was, you didn't think Mr. Diaz was in danger?"

"I did not. That is correct."

I am sure that Carnow is a sympathetic witness to Pete; he is just there to tell the truth, and not happy about it. So I give him a chance to help us.

"Tell me if this statement is true, Chief Carnow. You weren't worried for Diaz's safety, because you considered Captain Stanton a fine cop who would not take the law into his own hands."

"That is true."

"Thank you, Chief."

Sam is waiting for me when I get home.

I've asked him to work his computer magic from here today, because the timing is so important. He is monitoring Blackman's phones, to see if he calls Reynolds, or anyone else relevant to our investigation. Laurie is with him, and has obviously already heard what I'm about to hear.

"He called Reynolds," Sam says. "About an hour ago."

"Did he call anyone else we care about? By that I mean us or the FBI."

"No."

I turn to Laurie. "You told Marcus, right?"

"Yes."

"Where is Blackman now?"

"Marcus said he's at home. Hasn't budged all day. No visitors either."

"Okay. He knows the drill." By that I mean that Marcus is to call us if Blackman leaves the house, or if anyone shows up to see him.

Blackman's calling Reynolds doesn't prove conclusively that Blackman is not going to cooperate with us, since he works for the guy. For all I know, they could be talking about a new Blaine drug to treat canine dandruff.

He also could be doing the honorable thing and giving Reynolds the courtesy of hearing that Blackman is going to the FBI. It's considerably less likely that this is what he's doing, but possible.

Rather than just pace and wait for a Marcus call that might never come, I decide to begin figuring out what I'm going to do in court Monday when the judge tells me to call my first witness. But before I do that, I head up to Ricky's room, where he's playing with his ever-expanding collection of toys.

I'm finding I'm enjoying spending time, short as it is, with Ricky. I'm more comfortable with him now than I was before, and more used to having him around. This may reflect badly on me, but I'm seeing him more as a person, and less as a child object.

He's smart and has a pretty good sense of humor for someone his age. Of course, he's the only person his age I've known since I was his age, so I may not be the best judge of age-appropriate smartness and humor.

I feel bad that he's been cooped up in our house so much. He's almost under house arrest as much as Pete is, and neither deserve it. It's only fair that he get on with the rest of his life, though it's still to be determined where and with whom that life will be lived.

I figured I'd spend fifteen minutes with him, but it turns into forty-five, as he ropes me into another video game. He destroys me three straight times, but I don't bother claiming he was lucky. Both he and I know better.

I finally leave and start working on the case. I'm certainly going to try and tell the jury the story of Daniel Mathis and his euthanasia drug, and how I believe it has been used to commit murders. They need to know about Reynolds, and Parker, and all the rest.

But even assuming the judge admits it, I still need people to get up on the witness stand and answer my questions. That is the way stories are told in trials. And I have a real shortage of witness possibilities, and maybe none who know the whole picture.

I certainly can't rely on Blackman, at least not yet. I guess the closest I have to the right person is Lieutenant Coble, though I have kind of frozen him out by going to the FBI. I call him, so that I can bring him up to date. I need to stay on his good side, to get him to testify for us.

"You went to the FBI, asshole?" is how he gets on the phone. I don't think the Andy Carpenter charm is working on him so far, and it is certainly not overcoming the natural distrust that local and state police often have for the Feds.

"They were already on it," I say. "A friend of Daniel Mathis went to them."

I don't think he buys it. "So why are you coming to me now?"

"To let you know what's going on. That was our deal, right? We exchange information, so you can solve this thing, and testify for me."

"Good luck with that," he says.

I let that slide. I'll be calling him, but this is not the time to argue about it. Instead I tell him almost everything, though I certainly leave out the part about believing that Blackman might be killed, and sending Marcus to prevent it.

"I think we can blow this open," I say.

"We?"

"Yes, we. I don't trust the FBI to do anything fast, or anything at all, for that matter. I need your help. We need to stop these people. You need to stop these people. And starting Monday, the world finds out about them, and what they have done."

We talk for a while more, and I actually think I make progress with him, probably for three reasons. One is my legendary power of persuasion. Two is the fact that his job and his goal is to put bad guys in prison. And three is the obvious fact that if he can take the credit for ending a murder ring of this magnitude, he will be hailed as a hero.

So for now it's back to going over the documents for what seems like the hundredth time, and waiting for Marcus to call.

And then, at nine-thirty p.m., he does call. Laurie answers, since she's basically the only person who can understand a word he says. When she gets off the phone, the message she relays is a simple one:

"Blackman is on the move."

Marcus said that Blackman is heading in the general direction of Alpine.

I'm going to assume that he's going to Reynolds's house, so Laurie and I get in the car and head toward there as well. She has her cell phone, and if Marcus sees that Blackman is going somewhere else, he will call her, and we'll adjust.

Sam is staying back with Ricky. He's not thrilled about it; he wants to be where the action is. I had to choose between Laurie and Sam to go with me, and it was not a tough choice. Laurie carries a gun, and Sam carries a computer. Besides, Ricky is already asleep, so it should be fine all around.

Marcus calls back, but only to report that Blackman has made a turn that confirms he's heading toward Reynolds's house, so we continue there as well. Laurie says that we should park nearby and approach the house on foot, because we won't know what we're walking into, or what Marcus is doing. So that's what we do.

I'm not too worried at this point, as we are walking up the dark street toward Reynolds's house. I've got Marcus and Laurie with me, and the other side has two middle-aged businessmen. That's not to say I'm thrilled with the situation, but I do feel like I should be here.

That feeling changes rather quickly, and all it takes is the sound of one gunshot. In the otherwise completely silent night air, it sounds like an explosion, and the echoes from it almost make me think that there are subsequent shots. But there were not, or at least I think there were not.

Almost as if the gunshot were from a starter's pistol, Laurie is running toward the house. I assume she has her gun drawn, but she's in front of me, and it's dark, so I can't be sure.

The fact is that it is not my instinct to run toward gunshots; my natural tendency would be to run the other way, or curl into the fetal position and whimper. But I'm also not thrilled to be left alone in the dark surrounded by dangerous people with guns, so I take off at something less than a full sprint after Laurie.

The house comes into view, which doesn't clear up much for me. I can see that there are lights on inside, and I can see Laurie approaching the house, but there are no other people around, not even Marcus.

Laurie reaches the front of the house and looks in through a window, and I can see the gun in her right hand, against the backdrop of light from the window. She quickly moves toward the front door and goes inside, apparently leaving me as the only dope outside.

I reach the house but don't go to the window; I'll take Laurie's unspoken word for the fact that the place to be is inside. So I go in the front door, and hear noises coming from the same den where I had met with Reynolds and his lawyer.

The scene is somewhat different this time. Reynolds is sitting upright in a chair, but while his body is vertical, his head and neck are horizontal. It is one of the most disgusting sights I have ever seen, which unfortunately makes it one that I will remember for a very long time.

Looking away, I see Blackman standing against the wall, looking even more scared than I am. Laurie and Marcus are both standing and holding guns, while another man lies on the floor with a gun still in his hand and a bullet hole in his forehead.

I've never met the dead man, but I've seen his picture.

Alex Parker.

Which is somewhat surprising, since this represents the second time he has died.

Blackman is almost too scared to speak, and Marcus is Marcus, so it takes a while to extract the story of what happened. As best I can understand, Blackman came to see Reynolds, who was already dead when Blackman arrived.

Parker was also on the scene, and was just about to make Blackman as dead as Reynolds, when Marcus intervened. Parker attempted to shoot Marcus, but that became moot when Marcus put a bullet in Parker's head.

We need to call the police, to have them sort this out, and present our side of what happened. Rather than bring in local cops, I call Lieutenant Coble. He'll come in educated as to the players, and will easily understand what happened, and why.

People have lost their lives here, and I suppose on some level I should be reflecting on that, but Reynolds and Parker were slimeball murderers, and I just don't see their deaths as tragedies.

All that I really care about is what impact this has on our case. It's probably positive: Reynolds was not going to testify for me anyway, and I hadn't even known Parker was alive. Certainly he would be no help, although I'd love to know who got his head bashed in, and how Parker got the fingerprints to match.

The good news is that Blackman will certainly testify and tell everything he knows. There is no longer anyone for him to protect, or be afraid of. His interest will undoubtedly be in keeping his own ass out of prison, and cooperating will be the only way to do that. I tell him this in no uncertain terms, and we agree to meet tomorrow, at his house, to go over what will be lengthy testimony. I especially need him because he tells me that the records of Mathis's work are also gone, so he is the only one who can vouch for it.

Blackman is also going to have to talk to Akers at the FBI, and he understands and accepts that.

Coble shows up with a small army of state troopers. He takes one look at the carnage and says, "You're different than most lawyers I know."

"Shucks, thanks," I say.

Coble sees Parker lying on the floor, and his look is appropriately puzzled. "Parker?" he asks.

I nod. "Parker."

He shakes his head. "Son of a bitch," he says softly, under his breath.

Three hours later, we are finally given the okay to leave. All in all, the evening has gone fairly well, unless you're the guy with the broken neck, or the bullet in his head.

It's going to be a long weekend.

I've got a lot to do, both in getting our case ready, and more importantly in convincing the judge that the outside conspiracy is relevant to Pete's trial. I'm feeling somewhat confident about getting it admitted, but I'm still anxious about it.

So the weekend will seem longer because of how important Monday is going to be. If I get the testimony admitted, we have a shot. If I don't, the jury might as well phone the guilty verdict in.

The newspapers are playing up the death of Carson Reynolds, probably because he was so rich. I hope the jury is reading it, and that they will connect it to what they will be hearing in court.

The stories on Reynolds are glowing, speaking about the tragedy of such a wonderful philanthropist cut down in the prime of life. They also point out that he and Katherine had no children, and neither had siblings, so there is speculation over who might get their money. I know that his mistress Susan Baird won't be the one; the gravy train has come to a stop moments before it reached her station.

I spend some of Saturday morning on the phone with Mitchell Blackman. He is still shaken up, but with Reynolds out of the picture he seems comfortable about testifying. I'm surprised that he hasn't "lawyered up," but so far, so good. He claims not to have been part of any murder-for-hire conspiracy, but knows all about Daniel Mathis and his pills, and will testify to Reynolds's covering up the theft of them.

He also will say that Reynolds had a key to the company offices, and was listed in the security log book as having been in the building on the day the pills were stolen. With Blackman setting the table, and then Lieutenant Coble coming in to finish the story, I think we have a compelling case, and a definite ability to create reasonable doubt as to Pete's guilt.

Coble told me yesterday that he is going to interview Blackman as well. "So you can coordinate your testimony?" I made the mistake of asking.

"Yeah," he said. "I told my boss that all that matters is Carpenter's case. Whether we can figure out what happened with the murder of half the people in our state is unimportant. It's Andy Carpenter that we should worry about."

"You catch on quickly," I say.

Click.

I call Blackman in the afternoon, just to make sure he's not getting cold feet, and still planning to testify. "You doing okay?"

"Yes, just wiped out. I'm not used to this kind of stuff."

"Get some rest."

"I will," he says. "That state cop is coming back later to ask me some more questions. In the meantime I'm going to try and take a nap."

"Good idea. I'll call you tomorrow so we can go over a few final things."

Laurie comes in and says, "You busy?"

"Is that one of your sexual come-ons?" I ask.

"No. It was a totally asexual attempt to find out if you were busy."

"Oh. Amazingly, I'm not. I'm in pretty good shape. I may even watch the Mets game."

"There's a new Disney movie that just opened," she says.

"Good. That will make the 728th one in a row that I missed. But I definitely plan to get around to them; probably on DVD."

"I thought we could take Ricky."

Suddenly, as if from nowhere, Ricky is standing at Laurie's side. "Can we go?" he says. "Is it okay?"

"Sure," I say, although it's hard for me to speak between my clenched teeth. "Unless you'd rather watch the Mets game?"

"Nah," he says.

"Nah," Laurie says.

"They're playing the Yankees in an interleague game. Harvey is pitching."

"Nah," Ricky says.

"Nah," Laurie says.

"Super," I say. As I get up to head out the door with them, I whisper to Laurie, "Any chance the film has gratuitous nudity and violence?"

She smiles. "Probably. You should watch for it."

We get to the theater, which is an absolute madhouse, with what seems like thousands of little people running around like ants, yelling and inhaling candy and soda. I feel like Gulliver, having wandered into a cinematic Lilliput.

There are other adults like Laurie and myself, but our role is simply to provide cash for refreshments. Ricky, Laurie, and I each get popcorn and a soda, and for the money it cost me, I could buy a serviceable used car.

The film itself is not bad, with some sophisticated humor obviously designed to make it barely palatable for adults. But Ricky certainly seems to love it, and he tells us that it is the first movie he has ever been to.

"That was great. Thanks for taking me," he says, as we get into the car.

"Thanks for going with us," Laurie says to him. "We had a wonderful time. Didn't we, Andy?"

"We certainly did," I say, and I'm only partially lying.

Lieutenant Coble arrived at Blackman's house at six-thirty in the evening.

He brought with him State Police Lieutenant Nick Vasquez, probably the most skilled interrogator in the department. They weren't going to grill Blackman, but they planned to fully debrief him, so that nothing he said in court on Monday would be a surprise.

It was important to get it on the record before that testimony, since once he spoke publicly, everything after that would be somewhat tainted.

Blackman was the key to their case, as it was to Carpenter's. With him filling in at least some of the blanks, they would have a clear picture of what went on, and at a minimum would be able to claim partial credit for having stopped it.

The first sign of something being wrong was that Blackman did not come to the door when they knocked. His car was outside, and there were lights on, but no signs of movement.

The second, more significant indication of trouble was when they peered in the window and saw Blackman's body lying, face-down, on the hardwood floor in the hallway adjacent to the den.

At that point they felt free to enter the house, and once Coble called for backup, they did so by breaking windows on either side of the house and climbing in.

Having seen a number of recently deceased bodies, Coble and Vasquez each estimated that Blackman had been dead for perhaps three hours. There were no signs of violence, either on the body or in the house. No apparent break-in, no blood, no signs of a struggle . . . nothing. No sign that anything was amiss, except for the human being on the floor that was no longer alive.

Coble made another call to add a homicide team and coroner to those that would descend on the house. Once they arrived and assessed everything, it certainly seemed like Blackman's death was from natural causes.

Coble knew all too well that there was no such thing as obvious death by natural causes anymore, and he knew that Carpenter would understand that when he called him.

Which he did at eleven-thirty that night.

It's been a while since I've had a phone call that awful.

Lieutenant Coble called me about an hour ago to tell me that Mitchell Blackman was found dead in his house early this evening, and Laurie and I have been talking about it ever since. I haven't called Pete yet, although I probably should. I'm sure he's sleeping, and there seems to be no upside in keeping him up worrying the rest of the night.

Coble told me that the coroner's early opinion is that Blackman died of a heart attack, but he won't know for sure until he performs the autopsy. If he's right about the cause of death, and I suspect that he is, it obviously has significant implications unique to this case.

It's possible that Blackman's heart naturally failed; perhaps he had a condition that was aggravated by the substantial stress he was under. He looked healthy to me, but that doesn't mean he was.

But I don't believe in coincidences this great. I believe that his death was caused by one of Daniel Mathis's stolen magic pills, and that he either committed suicide, or it means the conspiracy is ongoing. I had thought the death of Reynolds and Parker had eliminated all the bad guys, but if Blackman didn't cave from the pressure and take his own life, then I was wrong.

If in fact the conspiracy is ongoing, as seems most likely, then there are all kinds of very negative things that flow from that. Not only is there the likelihood that the murder for hires might continue, but there is also the personal danger to myself and our team.

We have done more investigating of this than Pete ever did, and they have gone to extraordinary lengths to put him and many others out of commission. There is no reason to believe that they wouldn't ultimately want to eliminate us, either now or later.

Sitting with the belief that there are ruthless people intent on killing me and people I care about is not my favorite situation.

In terms of the more immediate consideration, the trial, Blackman was a key witness for me, even more than Lieutenant Coble. He put a face on the conspiracy; he knew the players and was involved in the process, unwittingly if not criminally. His death of a heart attack would actually lend some credibility to my claims, but not nearly enough to offset the loss of him as a witness.

But in presenting our case, I've got to go with what I've got. It's a compelling story, if I can just get it in front of the jury. Coble seemed sympathetic to my plight, and agreed to be there when I need him. I will certainly need him, and more.

I call Hike first thing in the morning and ask him to come over around noon, so we can talk about witnesses and start lining them up. Then I head over to Pete's house to give him the bad news.

"Where was Marcus?" is Pete's first question when I tell him that Blackman had died.

"I pulled him off the job of guarding Blackman," I say. "I thought with Reynolds and Parker dead, there was no one to protect him from." It was a stupid move on my part, and I tell that to Pete.

"I would have done the same thing," Pete says, with incredible generosity considering the circumstances. "You couldn't have known."

"I couldn't have known is the exact reason I should have kept Marcus in place," I say.

"Probably wouldn't have mattered," Pete says. "Marcus doesn't protect people from pills. Blackman either had a visitor, or more likely he committed suicide."

I nod. "Suicide is a definite possibility. Maybe he had kept one of those pills for himself, and was afraid he'd be going to jail."

Now it's Pete's turn to nod. "Speaking from experience, the prospect of going to jail is very unpleasant. So what do we do now?"

"Monday morning I start presenting our case. Richard will say it's a fantasy and has nothing to do with the murder of Danny Diaz. Then we fight it out."

"And if we lose that fight?" he asks.

"We cannot lose that fight."

I head back home to meet with Hike and go over our strategy and witness possibilities. We quickly agree on the witnesses, some of whom may not be thrilled to be called. But they'll have no choice; we can subpoena them, even though I doubt that will be necessary.

Our witness choices are designed to surprise Richard. He will be expecting them to testify to something totally different, and therefore he will be less able to prepare challenges to them.

Lieutenant Coble will be our last witness. He'll lend credibility to the proceedings, and hopefully will be able to tie it all together. I'll then retie it in my closing argument, and then it's in the hands of the jury gods.

Let us pray.

"The defense calls Janet Carlson."

It is not exactly unprecedented to call the coroner in a murder case, and although Richard probably can't imagine how Janet can help our defense, I doubt that he's particularly worried about what she is going to say. I've already announced that I will be recalling Chief Carnow to the stand as my second witness, and he is also not likely to strike fear in Richard's heart.

The gallery is packed, and I see more members of the media than usual. Obviously the start of the defense case is the catalyst for the increased interest, though it's been pretty crowded throughout.

"Dr. Carlson, was I in your office last month?"

"Yes."

"And was I there to discuss an autopsy you had conducted?"

"Yes, that of William Hambler."

"And did I ask you to also look into an autopsy done on Katherine Reynolds?"

"Yes."

Richard is out of his chair. "Objection, Your Honor. Who are Katherine Reynolds and William Hambler?"

I respond quickly. "Your Honor, unless I missed a class in law school, I don't think 'who are Katherine Reynolds and William Hambler' is a valid objection."

Richard doesn't seem amused by my comment. "Objection, Your Honor, as to relevance."

"I will certainly establish relevance, Your Honor. And I will also answer the 'who is Katherine Reynolds' question, if I may just continue presenting my case."

"Proceed," the judge says, but then adds the unwelcome caveat, "For now."

"Thank you, Your Honor. Dr. Carlson, can you please describe our conversation?"

"Yes, I told you that Mr. Hambler had died of a heart attack, and you asked me if perhaps he was murdered, if the heart attack could have resulted from other than natural causes."

"And you said?"

"That there was no evidence of that. I qualified it by adding that certain naturally occurring chemicals, taken in combination, could induce an attack of this kind, but that they would have dissipated long before the autopsy took place."

Richard renews his objection, but Judge Matthews overrules him again, though I think her patience is wearing thin. At some point she is going to stop me, but the more I can get on the record, the better.

"And did I ask you to analyze two other autopsies, ones that you had not conducted yourself?"

She agrees that I did, and goes on to describe the cases, and her acquisition and analysis of the autopsies.

"Were they deemed to have been heart attacks as well, with no evidence of foul play?"

"Yes, although there were certain levels of chemicals consistent with the Hambler case."

"Enough to cause you to believe them to be murders?"

"No, I wouldn't go that far," she says.

Richard is up again. "Your Honor, I must object again as to relevance. Mr. Carpenter needs to explain what three heart attack deaths, all ruled to have been natural and not the result of foul play, have to do with the shooting death of Danny Diaz."

"I'll see lead counsel in my chambers," the judge says. "The jury will retire to the jury room."

As I get up, Pete touches my arm and leans over. "Try not to screw this up."

I smile. "It feels good to be so respected."

Once we're back in chambers, Judge Matthews says to me, "Okay, Mr. Carpenter, what are you doing?"

"I am establishing reasonable doubt, Your Honor, by pointing to other people who are more likely to have killed Mr. Diaz than Captain Stanton."

Richard is obviously annoyed by my actions, which at this point is pretty much too bad for Richard. I like him, but I like the idea of keeping Pete out of prison considerably more.

"What is Chief Carnow going to testify to next? That other dead people were not murdered either? Or are you going to argue that Danny Diaz died of natural causes like everyone else, and that the bullet had nothing to do with it?"

I ignore Richard, because I don't want to be drawn into a one-on-one argument with him; my audience right now is only Judge Matthews. "Your Honor, there has been a conspiracy to commit murder. I know of seven people who have died already, including Danny Diaz. But I need witnesses to tell the story, and they and I will make the connection to this case. I just need you to give me a little latitude."

"It is reasonable to require an offer of proof," Richard says.

I shake my head. "This is an unfolding conspiracy, Your Honor. Just this weekend, one of my key witnesses was killed."

"Who was that?" Richard asks.

"Mitchell Blackman, CEO of Blaine Pharmaceuticals." I'm sure Richard read about Blackman's death in yesterday's paper, and the judge probably did as well. Neither of them have any idea how it ties into this case, but it really wouldn't matter if they did.

I continue, "The point is, I need to present my case in the best way I can. I can vouch to the court that it will be obviously relevant to the Diaz murder, and all of my witnesses will be respected, credible people. Captain Stanton was considered a danger to the conspirators, and they acted to put him out of commission.

"But if you find that it is not relevant, Judge, then you can so rule, and you can direct the jury to disregard the entire defense case. That would be within your discretion."

I have an advantage here, and though judges would never admit it, it is one that the defense in a case of this magnitude almost always enjoys. And that has to do with a judge's natural dislike of being overturned on appeal.

If a defendant is acquitted, the prosecution cannot appeal; the case is over in all but the rarest of instances. But if a defendant is convicted, then the defense can appeal to their heart's content. Therefore, a judge is inclined to give extra latitude to the defense, so as to limit his or her chance of being overturned by the appeals court.

Additionally, since the penalty for conviction in cases of this type is so severe, judges generally want to bend over backward to give the defendant, if not the benefit of the doubt, then an unquestionably fair shake.

For all of these reasons, I'm hopeful if not confident that Judge Matthews will rule in our favor. To cut off the defense case as it is just beginning would be a dramatic and dangerous move.

And for once I'm right. Judge Matthews says, "I'm going to allow it on a witness-by-witness basis, but I am not giving you carte blanche, Mr. Carpenter. You need to quickly establish relevance; I can't have the jury confused and thinking they walked in on the wrong movie."

Richard gets it on the record that he renewed his objection, but the boat has sailed.

We head back into court, and I conclude with Janet Carlson. She won't give me an opinion that the cases we're talking about were murders, but she helps me get the deaths on the record for the jury to hear.

Richard's cross-examination is quick and to the point. "Dr. Carlson, is it your professional opinion that the three people Mr. Carpenter asked you about died of natural causes?"

"Yes."

"And what was the cause of Mr. Diaz's death?"

"A gunshot wound."

"Thank you. No further questions."

Chief Carnow jumped at the chance to testify for us.

He had been unhappy at being part of the prosecution's case against Pete, but obviously felt an obligation to tell the truth. He's still going to tell the truth, but it'll be our truth this time.

I start out by having him talk about what a terrific cop Pete has been throughout his career. In the process, he refers to Pete as a "valued right hand." This is not a guy who bails out on his friends.

"In the space of seven years, is it accurate that he has been promoted from detective, to lieutenant, and then to captain?"

"That's correct," he says.

"Is that unusual in any way?"

"Absolutely. It is rare that someone advances that fast," he says.

I take him to one month before the Diaz murder, and ask him if Pete came in to see him about a case. He says that he did, that "he was becoming convinced that a series of deaths he was looking at were murders, even though they did not appear to be."

"Were you skeptical of his point of view?"

"I was, but I have learned to trust Captain Stanton's judgment."

"What was he asking you to do?"

"To assign manpower to work with him, to try and learn if there were other deaths that might fit the pattern."

"Would you describe him as determined?" I ask.

"Captain Stanton was always determined."

Carnow goes on to say that manpower was particularly limited at that point, but that he was reassigning personnel to work with Pete, within limits. "Much of it was out of our jurisdiction," Carnow says. "But Captain Stanton was breaking down those walls."

"Did the arrest of Captain Stanton put an end to the investigation?"

"In terms of our department, yes. But the state police were working on it."

I turn him over to Richard, who once again comes right to the point. "Chief Carnow, did we talk about this case before you testified for the prosecution?"

He nods. "We did."

"Did you mention anything about these other deaths as possibly being relevant to this case?"

"No."

"Did you hold that view, but for some reason decided not to mention it?"

"No."

"Thank you."

I'm not good at reading juries; I'm not sure anyone is. You see pundits talking about whether juries took notes, or looked at the defendant, or seemed particularly attentive, as a way to determine which way they were leaning.

I've never bought into that, and I've never seen any correlation between any of that subtle conduct and the ultimate verdicts. But if I was into reading juries, I would have to say I am not thrilled with the story this jury is telling.

I expected them to be confused, and unsure where we were going with this. But they also seem to be less attentive, maybe even tuning out, as the case drags on.

During the lunch hour, I discuss my concerns with Pete and Hike. "I think we're losing them," Pete says, even before I state my view.

"Losing them? We're losing me," Hike says. "We're talking about rich people dying of heart attacks, and they don't see what this has to do with Danny Diaz lying in his living room with a hole blown into his chest."

We kick it around some more, but the view is unanimous.

We need to step up the pace.

Jane Michael thought she was off the hook.

She is the phone company employee who put together the phone records of Reynolds, Parker, and Danny Diaz, in response to our subpoena. She was performing work legally that Sam had already done illegally, but of course we couldn't tell anyone that.

When she originally brought the records in, both sides stipulated as to their legitimacy, and she didn't have to take the stand. She confessed to me that she was relieved, that public speaking was not her thing, especially in a situation of this importance.

So she was less than thrilled when I called her to tell her we would be calling her as a key witness, to testify at length and in detail about the records. I sent Hike to spend a few hours with her, to go over specifics about what we'd be asking her.

When I called her afterward to ask her how it went, she said, "Mr. Lynch seemed pretty worried."

"Mr. Lynch is always worried," I said. "It worries him not to have anything to worry about. Are you comfortable that you know the answers to the questions we have?"

"I am. It's all in the records."

"Exactly. We just want you to tell the truth. You'll be there because the records can't talk themselves, and they need explanation."

I'm worried that her nervousness will make her appear unsure and indecisive, but that's not what I see as she takes the stand. I see a composed and confident woman. She has no stake in the outcome; she is simply here to present the facts, and to represent her company and herself well.

My problem is that there is a lot of detail here, but I need to move through it quickly. If I don't, I'll start to see jurors' eyes close, and heads nod. To assist in the demonstration, I had Sam prepare the records on slides, which we project side by side on a large screen that we set up in the courtroom.

I have Michael verify them as the records of Reynolds, Diaz, and the man we identify as Alex Parker. Coble will cement that identification when he testifies, but for now it's only important that the jurors see him as a bad guy; his name doesn't matter.

But I have to take some time to set it up, especially the GPS portion. Not many people know that their cell phones contain the GPS signals, and based on the biographies they filled out during jury selection, this group of twelve does not represent the cream of the technology crop.

I can see the surprise in most of their faces as they learn about it; one woman even seems to look up, as if hoping to see the satellite that is keeping tabs on her.

Once that is out of the way, I have Michael focus on the connection between the three phones. The key fact is that both Diaz and Reynolds were in touch with Parker. Also significant is that both Diaz and Parker were in touch during the same period of time with Wally Reese, who was holding the ill-fated Juanita Diaz hostage.

Next I move to the GPS data, which is at least as important. I direct Michael to the day that Diaz was killed, and the fact that the cell phones of both Diaz and Reynolds were in the same place that morning. "What is located at that address?"

"That is Captain Stanton's house," she says, and maybe it's my imagination, but the jurors seem to sit up a little straighter.

"Are you saying that Danny Diaz and Alex Parker were both at Captain Stanton's house that morning?"

Michael shakes her head. "No. I'm saying their cell phones were there."

"You're certain of that?"

"Yes."

"Could one person have been carrying both phones?"

"I don't see why not," she says.

There are a lot of facts that I wish I could tie together now, but Michael is not the person to make that happen. For example, I wish I could remind the jurors that Diaz once stayed at Pete's house, and likely had a key. Hopefully I'll be able to get those things in through Coble; if not, it will have to wait for my summation.

Next I have Michael talk through how Alex Parker's phone was at Blaine Pharmaceuticals the day that Daniel Mathis went missing. The jurors don't know who Mathis is yet, but they're about to find out.

Richard's cross-examination focuses mostly on the technology—for example, questioning how exact the GPS data can be. Michael cannot say that it is completely precise; there is always the chance that the cell phones were not at Pete's house, but at the house next door.

He can't get into the meaning of it all, because that wasn't her job, and we didn't talk about it on direct examination.

That is for others to do, and they're about to.

Sharon Dalton is raring to go.

Unlike Jane Michael, who would rather have been anywhere else on the planet than on the witness stand, Sharon Dalton has been waiting a very long time to tell her story. She is going to be the voice of Daniel Mathis, and she is going to yell as loud as she can.

"Daniel is a wonderful man," Sharon says on the stand. "Smart, and funny, and caring. That's what his work was all about. Caring."

"Did he discuss with you the project he was working on in the months before his disappearance?"

"Yes, many times." She goes on to describe his work on the euthanasia drug in some detail. The portrait she paints is of a guy whose total dedication was to prevent the suffering of animals. It sounds good, and I'd like to believe it, but I have no idea if that was true. He could have just been doing his job, which wouldn't make him a bad person, either.

I lead her into telling the court about the theft of the pills, and the torment Daniel suffered over it. "Mr. Blackman kept telling him not to talk about it, that it would be bad for the business, and that they were probably just misplaced. But Daniel knew better."

"Is that the Mitchell Blackman who according to the media was murdered this week?"

Richard objects, and Judge Matthews both sustains and warns

me to be "very careful." Of course she and Richard both know that I was very careful; that's how the jury got to hear that Blackman was dead. It's now in their mind; you can't unring a bell, and you can't un-kill a CEO.

"What did Daniel tell you he was going to do the day before he disappeared?"

"He was going to tell Mr. Blackman that he had made a decision: he was finally going to the FBI and telling them what had happened."

"Was he worried about doing that?"

"I think he was relieved. I was very proud of him."

"Do you know if he ever got to tell Mr. Blackman his decision?"

"I don't know," she says.

I've gotten all I can out of Sharon; she has been a very credible and sympathetic witness. She doesn't make the case for us, but she takes care of a big piece, which is showing how it is possible that all of the "heart attack" deaths were actually induced.

I expect Richard to treat her cautiously, but he surprises me by going right at her. "Ms. Dalton, was Daniel Mathis worried that he himself might be accused of a crime for not reporting the theft?"

"Yes, that was one of the considerations."

"And in fact, did you delay reporting him missing, because you didn't want to open him up to those same possible criminal charges?"

"Yes, for a day or so."

"Are you aware that some people, when worried about going to jail, sometimes don't come forward and confess, but instead go on the run?"

She shakes her head. "Not Daniel."

"Because he was a moral, upstanding citizen?"

"Yes."

"Was it moral to not report the theft for so long, while believing that people could be dying as a result of it?"

"You're making him look bad," she says.

"I'm sorry about that, but I am just repeating what you testified to."

"He wouldn't have left without telling me, without contacting me."

"Are you and Daniel married?" Richard asks.

"No."

"Engaged?"

"We were in love," she says.

"And you'd do anything to protect him?"

She takes a deep breath. "I only hope it isn't too late to do that."

When Sharon finally leaves the stand, Judge Dalton sends the jury out of the room and asks me how much longer the defense case will go on.

I have a big decision to make. I can call witnesses to rebut some of the testimony of the prosecution witnesses, but I can't prevail like that. Their witnesses were telling the truth, and presenting real evidence. My challenge to it is not that they are wrong, but that the evidence was planted.

If I don't put on that testimony, then I am counting solely on my conspiracy theory, hoping that the jurors will first understand it, and then buy into it. It's a gamble, a roll of the dice with Pete's life on the line.

"We have just one more witness, Your Honor. Tomorrow I will be calling Lieutenant Simon Coble of the New Jersey State Police."

All or nothing.

I'm pleased with Lieutenant Coble's attitude.

He and I have had our disagreements, and I was concerned that his testimony might be less than enthusiastic. But he has shown up this morning fresh and raring to go, promising he'll do his best to prevent the injustice of Pete being convicted.

"The defense calls Lieutenant Simon Coble," I say, and he strides to the witness stand with confidence and purpose.

I take him through a description of his career path, and awards he has won. He's an impressive guy in this setting, and seems to have a presence that makes the jurors sit up and take notice.

"Lieutenant Coble, how did you and I first come to speak about this case?"

"You called me. You said that Captain Stanton told you he had discussed the death of Katherine Reynolds with me, and his suspicions about it. And I confirmed that."

"And how did you come to speak with Captain Stanton about Katherine Reynolds in the first place?"

"Her niece had contacted me with her own concerns that it might have been a murder, and I checked into it. When I heard that Captain Stanton was then investigating it as well, it seemed the logical thing to do would be to have a conversation with him about it. To compare notes."

I have rarely been stunned and speechless in a courtroom; in fact, this may be the first time. Coble has just said something that caused a set of facts I had in my mind but couldn't really see to come flooding forward. He had said the same thing before, but I hadn't thought about the implications of it.

And all of it has convinced me of one thing:

I am talking to a murderer.

I am flustered; and I take a moment to compose myself by drinking a glass of water. Coble sits on the stand looking at me, and there is a slight smile on his lips.

I can't be certain of this, yet I am:

He knows that I know.

There is nothing I can say in the moment, no questions I can ask, to demonstrate what I am positive is the truth. And the horrible irony is that attacking Coble right now would be completely counterproductive. I desperately need his testimony to save Pete.

So I force myself to focus as I take him through the story. It is one of the hardest things I've ever had to do in my life, but I get through it.

And Coble is great, the perfect witness. He helps me tell the story economically and with clarity; together we tie up every loose end we can find.

Richard tries valiantly to attack Coble in his cross-examination, but he makes very little progress. Everything that Coble is testifying to is the truth. The events happened exactly as he is describing them. What he leaves out is that he helped orchestrate them.

But because they are true, Richard can't make a dent in them, or in him.

When he finally gets off the stand, Coble passes me on his way out of the courtroom. He leans in and whispers, "Don't be a hero, Counselor."

I don't answer him. I don't know what I could say, but in any event, the judge has already asked Richard to begin his closing argument. I force myself to try and listen, but it's very hard.

"Ladies and gentlemen, you've been treated to quite a show in this courtroom," Richard says. "You've been empaneled to decide who shot Daniel Diaz to death in his home, and you've heard a lot of clear and I believe compelling evidence that says it was Peter Stanton that committed the crime."

He goes into the evidence that the prosecution presented, clearly and concisely summarizing it. Just listening to him, I think that even I would vote to convict Pete.

"But that's not all you heard," Richard continues. "You heard about a huge conspiracy, about dog drugs that murder people, about kidnapped wives, and dead executives, and missing researchers.

"And what does this have to do with the case you are here to judge? Not a hell of a lot, I'll tell you that. All that connects that bizarre world to this case is a line on a phone bill. That's it.

"Maybe it was a wrong number, and maybe the GPS satellite was off. I don't know about you, but I've followed my GPS into more than a couple of dead ends. It's an imperfect science, and it should not be misused to ignore all the facts you've had placed before you.

"Captain Pete Stanton murdered Danny Diaz. He had opportunity, and he had motive. Don't be fooled into believing otherwise. Follow your heads, follow the logic, and please give justice to Danny Diaz and his son.

Thank you."

I wish like hell I could delay my closing argument until tomorrow.

It's not that what I would have to say would be any different, it's more that I could calm down and focus on what is important in the moment. There will be time to consider what I have just realized, and figure out how to deal with it.

Pete's entire life is on the line, so I need to get a grip and do what I have to do. Composure has never been a problem for me, and I can't let it be one now.

And I won't.

"You okay?" Pete asks. He can tell something is wrong, but obviously has no idea what it is.

"Fine," I say. "It's show time."

I get up and say, "Closing arguments are supposed to be a summary of the case. We lawyers have been bombarding you with different facts and theories, and all you've been able to do is sit there and listen. You aren't even allowed to ask questions, so there is no way for you to possibly remember and connect everything, especially in a case as complicated as this.

"So my job now is to summarize what I have tried to get across, in a clear way, supported by the facts.

"Mr. Wallace presented a great deal of evidence to you, and if it had gone unrefuted, you would be justified in deciding that

Captain Stanton was a murderer. So let's analyze those facts, and see if it is reasonable to doubt that they are accurate.

"Captain Stanton was on the scene the night of the murder. We do not dispute that, and we even showed you the text message that brought him there. It was from his friend Danny Diaz's phone, and it sounded like Diaz needed help. So he rushed there, just as the real murderer knew he would.

"But Danny Diaz did not have his phone; you heard evidence that it still hasn't been found, to this day. So what happened to it? Did he text Captain Stanton, then throw it away? Why would he do that? Did Captain Stanton take it? Why would he do that? The text would be on his own phone as well, and in the phone company's records. No, Danny Diaz did not have his phone because it was taken from him by his killer."

I go on to point out the weaknesses in the evidence regarding the fingerprints and the gloves, and then move on to the drugs. "And how did they get there? Did Captain Stanton store them there, not under lock and key? Why would he do that? And why would he have all those drugs, without there being the slightest shred of evidence that he ever used or sold them? And why would he have wiped the package clean of fingerprints, and then store them in his own house?

"None of that makes sense, certainly not from a smart cop like Pete Stanton. And even Chief Carnow told you that Pete is one of the smartest and best cops he has ever met.

"We know from the GPS records that people were in Captain Stanton's house the day of the murder, possible even Diaz himself, but certainly someone who had Diaz's phone. There was no doubt it was Alex Parker, and if he took Diaz's phone, surely he could have had the key to the house that was in Diaz's possession. Why was he there? Isn't it reasonable to believe that he might have planted the drugs?

"So I believe that just based on the prosecution's evidence, we did enough to make a not guilty vote the correct one. But then we did more: we pointed to a real-life massive conspiracy of murder, one that has left many bodies in its wake.

"Lieutenant Coble and the other witnesses told you all about it, in probably more detail than you needed. But the facts are the facts, and the facts show that Pete Stanton was framed so that he would not be able to continue investigating that conspiracy of murder."

I go into some detail about Parker, Reynolds, Mathis, et al., but not too much. Coble had done much of that work in his testimony, and I also feel like I have the jury now, and I don't want to lose them.

"But I would submit that after all that, you should consider the character of the man that is Captain Pete Stanton. He has spent his entire life upholding the law and protecting all of us. He is possibly the finest public servant I have ever known, and I am proud to call him my friend.

"He doesn't deserve what has happened to him, not one bit of it. But you have a special power, and only you have it.

"You have the power to make it right.

"Thank you."

As I head back to the defense table, I see Laurie, and Sam, and Willie, and Vince Sanders. They are staring at me, smiling and giving me gestures of support, from Laurie's thumbs up to Vince's clenched fist. Pete claps me on the shoulder and mouths a silent "thank you."

They think I have done well, and that I should be pleased.

Maybe they're right.

But they don't know what I know.

I'm usually a total basket case when waiting for a verdict.

I don't talk to anyone except Tara, I don't do anything except walk Tara, and I become a mass of superstitions.

But this time is different; this time I call a meeting of the entire investigative team at our house. I want to tell them what I know, both because I am not positive what to do, and because I don't want to be the only one who knows it.

I start by saying, "I believe that Lieutenant Simon Coble was a leading member of the murder-for-hire ring; he may have been the leader, but more likely his role was to provide cover for them.

"It hit me when I caught him in a relatively minor lie: he said he was looking into the Katherine Reynolds's death because her niece asked him to. But Katherine Reynolds lost her family in a car crash; she had no other family at all. And Carson Reynolds was an only child. Therefore, it is not possible that Katherine Reynolds had a niece at all."

"You've got more than that, right?" Hike asks.

"I do. Alex Parker obviously faked his death; I don't know who the actual poor guy was who had his head beaten in. But Coble said the deceased's fingerprints matched Parker's army record. But they could not have; so Coble must have changed them.

"I told Coble that we knew Reynolds and Diaz had been in

phone contact with Parker, and that we knew where Parker lived in Hackensack. The next day Parker was out of there, and the phone was never used again.

"When I talked to Blackman the day he died, he said that the 'cop was coming back,' to question him. It didn't mean anything to me at the time, but the cop had to have been Coble, and when he was there earlier, I'll bet he slipped Blackman the heart attack pill. When he came back, he knew he would find Blackman dead.

"But maybe most important is that Coble is the reason they went after Pete. He knew from his meeting with Pete that Pete had a gut feeling that these were murders, and he wasn't going to drop it until he found out the truth.

"He was afraid that if they killed Pete, his fellow cops would pick up the trail. But if they got rid of him by sending him to prison, no one would follow up on his cases. They'd be home free."

"Why did he testify like he did?" Hike asks.

"I'm not sure," I say. "But I think that he knew if Pete was convicted, I'd never let it drop. I'd keep trying to prove the conspiracy, and he was the only one left that the truth could bring down."

"So what do we do now?" Sam asks.

"Let's get the son of a bitch," Willie says.

I shake my head. "My instinct, and tell me if anyone disagrees, is to let this sit until the verdict comes in. Pete gains nothing if we announce to the world that our star witness is himself a murderer. Once we have a verdict, either way, we try and prove the case against Coble."

There is general agreement that this is the correct approach. Laurie and I discussed it last night, and she feels firmly that what is best for Pete must be the immediate priority. So that's what we'll do.

"There's one other complication," I say before everyone leaves. "I think Coble knows that I know. It's the way he looked at me and smiled the moment I realized it."

The rest of the day goes by without a verdict. I try and take my mind off everything, but it's an impossible task. Laurie recommends that I take Ricky down to the Tara Foundation building so he can see the dogs we have for rescue, but I don't really want to. I want to just sit by myself and worry.

"He loves dogs," Laurie says.

"So?"

"So take him, Andy. Please."

So I do, and when I see his face when we walk in, I'm instantly glad that I did. Within two minutes he's rolling on the floor with four of the dogs, laughing the most carefree laugh I've heard out of him since all this started.

Willie's wife Sondra is there, but she says that Willie is out. "I know I shouldn't ask this," she says. "But is Pete going to win?"

"I know I shouldn't say this," I say. "But I think he will."

It's on the way home that I remember something about the case that I had forgotten. Rozelle, the manager of the dump apartments where Juanita Diaz was imprisoned, had asked me if we "ever talk to the cops." I glossed over it at the time, but it might mean that he had dealt with Coble before we got there.

If he had, then there are two credible possibilities. One, that he might have some information about Coble that could be helpful when we go after him. And two, that he might be in danger, since Coble seems to have a desire to eliminate loose ends.

For that matter, I am the loosest of the loose ends. If I don't put Coble away, every time I eat a meal I'm going to wonder if there's a little white pill tucked away in it.

Not the best way to live.

It's been one day and I'm going insane.

I just can't sit around and do nothing, even though I told the team we needed to wait for a verdict. So I take a ride up to Spring Valley to talk to Rozelle. Laurie wants to go with me, but Edna is not at the house, so she needs to stay home with Ricky.

I drive up there and when I reach the building, I go around to the back where his office is. The door is locked, and no one answers when I knock. I'd called ahead, and Rozelle had said that he'd be here. I'm annoyed by this, but that annoyance dissolves into fear when I feel metal jammed into my back, and I hear Coble's voice.

"Couldn't let it alone, could you?"

"I don't know what you're talking about," I say, feebly.

"You looking for Rozelle? Come on, I'll take you to him."

He half pushes me toward his car, which is not a police car. He makes me drive, and sits in the passenger seat with his gun pointed at my head.

I am scared out of my mind.

We drive ten minutes, and he tells me to take a small dirt road for about half a mile. We get out, and we walk into a densely wooded area, about two hundred yards from the road. All of this time I am making plans to make a break for it, and then not doing it. There just doesn't seem to be a chance at any point for me to make it.

I am going to die here.

There is a clearing, empty except for Rozelle's body lying there, a gunshot wound in the head. "He told me you were coming to see him," Coble says. "He thought telling me that would save his life. Instead it ended yours."

At this point I am past panic. I am going to run, into the woods, but they are twenty feet away, and I will be dead before I get there. I know this with certainty, but I simply cannot think of anything else to do.

"You gonna make a break for it, Counselor?" Coble asks, smiling as he reads my mind.

My legs are weak and shaking. "No." It's a lie, or at least I think it is. If I can get my damn legs to support me, I'm going to try.

In the interim, my only plan is to rely on what I usually rely on, which is my mouth. If I can keep him talking, then he won't be shooting. It's like being down ten points with thirty seconds to go in a basketball game and constantly fouling. The cause is hopeless, so all you try and do is extend the game.

"Was this whole thing your idea?" I ask.

"I wish," he says, then laughs. "I'm not that smart. It was Reynolds. He brought in Parker, and Parker brought me in to cover for them. Parker and I go back a ways in the service."

"Was it all about money?"

"What difference does it make to you? You know as well as I do that you're not getting out of here."

"I guess I just want to know why."

He shrugs. "It was about money to me and Parker." Another laugh. "Lots and lots of money."

"So why did you get rid of your partners?" I ask.

"Same reason I'm getting rid of you. Self-preservation." He raises his gun. "Counselor, if you're going to make a break for it, now's the time. Or, you can choose to die with some dignity."

I'm staring at the gun, and then I hear an incredibly loud noise as he fires it. But I don't get hit, and he starts to lower the gun. Then I realize that it wasn't his gun that fired it at all, and as it is being lowered, it is being showered in blood.

Coble's blood.

So I look up, and there are three men standing there, two with guns. The third man is Joseph Russo.

"You okay that we killed him?" Russo asks.

"Yeah," I say, trying to control the tremor in my voice. "But don't let it happen again."

"Willie asked us to follow you," Russo says. "Willie's my man."

I nod, feeling an urge to cry as the full impact of what happened hits me, but trying not to. "Mine too." Then, "What do we do with them?"

"Not for you to worry about," Russo says, so I won't. I just thank him about four hundred times, after which one of his guys drives me back to my car, and I head home.

Laurie's waiting for me on the porch when I pull up. The look on her face is one of concern and stress, and I figure that she must know what happened.

She doesn't. "There's a verdict," she says. "They're waiting on you." The she looks at my disheveled clothing, and she says, "Andy, is that blood?"

Apparently a small amount of Coble's blood sprayed on me, and I hadn't noticed. "It's a long story," I say, and then I run into the house to get dressed in about two seconds flat.

I tell Laurie the story on the way to court.

She is horrified, and starts to cry for only the second time since I've known her. She's apparently a lot tougher for herself than she is for me.

We arrive at the court, and everyone is in place except me and Judge Matthews. The gallery is packed and restless. "Glad you could make it," says Pete, smiling. How he can smile at a moment like this is beyond me. Then he sees my face and asks, "You okay?"

"I'll let you know in a few minutes," I say.

Judge Matthews comes in moments later, staring at me in a silent reprimand. If she only knew.

She brings the jury in, and asks if they have reached a verdict. They say that they have, and I can feel Pete tense up next to me. Smiling time is over.

The foreman gives the verdict sheet to the clerk, who gives it to the judge to look over. The judge hands it back to the clerk to read aloud, and Pete, Hike, and I stand. All of this takes about twelve hours, or at least it seems like it takes that long. I put my hand on Pete's shoulder, and we wait to hear if he is going to spend the rest of his life behind bars.

She reads in a low monotone, a jumble of barely intelligible words about the state of New Jersey, and various counts, blah, blah, blah. But two words come ringing through loud and clear.

"Not guilty."

Pete turns to me and we hug. Hugging is not something that Pete and I do, but here we are doing it in public. They're even snapping pictures of it. It's going to be tough to live this one down.

"You did it," Pete says.

"The team did it."

"I've never been that scared in my life. I thought I was going down."

"Never in doubt, buddy. Never in doubt."

"I need to calm my nerves," he says. "How about buying me a beer?"

Richard Wallace comes over to offer us both his congratulations. Pete shakes his hand warmly; if there are any hard feelings, I don't see them. And I'd bet anything that Richard is glad he lost.

Laurie waits until after we have dinner, tuck Ricky in, and then make love, before she brings up the issue that has been hanging over us. "Andy, I know what you've been through, so if this isn't a good time, I'll understand. But at some point we need to talk about Ricky."

"There's something I need to tell you," I say. "I was positive I was going to die today. You know how they say your life flashes in front of you? Well, mine didn't. What flashed in front of me was my obituary. And it said that Andy Carpenter had died, and that he was a lawyer. A prominent lawyer."

"So?"

"So I realized what I really want my obituary to say. I want it to say that Andy Carpenter was a loving husband and father."

"Husband and father?" she asks, emphasizing the word "husband."

"Husband and father."

"That's your idea of a wedding proposal?"

"No good?" I ask.

"Plenty good," she says, and her smile says she means it.

This beautiful, incredible woman actually wants to marry me.

Go figure.

Charlie's has never had an event as classy as this.

There are balloons everywhere, paper tablecloths on the tables, and the beer is flowing like, well, beer. It's the first wedding in the history of the place, so we're pulling out all the stops.

It's hard to believe we planned all this in two days; it must have taken almost that long to blow up the balloons. But once we confirmed with Ricky that he and Sebastian were okay with the plan, we sprung into action.

I had been worried about the conversation, so of course I let Laurie take the lead. "Ricky," she had said, "we love you and want you to be part of our family."

He didn't respond, so I added, "Forever."

"Sebastian too?" he finally asked.

Laurie smiled. "Of course. Sebastian too."

"Cool," he said, and that was that.

We do the wedding ceremony first. Ricky gives Laurie away, Tara is her maid of honor, and Sebastian is my best man. Ricky has dressed Sebastian in a top hat, but Tara doesn't wear anything except a rose in her collar. Tara is a no-nonsense girl.

There are about fifty people there. Our whole team, of course, and Pete and Vince, and a bunch of our friends. Cindy Spodek has come down from Boston with her husband. I invited Richard Wallace, and am glad that he showed up.

It's a quick ceremony, and before I know it I am kissing the bride, as the place erupts in applause. "I love you," Laurie says, and I say, "That makes us even."

"Is this going to change anything?" I ask.

She nods. "We'll stop having sex." And then she smiles. "But we can start the new policy tomorrow."

As soon as the ceremony is over, we take a picture of the five of us: me and Laurie, Tara, Sebastian, and Ricky, our son. I probably should have worn my new sneakers, but I think Tara will block them in the photo anyway.

Then we have a great party. The TVs are turned to the Mets game, and they are winning. All is right with the world.

Edna tells me that she has decided not to retire after all, that she thinks she can do both, maybe even train for her crossword puzzle tourneys in the office, when we're not busy. Since I have no intention of taking on any clients, I tell her it's workable.

She also has an idea. "Maybe I can wear a sweatshirt at the tournaments with your name on the back, like 'For a great lawyer, call Andy Carpenter.' You know, like advertising."

I tell her that may not be workable.

Marcus has brought his wife, Jeannie, to the party. This surprises me in a couple of ways. For one thing, I had no idea that Marcus was married, and for another, she refers to him as "my Markie" when I'm talking to her. She makes it sound like he's a poodle. Jeannie is spectacular-looking, but I would doubt that too many people would try and hit on her with "her Markie" around.

Hike pulls me aside at one point and sincerely wishes me a long and happy marriage, but adds, "although based on the statistics, the odds are against you."

Willie apologizes to me for telling Joseph Russo to follow me, but in light of subsequent events, I decide to forgive him. I'm very gracious that way.

Pete has been reinstated in full to the police force, and tomorrow is his first day back on the job. "You did good," he says to me. "You were worth every penny."

"You didn't pay me," I say.

He nods. "My point exactly."

All in all it's a great night, but one highlight sticks out. I overhear Ricky and Vince talking, and I hear Ricky call him "Uncle Vince." But then he refers to "my dad."

And he's talking about me.

Turn the page for a sneak peek at
David Rosenfelt's next novel

WHO LET THE DOG OUT?

Available July 2015

This was not going to take a master thief. The difficulty of robberies, Gerry Downey knew, was directly proportional to the fear and expectation that the targets had of being robbed. No one goes to extremes to protect property unless they think someone might want to take that property. That's why banks and jewelry stores are tougher targets than hot dog stands and city dumps.

It's Robbery 101.

That was why Downey, who over time had accumulated enough real-world robbery credits to earn his master's, had no concerns about his current job. But that did not mean he was careless about it. He was a pro, and knew it was the easy ones that could occasionally throw you a curve. Which is why he had staked this one out for three days. After all, he was a professional and would act like one, despite the demeaning nature of this particular job.

Of course, the job wasn't just demeaning; it was also strange. Downey had never stolen anything like this before, and likely never would again. But if the payoff was always going to be this good, he'd happily sign on for a repeat performance anytime.

The building was on Route 20 in Paterson, New Jersey, a heavily trafficked road that had a number of commercial businesses on it. Part of that time he had been watching from a hamburger place across the road, which turned out to be bearable, because the burgers were charcoal broiled and damn good, and the French fries were crisp.

The guy who ran the place he was watching, Willie Miller, left with his wife most days at around five o'clock in the evening, sometimes a little later. The exact timing seemed to depend on whether they were there alone, or whether a customer was on-site. But so far neither Willie nor anyone else had come back once they left, and Downey had watched until eight o'clock each night.

Downey had gone inside the target building the previous morning, pretending to be a customer himself. He needed to learn whether there was a burglar alarm (there was) and whether there were indoor cameras (there were). Neither would cause him any concern.

On this day Miller and his wife didn't leave until five-fifteen, so Downey waited twenty minutes and then drove over. There was no reason not to do it in daylight. If for any reason anyone was watching, a car pulling up to that building would seem more natural then than at night. And besides, he would only be there a few minutes.

Downey picked the lock in less than ten seconds, and went inside. He knew the silent alarm would be going off, but he'd be out long before anyone could respond. He pulled his jacket up over his head and headed for the electrical box to turn off the cameras. This was accomplished in a few seconds as well.

The only thing that was annoying Downey at that moment, other than the indignity of having to do such an easy job, was the noise. The barking was deafening; he had no idea how Miller could stand it every day.

Downey went directly to the dog runs, stopping at the fourth one on the right. Inside was a large dog, matching the photo he had been given. He didn't know what kind it was, and didn't care. Dogs didn't interest him one way or the other, and it amazed him how some people talked about them like they were human.

He opened the cage, pulling the leash out of his pocket. The dog seemed friendly enough and not inclined to attack, which was a plus, since if Downey had to shoot her, it would have defeated the purpose of his being there.

But her tail was wagging, and she came over and lowered her head, as if she wanted Downey to pet her. That sure as hell wasn't going to happen, so Downey just put the leash on her and led her out.

Downey took her to his car and she hopped right in. The entire thing hadn't taken more than three minutes, a very profitable three minutes at that.

The man is pure evil. He must be stopped."

"That might be overstating it a bit," Laurie Collins says. "He's a baseball coach, working with nine-year-olds."

I point toward the field. "Do you see where Ricky is? Do you?" I'm talking about our recently adopted son, currently positioned in the outfield.

"Of course I do. He's in right field."

I nod vigorously. "Exactly! Right field! That's where they put the losers, the guys they're trying to hide. Nobody good plays right field."

"Ruth, Aaron, Kaline, Clemente, Frank Robinson, Andre Dawson . . ." The only team sport that Laurie likes is baseball; she loves the history and tradition, and she's a student of it. If I don't interrupt, she'll name fifty great right fielders.

"Believe me, those guys didn't play right field in Little League," I say. "They pitched or played shortstop. In the majors, right field is fine; in Little League it's Death Valley. This coach has no idea what he's doing."

"Don't talk to him, Andy. Don't be one of those parents."

The coach is Bill Silver, and since he's at least six-two and 210 pounds, there's no way that I, Andy Carpenter, am going to confront him. I can't be one of "those parents," as Laurie put it, because "those parents" usually aren't cowards.

Laurie and I have been married five months, and we adopted Ricky at the same time. It was too late to get him involved in peewee football, so this is my first chance to see him on an athletic field.

The next batter hits a fly ball to right field. Ricky doesn't panic, just circles under it, waiting patiently for it to come down. And it does in fact come down, about eight feet to the right of where Ricky is standing. Displaying keen baseball instincts, he runs over and picks it up, then throws it to no one in particular, but in the general area of the infield. And it almost reaches the infield by the time it stops rolling.

"Good try, Rick!" Laurie calls out.

"He's a shortstop," I say to no one in particular. "Shortstops don't catch fly balls. You put Derek Jeter out there, and he embarrasses himself. You ever see Cal Ripken try to catch a fly ball? Pathetic."

"Andy, Ricky's having fun."

"You don't get to the majors by having fun," I say.

"Majors?" Laurie says, her voice both incredulous and disapproving. "Is that your plan?"

"Why not? I could have made it to the majors myself, if I had the breaks, and the dedication, and the ability. Why can't Ricky make it?"

"Well, for one thing, maybe he isn't good enough."

"That's because he's not focused on baseball. You need to stop bothering him, cluttering his head with that other stuff."

"What other stuff?"

"You know . . . like reading and math. When is he going to need that junk in his life? Nobody reads anymore; everything is video."

"Andy . . ." I've got a hunch that the next words out of Laurie's mouth are not going to be "I agree with you completely." But I don't get to hear them, because my cell phone rings and she stops in mid-sentence.

Caller ID tells me that it's Willie Miller, my former client and current partner in the Tara Foundation, our dog rescue operation. Willie and his wife Sondra are completely dedicated to finding loving homes for the dogs we bring in.

"What's up?" is the way I answer the phone.

"We've had a robbery," he says.

"At your house?"

"No, at the foundation. Sondra and I went to get something to eat after work, and when we got home I noticed that the alarm had gone off. So I came down here to see what was going on. There was a break-in."

I'm a little confused, because there is really nothing to steal there. We don't keep money or valuables in that building, just dogs. "What did they steal?"

"The shepherd mix. Cheyenne."

"I'll be right there," I say to Willie, and then turn to Laurie, who has overheard my end of the conversation. "Somebody stole a dog from the foundation."

"That's bizarre," she says, which is true. These are dogs up for adoption; there should be no reason for someone to steal one. "You go down there; I'll get a ride home with Sally."

Sally Rubenstein is our neighbor, and her son, Will, is on the same team as Ricky. They are best friends, but unfortunately, Will is playing shortstop, and he fields grounders like Ozzie Smith.

"Okay. If you get a chance after the game, talk to Coach Silver about Ricky."

"What do you want me to say?" she asks.

"Tell him Ricky should play in the infield or pitch. Don't overtly threaten him, but make sure he sees your gun." Laurie is an ex-cop and the private investigator for my law practice, and she carries a handgun.

"Goodbye, Andy."

The guy shut the cameras off. And he picked the lock. He knew what he was doing."

I have to agree with Willie on his assessment, though it seems to make very little sense. Why would an accomplished thief come in and take a stray dog that was already up for adoption?

"You look at the tape?" I ask. "We get anything before he shut it off?" The cameras were not designed to capture thieves in action; we never contemplated that there might be a need. They were actually set up as a webcam, so Willie can see from his home what's going on with the dogs, in case any are sick. Cheyenne's run would therefore be within the view of one of the cameras.

"Nah. He had his head covered with his sweatshirt; from some kind of college, I think. But we've got the GPS, unless the guy removed it."

They make inexpensive GPS devices that are small and attach to dogs' collars. We started using them about six months ago, when one of the dogs we adopted out escaped from his new owner. We searched for three days before we found the poor dog. If a dog is going to get away, it is likely to be before he or she is acclimated to the new home, so now we do the GPS thing as a service to protect both the dog and the adopter.

"Let's take a look."

We go into the office, and Willie takes the tracking machine out of the cabinet. He turns it on, and we wait the few seconds until it's ready. Once it is, Willie punches in the number that identifies it as Cheyenne's collar.

"We got it," he says. "Twenty-sixth Street, off Nineteenth Ave. Let's go."

"We should call the police," I say. "Have them meet us there."

"The police? For a stray dog? We can handle this."

Willie is a black belt in karate and one of the toughest people I've ever met. He can also be very nice, as evidenced by the fact that he used the pronoun "we." He knows very well that if there is any "handling" to be done, I'll be of little use.

"I'm not saying we can't handle it, but—"

"Andy, if he takes the GPS collar off and then leaves with the dog, we could lose him. Let's go; you can call the cops on the way if you want."

We head for my car, and I call Pete Stanton as we drive. Pete is a Paterson Police captain, and a very good friend of mine. I reach him on his cell and tell him what's going on.

"So what do you want from me?" he asks.

"To meet us there, arrest the bad guy, do your job, protect the public. That kind of thing."

"Willie can handle it," he points out.

"That's what I'm afraid of." Willie has been known to be somewhat protective of our dogs. If this guy has hurt Cheyenne, Willie might impose the death penalty on him. "What else have you got to do?"

"Not much; I'm just trying to apprehend a murderer."

There was a local murder last week, and the suspected perpetrator, Eric Brantley, has eluded capture despite an all-out manhunt. He is accused of killing his business partner with a well-placed bullet in the back of the head.

"The only way you're going to catch him is if he comes in voluntarily and surrenders," I say. "And even then you'll probably screw it up. Come on, this won't take more than twenty minutes."

"You're a pain in the ass, you know?" Pete asks.

"I am aware of that." I'm also aware that Pete could never turn me down for anything, since it was just a few months ago that I successfully defended him when he was wrongly accused of murder. I am ridiculously wealthy, mostly through inheritance, so I didn't charge him for the defense. Therefore he will owe me until the end of time, and I intend to take advantage of it for even longer than that.

I give him the address, and he agrees to meet us there. We're going to get there before him, but we can decide how to handle things when we arrive.

The house the GPS leads us to is modest and a little run-down, but no more so than the others in the neighborhood. This is not a wealthy area; most of the residents are honest, hardworking people who struggle to make ends meet. I never thought of them as a particularly dog-thieving group.

There is still daylight left, so the fact that there seem to be no lights on in the house is not particularly significant. Nor is the fact that there is no car in the driveway; there are plenty of cars parked on the street, and one of them could be the car that brought Cheyenne here.

We park and get out of the car. Willie starts toward the front porch of the house, showing no hesitation whatsoever.

"Let's wait for Pete," I say.

"We don't need Pete."

"I'm sure that's true, but there's no downside to waiting. He'll be here in five minutes, and it's not like they can leave without us seeing them."

"Come on, Andy. I want a shot at this guy. He won't tell the cops why he did it."

"He won't tell us either."

"Oh, yes he will," Willie says, and I believe him.

But I convince him to wait, and my job is made easier by the fact that Pete pulls up within two minutes. He gets out of the car, and we update him on the little that has happened so far.

Pete frowns at the indignity of having to deal with this as he starts up the steps. Willie is right up alongside him, and I'm a couple of paces back. I'd just as soon wait in the car, or even better, at home, but I'm actually not that afraid. Unless there's a Russian battalion setting up an ambush in that house, Pete and Willie can handle this.

Pete rings the bell, and immediately a dog starts barking.

"That's Cheyenne," Willie says, immediately.

"How do you know that?" Pete asks.

"I recognize the bark," Willie says, but I think he's lying. There's nothing about the bark that is distinctive, and we've only had Cheyenne for a few days. Besides, when one dog barks at the foundation, they all do, so I doubt he's ever heard Cheyenne's bark when it wasn't drowned out by all the others.

The barking stops, but no one comes to the door. Pete rings the bell again, which restarts the barking, but once again fails to turn up any humans.

"Nobody here," Pete says.

"Cheyenne's here," Willie points out. "Let's go in and get her."

"You've got probable cause for a robbery," I point out to Pete. "The stolen merchandise is barking."

He turns to Willie. "How do you know it's your dog?"

"Because it's MY dog. So I know her bark."

Pete rings the bell again, with the now predictable result . . . more barking, but that's it. After a few moments, he takes out his gun, which I assume is proper procedure when entering a crime scene in this fashion.

He reaches for the door handle, and seems surprised to find that it turns and the door opens. "Wait here," he says, which I am quite happy to do.

Willie is less inclined to follow the order, and when Pete enters the house, Willie is right behind him, leaving me alone on the porch. Alone is not my favorite state of being in situations like this, so I belatedly join the procession.

There is a staircase directly across from the door, off the foyer, and since I'm a few seconds late, I don't know whether Pete and Willie went into the room to the left of the staircase or the room to the right. I'm about to call out to them when I hear a bark, which is clearly to the left. So that's where I go.

Huge mistake.

Cheyenne stops barking when she sees me. She is sitting on the floor about five feet from a recliner chair in what probably passes as the den, with a leash still around her neck. The room has a sofa, a table with a small TV resting on it, and the chair.

In the chair is a dead body. As a criminal attorney, I have seen way more than my share of them, both in photographs and sometimes in person. While I don't make it a practice to rank them, it's safe to say that this is not one I am soon going to forget.

The victim looks to be in his forties, well built, dressed in jeans and a Syracuse University sweatshirt. My guess would be that he's about six feet tall, but it's hard to tell because he's sitting down, and mostly decapitated. His throat has been sliced, and his head hangs to the side, only partially connected to his torso. His hands are behind him, probably tied behind the chair, but I'm not about to go back there to find out.

No one is going to have to feel for a pulse to know that this guy is history, and establishing time of death is not going to be a problem, because before I turn away I think I can see that the blood is still flowing.

It's hard for me to accurately take in the scene, because I'm trying to do it while gagging, screaming, and running out of the room. As I'm leaving, Pete and Willie have heard me and are running in.

They're going to understand my reaction soon enough; there's no reason for me to stop and explain it to them.

I run out on the porch and try to take deep breaths and avoid throwing up. I haven't thrown up since I was a kid, and just the memory of how awful it was makes me want to throw up. I can hear Pete yelling something inside the house, but I can't tell what it is.

Moments later, Willie comes out with Cheyenne on the leash, and he hands it to me. "Keep an eye on her," he says, and when I take the leash he goes back into the house.

So I'm left on the porch, simultaneously retching, gasping, panicking, and holding a leash. Fortunately, I'm a multitasker.

It's less than five minutes before the police cars start to arrive, and there must be ten of them. Pete comes out to talk to two of the officers. Pete is a captain in robbery/homicide, so I assume he's in charge, and just consulting.

He hasn't said anything to me since we discovered the body, but when he sees me still on the porch, he comes over. "You and the dog should wait over there," he says. "You're going to need to give a statement."

"You know everything I know."

He nods. "We have to get it all on paper." Then he points to Cheyenne. "Too bad he can't talk."

"She."

"What?"

"She's a female. Her name is Cheyenne."

"Thanks," he says, with a slight frown. "That's just the kind of information we need."

"What's the victim's name?" I ask.

"According to his driver's license, Gerald Downey. You know him?"

I don't, and I tell him so. Then, "Any evidence of a break-in?"

Pete frowns again. "You conducting a formal investigation? Or maybe looking for a client?"

"No chance. My last client was such a pain in the ass, I'm retired." Since Pete was my last client, the dig isn't that subtle.

"The back door was open; that could have been the point of entry, and it's possible the perpetrator took off that way when we showed up. The wound was very fresh."

"I noticed," I say. "And after our statements, we can take Cheyenne back to the foundation?"

He nods. "Yeah. I don't see her as a suspect. Maybe you can represent her in a civil suit."

Crime scenes take forever to process, and when the crime is murder, then "forever" understates the case. It's almost three hours before Willie and I give our statements and are cleared to leave.

Willie has Cheyenne's leash, and he comes over and says, "I'm going to take her home with me, just in case."

"Okay."

"You get a look at the guy's face?" he asks.

"Not really. . . . Once I saw it wasn't attached to his neck, I didn't really focus on it."

"I did; he came in yesterday. Said he was interested in adopting a dog."

"Which one? Cheyenne?"

Willie shrugs. "I don't know; it never got that far. I asked him where the dog would sleep, and he said he had a doghouse, so I got rid of him."

"He was probably just checking the place out," I say.

Willie and Cheyenne leave, and before I go I find Pete and ask him if he's learned any more about the victim.

"Did I say anything to give you the impression that you and I were conducting a joint investigation?" he asks.

"A guy steals my dog and then gets murdered; I can't help but wonder if the two are somehow connected."

"Your dog wasn't the only thing this guy stole."

"He had a record?"

He nods. "That's understating it. Been a thief his whole life, spent a bunch of it doing time. Hasn't been arrested in the last two years, which is a record for him."

"What did he steal?"

"Let's put it this way: I think until tonight dogs were the only thing he *hadn't* stolen. Probably had it on his bucket list before he kicked it." He pauses, then says, "Just got it in under the wire."

There's nothing left to be learned from Pete tonight, so I go home to Laurie, who is awaiting my arrival so eagerly that she has fallen asleep with anticipation.

I take Tara and Sebastian for their nightly walk. Tara is a golden retriever and the greatest dog in the history of the universe. Sebastian is the basset hound we adopted as a package deal along with Ricky. It is poor Sebastian's plight to forever be the second-best dog in the house, but he seems to accept it and deals with the humiliation pretty well.

I plan a ten-minute walk, but they appear to enjoy it so much that I extend it to a half hour. When I get back, Laurie has awakened and is sitting up in bed waiting for me.

I had called her from the scene, but now I explain the night's events in more detail. "You think the murder and stealing the dog are connected?" she asks.

I shrug, which is what I do when I don't know something. I find that I shrug a lot. "Beats me."

"You going to look into it?"

"Maybe. I'm curious about it."

Unfortunately, the conversation doesn't get any more insightful than that, and finally she brightens up and starts telling me about the rest of the baseball game. "Ricky hit a home run!"

"He did?"

"Well, I'm not sure it's officially a home run. He hit it about five or six feet toward third base, and then the other team kept throwing the ball away, and he ran all the way around the bases. Then he started going to first again; he thought he could just keep running until they tagged him. It was adorable and he was so excited; I wish you had seen it."

"Aggressive on the bases, and always looking for that extra edge: that's what I like to hear," I say. "I worked with him on that."

"Don't tell him I told you about it," Laurie says. "He wants to tell you himself in the morning."

"Did you talk to the coach about the right field thing?"

She nods. "I did more than talk. I pointed my gun at him and told him either Ricky plays shortstop or the team will be minus one coach."

"Perfect. What did he say?"

"He refused, so I shot him."

"That's my girl."